CW01638076

Deneer was faster in her reactions. She swooped in with a terrible war cry. Her shrieking Whistler flashed in the sunlight and the man's head fell from his shoulders in the same manner that the two who had been vanquished by Kaz Oshay had done. But the enemy Death Machine was spinning out of control, and in a great screaming flash of anti-matter, it dissolved into an empty nothingness, shattered by Deneer's blaster pod into its constituent atoms . . .

Deathsport

WILLIAM HUGHES

**Based on a screenplay by
Henry Suso and Donald Stewart**

SPHERE BOOKS LIMITED
30/32 Gray's Inn Road, London WC1X 8JL

First published in Great Britain by
Sphere Books Ltd, 1978
Novelisation copyright © Sphere Books Ltd 1978
Based on a screenplay by Henry Suso and
Donald Stewart
Published by arrangement with New World
Productions Inc.

TRADE
MARK

This book is sold subject to the condition that it shall not, by way of trade or otherwise, be lent, re-sold, hired out or otherwise circulated without the publisher's prior consent in any form of binding or cover other than that in which it is published and without a similar condition including this condition being imposed on the subsequent purchaser.

Set in Intertype Baskerville

Printed in Great Britain by
Hunt Barnard Printing Ltd.,
Aylesbury, Bucks.

'The Greatest Miracle is Unity'

Yogi Bhajan.

CHAPTER ONE

Long ago, in the times of great darkness that fell between the first millennium and the new millennium that surrounds us today, the twin planets of plenty that we call home, the Earth and the Moon, were very different places from the surroundings we now know. There is little fact, but much legend, known of those times, though the antiquated dating system we still use was carried on during this period and the memories of stories handed down from generation to generation recount the folk-memories of the great tragedy that once overtook our world, plunging it into the dark age of which I now write.

This much is known to us; that in the first millennium of plenty, man took his dating from the Birth and Death of one of his own number, believed to be the son of that mystical force we know as the consciousness. For some two thousand years from the death of this mystic, man sought to attain greater and greater heights of prowess and learning, even creating a technology that could reach out beyond our own universe in huge fuel-powered machines, so that man could carry his seed to the ends of time and space.

This may seem a strange concept in our world, where we know that the power of the mind can accomplish the journey for us and tell us all we need to satisfy our curiosity without such mechanical endeavour and the great cost it would bring to us; but these were indeed primitive and physical times for our ancestors.

But, like now, the Earth was rich and green and giving of plenty to the peoples and animals that roamed upon it. The moon was smaller, barren and without life as it is today. Its size was augmented only by the fall-out of material that came with the coming of the great tragedy of the people of the earth, a fall-out which gave the life forces to this barren rock and, the hand of man not being there to interfere, allowed life to evolve and grow and an atmosphere to assert itself over the face of our twin planet.

For while man was striving ever upwards for knowledge and enlightenment, there was also a darker side of his nature made manifest in his strivings, strivings that were luring him all the time on the downward path that led almost to his own destruction.

His darkest sin was that of pride, a force which came upon him in collectivity down the centuries. He formed societies which tried to rival one another in strength and power and that was the start of his undoing. For the only settlement between any one or group of these states and another was that out-moded concept that the history computers tell us was called 'war', and all through the history of this primitive world, wars raged unabated, each side trying to produce weapons that would stun their enemies into a total submission to their power. And as expertise and learning increased, so too did the weapons and their destructive powers, until the weapons became so powerful that they controlled man instead of he controlling them.

As near as it is now possible to date it, the great holocaust came in the twenty-first century after the death of the great mystic of the consciousness. It was another war, one so dreadful that the whole of the earth was laid waste and unproductive and, had it not been for the tiny gleam of foresight in the minds of a few of the leaders, mankind might have died along with the world and we would not have been here to tell this story.

Those who had the intelligence to see that the devastation would be beyond imagining gave wealth and authority to their technicians for the building of great cities, protected by domes of metal from the outer air, the main body of them hewed from the solid rock beneath, wherein whole communities might be housed, complete with all their social systems and professional needs to perpetuate their society, so that many people could survive the poisoning that was being spread across the planet.

By the time this last great war ended, there were none who could remember why it had been fought and the world was now a place of poisoned desert and polluted water as the globe slid back into a new dark age that was to last for nearly a thousand years.

It is more by a miracle than by his own endeavours that

man has survived and lived on into our own age of renewed plenty and the peace that only the true enlightenment of the consciousness can bring.

For a century or more after the devastation, the survivors and then their children and their children's children dared not venture forth beyond their protective domes, living entirely off the stores of fuel and food that their leadership had provided in their wisdom, their main work being to tend the great breeding tanks that kept their food supplies going. The memory of much of the technology they had previously achieved was slowly forgotten and with it the means of making weapons for further escalations of the destruction they had wrought upon themselves.

Outside these domes, in the great deserts that had been formed, the Flash Winds howled, bringing their great clouds of radio-active destruction with them, clouds that meant certain death for any who stood in their path.

But, in time, the memory of death died a little and man ventured forth to look, at least, at the new world his triumphs of technology had created for him and when he did so, the Stateman of the great Cities found that he was, after all, not alone upon the earth. Others, too, had survived: two distinct groups of descendants from man's ancestors. And to both groups, Statemen gave the name of 'Mutants'.

There were two sides to the coin of mutation, just as there had been always two sides to man's own nature. The largest of these groups were animal-like primitives, scavengers who survived by attacking and overcoming anything still living that they could find – others of their number included, if there was no other food to be had. They had developed a saliva that poisoned all who came into contact with it and two rows of sharp razor-like teeth so that they could poison and eat even living creatures when they fell upon them.

But there was another race also. These were the descendants of those we know to have been called the Combat Rangers in the last great war. Men and women of great individual courage who had fought that war in the open while the main body of mankind hid behind its technology of destruction. They too had developed and evolved in ways that were different from their cousins in the cities. Each was as strong as any three men, with all their powers and perceptions heightened. Their minds had found the key to the consciousness and while each one ranged for most of his life on the special horses they bred across the wastelands and deserts, they would sometimes come together in the temporary joining or union to fight their enemies, only in defence of themselves, I must hasten to add, and to propogate their kind.

While, in common with all mankind, they had the self-powering weapons that the old technology had developed, which were known as anti-matter blasters, their main means of defence was a sword known as a Whistler, after the sound it made as it sped through the air, cleaving its way, unerring, to its target.

To these strange men and women, who were much more than ordinary mortals, their minds joined in their enclosed order in which each was whole and free yet still part of a greater whole, the Statemen of the Cities gave the name of Range Guides.

For most of their time, they remained entirely alone, roving free across the devastated face of the planet, but, in special circumstances, they would band together for a limited period, splitting again only when their task of defence or procreation was completed. Even their children remained with their mothers only as long as youth kept them in inexperience. Once come of age, a Range Guide was his or her own master and the mother became merely another of their kind, to be joined with or parted from whenever necessary.

While they would kill the barbaric and primitive Mutants whenever they were seen, for a sighting meant danger and an attack, over the centuries an uneasy co-operation grew up between them and the Statemen, as the latter came to trust them and their powers.

In the nine hundred years that followed the great devastation, a sort of trade sprang up between many of the Cities, where caravans of Statemen, guarded by the Guides who were available and agreeable, would journey from City to City to make contact and trade. For not only were these strange beings able to protect the Statemen caravans from the Mutants, they were also able to warn of the coming of the Flash Winds, smelling them on the light breezes hours ahead of their coming and warning the Statemen to take shelter from them.

And so it came to pass in the ninth century of the dark ages of the great devastation that there came one of the

Guides who held within him the seeds of the great truth and renewal that have led to our world. A special man whose descendants led the first faltering footsteps of the new mankind up to its present plateau, where the Guide descendants and the descendants of the Statemen are merged into one strong people within the protection of the consciousness. He came at a time of great danger, the greatest danger that mankind had faced since the holocaust, and mankind had waited almost too long for his coming. This is his legend, his story – the tale of Kaz Oshay, son of Oshay, Father of the worlds.

The vast complex of Helix City was similar to many of the other great domed places of protection that had survived the holocaust. Only in the forging of relationships with the other Cities had it remained aloof. True, its caravans traded with them in a normal and peaceful manner, but it had held itself apart from the Federation that had been agreed between the other Cities, that Federation which had agreed to outlaw the concept of war for all time.

Physically, it resembled the others, with its vast metal dome protecting it from the outside atmosphere, the small domes of its extensions grouped around it on the plain. The main part of the City was made of the old metals, lining the solid rock from which the shape of it had been cut, the light and air provided by the great humming power plants that worked from the stores of liquid fuel that had been provided by the foresight of its founders.

But now, after nine hundred years, the stocks of fuel were running dangerously low and the Lord Zirpola, the hereditary ruler of Helix needed all he could conserve for the coming to fruition of his great plan.

He marched now down a wide corridor in one of the lower levels of the City, the only sound the swishing of his great emerald cloak of office on the metal floor as he walked, and the ringing of the metal hobnails in his boots and those of his two companions as they went forward in step with a military precision. They turned a corner and entered another wide and deserted corridor, as brightly lit as the last had been. It ended some way in the distance in a huge metal door, closed now and with a large barring wheel at its centre, a secret light-code panel at its side – one of the great security doors that the Lord Zirpola had had fitted to seal off his secrets from the eyes of most of his subjects.

Feeling the pain that was now almost a constant companion streaking through his head once more, Zirpola angrily shook the mane of white hair that tumbled down over the back of his cloak and his pale, watery blue but compelling eyes were screwed up painfully at the excess brightness that assailed them from the corridor lights.

More and more, these days, were his senses a source of pain and distress to him, but this served only to fuel the urgency of his cruel ambitions, for he had never been a kindly man or a benevolent ruler, but always fuelled by hatred and suspicion of his fellow man. Now he was close to the fulfilment of his cherished and well-guarded plans and he could only hope that the weaknesses of his body were not going to dash the cup of triumph from his lips.

His face was etched with lines of strain and tiredness well beyond his fifty years of life, the skin wrinkled and pasty, glistening in the light from a cold sweat of pain that seemed to ooze from the pores of his oily skin. The thin prominent blade of his nose was his most imposing feature and in his youth it had given him that special look of distinction that he felt all rulers required, but its strength now merely served to emphasise the suffering that was mirrored in his other features.

He moved forward quickly, anxiously, as if the pain was driving him to even greater speed. His moods had become more and more mercurial of late and this sudden thrust forward came as no surprise to the men at his side, who lengthened their stride to compete with his own.

Both of them were taller than the Lord Zirpola and stood more erect, walking with the ease of Hunters. Between the two, one stood even taller and broader than the other. Both wore the tight metallic fabric suits that singled them out as Obedience Enforcers, the cruel band who policed the City and did the Lord Zirpola's bidding. The shorter of the pair was dressed in the conventional black, but with the silver flashes on his arm that designated a high seniority of rank. This was Polna, the man who ran the day-to-day affairs of the Enforcers.

The other man, Ankar Moor, was the Head of the Enforcers and second in power in the City to the Lord Zirpola himself. His attire was made entirely of silver garments. He was taller and broader than any other man in the City and none knew from whence he had come. There were those who said that he had come from another City far away that bred such men, but there were others that whispered that he was a man who had deserted the Guides for a life of protection.

Whichever was the right answer, there was a great visible mystery about him. For Ankar Moor's head was completely encased in a great and frightening mask of leather, with just two slits for his burning black eyes and another where a normal man would have his mouth. Again rumour was the only guide, but it was said that Ankar Moor's face had been destroyed in a great battle and was too frightening to look upon. Whatever was the answer, the man was possessed of a great intelligence and power.

As they strode towards the closed door, Ankar Moor spoke to his master, his rasping voice seeming to come through the slit from a depth greater than his own body, perhaps from the bowels of the earth itself:

'The plans move forward, My Lord. I will order the beginning of the training on the machines this afternoon.'

Zirpola tore himself away from the battle against the pain in his head and turned his watery blue eyes on his chief henchman:

'They must all be trained quickly.'

His voice was as deep and powerful as the other man's, giving no indication of the pain he was feeling.

Not for a second did the long strides of the three men falter as their conversation continued:

'I have given the orders that will take all my men away from their regular duties to make them available for their training. Is that acceptable to you, My Lord?'

It took a great effort for Ankar Moor to show deference to the other man in this way, for, in his heart of hearts, Ankar Moor deferred to no man; but his own ambitions made him wary for the moment.

'Most certainly it pleases me – we cannot afford to lose a single day. But tell me, how long do you estimate that it will take to train them to the proficiency that will be demanded of them?'

Polna, who was a simple man, and more pessimistic about the abilities of the clods that formed the main part of the force than was his superior, kept his silence as Ankar Moor boasted:

'I will make my men ride in one day. They will be expert in the use of the machines in one month.'

Zirpola gave a crooked smile that was totally lacking in warmth and humour. He put his head on one side, a sign of threat to those who knew his habits:

'I will hold you to that claim, Ankar Moor.'

'You will not be disappointed, My Lord.'

They marched the final distance in silence and it was then that chance struck, underlining the urgency of Zirpola's plans. The lights, until then so bright and steady, flickered for a moment, then died, throwing them and the whole City around them into total darkness. All three men stopped abruptly in their tracks.

Zirpola cursed, his voice suddenly thin with anger:

'Damn all scientists. That is the second time this week that the lights have gone out.'

It was Polna who gave patient reply. Polna always trusted and trustworthy, steady as a rock but lacking in the imagination that would have given him the burning ambition of his two companions:

'We will have to wait but a moment, My Lord, before the auxiliary power comes on.'

In the continuing darkness there came the rumble of a humourless chuckle from Ankar Moor:

'It is but a temporary thing. In a few months we will have the fuel for all the power we could ever hope to need.'

Zirpola echoed him:

'Yes, in just a few short months. But perhaps that is too long a time to wait. I wish we could make it sooner. I need it now if my plans are to be fulfilled.'

'Patience, My Lord, and all you desire will be yours.'

'Patience. Patience? Should I, the Lord Zirpola, the ruler of Helix, need to show patience? We must survive and grow stronger if we don't want to be overrun by those damned Mutants. They are the only ones who hold a real threat to our plans.'

Again Ankar Moor's voice rumbled out, confident and strong:

'The Mutants. They are no match for us in light or darkness. They will never overrun us, My Lord.'

'You make that boast when you cannot even keep the power going.' Even as the Lord Zirpola snarled out his reply, there was a flicker of light, another moment of gloom, then the lights came back on steadily, but at a lower level than before. The Lord Zirpola's face showed his dissatisfaction with the level of the power and he turned again to the tall commander of his Obedience force:

'So, the auxiliary power has not let us down this time. Now let us see if it will provide enough light for us to see these machines in which you place so much faith.'

Ankar Moor inclined his head and the three men resumed their march to the great door at the end of the long corridor. They halted a pace short and it was Polna who sprang forward to first tap out the special code on the light panel at its side before his huge strong hands gripped the wheel in the centre of the door, spinning it as easily as if it were a small child's toy, before opening the great door and standing aside for his masters to pass through.

He followed them and shut and secured the door behind them with a loud clang that echoed and re-echoed round the chamber into which they now passed. In the main part of the City, above, doors opened and closed by the mere use of palm or voice prints and simple light encoding. Only down here, in the lowest and most secure parts of the City, were these more complicated security measures in being.

The pair waited for him just inside the door and once he had stationed himself at the Lord Zirpola's left hand, they moved forward again. They were at the entrance to a huge workshop that had been planned and put in by the builders of the City, but, with the loss of technology and interest amongst the citizens over the centuries, the machines were now silent and unused. They passed down the centre of this chamber, past giant presses, lathes and all the other great machines from before the great disaster. Zirpola swung a hand in the direction of all this silent machinery:

'If only we had the science and knowledge still. We would be strong if we had the knowledge to work these things.'

'There are those who know, My Lord, those who still have the skills. But they use so much power. It was agreed not to use them any more in your great-grandfather's time, or so I have been told.'

Zirpola nodded.

'You speak truly. He was soft but he had great wisdom and foresight. But when we have the power, then we will need the skill to use these machines again.'

Polna said:

'There is Sarnoff. He can teach these skills.'

Ankar Moor said proudly:

'Sarnoff is leading our project now. He does have the skill.'

Lord Zirpola nodded. Sarnoff was the finest scientific brain now available to the City of Helix. In the past he had given all his skills merely to keep the power working, training technicians to work under him just as he had himself been trained. Perhaps his concentration on the great project had something to do with the repeated power failures over which his assistants seemed to have so little control.

'Yes, Sarnoff is a good and valuable man, but he is so slow.'

Ankar Moor boomed proudly:

'Yet he has told me this day that he has been able to assemble the first unit of the Death Machines from the parts already machined and stored away in the vaults. He also tells me that he and his men have inventoried enough parts to build up to one hundred more of them – and that, he estimates, is the maximum number we can fuel. He has done well enough so far, My Lord.'

He was puzzled by the shadow of anger that now passed across Zirpola's face. He was not to know that the Lord of Helix was fighting off yet another wave of pain.

'He seems to have done well enough for now. But let us see this great machine and decide.'

They had reached the far end of the huge silent workshop and stood now in front of a solid door as imposing as the first that had been opened for them to pass through. Once again, Polna went forward and went through the routine that opened the door, standing aside to let the others pass through before closing it again. They found themselves at once in another workshop, but one filled with activity. Ankar Moor, whose hearing was more acute than the others', heard Sarnoff's voice.

'Be quick. They are coming.'

There was more light in this shop than outside and Zirpola screwed up his eyes as he watched the activity before him.

He was standing at the entrance to a vast assembly shop. Even as he watched, two pairs of strong, trained hands were lifting up a huge rubberised tyre, attached to a gleaming chrome-spoked wheel, into its position on the front of the telescopic air-spring forks of the front of a gleaming black and silvered motor-cycle. The cycle was of the type that had been specially developed and built for the Combat Rangers of the third world war, some nine hundred years before.

Almost a thousand years of undisturbed storage had done nothing to dull the impressive look of the machine as it hung suspended in mid-air from its assembly carriage.

The same two overalled men, Sarnoff's assistants, their whites smeared with oil from their work, tightened the bolts on each side of the forks that held the huge wheel in place. As the Lord Zirpola stared at it, transfixed, it seemed to hang free in the air like a great flashing jewel on some huge metallic necklace. The strong hands spun the wheel to test it and it rotated freely in the air, sparkling in the artificial light like a moving diamond.

Now Sarnoff stepped forward to inspect the machine. His voice had the same tone as Ankar Moor had heard when they entered:

'Good, it is finished. Now stand out of the way.'

The two technicians immediately backed off and the wheel was left to spin unattended. Only when it had come to a natural halt did the Lord Zirpola step forward, his two companions following him, the door clanging shut behind them.

He walked straight forward, right up to the suspended machine, until it was directly above him and he was able to look up at it, much in the same way as Sir Galahad might have done during his vision of the Holy Grail or Arthur when he saw the great sword Excalibur for the first time, according to the ancient legends. To him this vision was every bit as powerful.

'It is beautiful.'

The other occupants of the room merely stood and watched him. It was Sarnoff who finally stepped forward, slightly impatient at this interruption to his work.

His face still held traces of youth, but Sarnoff was almost completely bald, a phenomenon that the people of the City put down to his great brain power, put to the use of the magic of the technology that was a closed book to most of them. In truth, his brain had never been stretched and his own opinion was that his hair had receded out of sheer boredom. A fastidious man, he regarded himself as a scientific genius and, though he would never give vent to such an opinion, he believed he was cleverer than even the Lord Zirpola himself. His whole life had been dedicated to keeping the machines that powered the city going and he was not surprised at the power cuts, which he put down as a result of his having to leave his post to blundering assistants. He now sighed his effete little sigh.

'Yes, My Lord, it does look rather nice, doesn't it?'

The looks he received both from the Lord Zirpola and from Ankar Moor told him that his opinion was not as enthusiastic as it might have been, and he recovered himself with his quick wits, going straight into a lecture, rather like a successful and confident salesman discussing his latest sure-fire product.

'It is powered by a single-cylinder, two-stroke, four-hundred-and-fifty cubic centimetre engine. Flat out, it will produce over one hundred horse power at about eleven thousand revolutions per minute. It has a top speed of well over a hundred odd miles an hour and, with the special mixed fuel I have prepared, it has a maximum cruising range of approximately six hundred miles with the new enlarged tanks.'

He paused, suddenly aware that he might have given his visitors more information than they could absorb in one bite, but they seemed to be merely waiting for him to go on. Now he really had to feign enthusiasm, for he mistrusted and abhorred weapons of destruction and these were the special feature of the machine. He pointed up to the front and then the rear of the great machine.

'As you can see, it carries four omni-directional anti-matter blaster bulbs, two fore and two aft.'

He let his hand drop to his side before glancing first at the frightening mask of Ankar Moor, then at the bland face of Polna, but their eyes told him nothing. He was not sure whether or not they were impressed.

As for the Lord Zirpola, he continued for the moment to contemplate the sparkling machine above his head, wrapped in his own thoughts. At last he dragged his watery blue eyes away and looked at the scientist.

'You have served me well, Sarnoff – very well. You will be rewarded substantially for this service.'

Almost purring with pride at the compliment, a rare occurrence from the Lord of Helix, Sarnoff puffed out his chest while blushing with an almost girlish modesty.

'Our ancestors designed and planned these machines, My Lord. I have only been the instrument of its assembly.'

Lord Zirpola hardly heard him as he reached out with a talon-like pale hand and set the front wheel of the great monster of death spinning round once more. After a moment of further contemplation, he reached up again and stopped the wheel, so that the machine merely swung from its assembly carriage.

'Amazing . . . Beautiful.'

Sarnoff relaxed inwardly. He had been a witness to too many of the Lord Zirpola's sudden changes of mood from sunshine to anger to be entirely at ease in his presence and he had been mortally afraid of failure when he had taken this assignment. He wished he were alongside his two assistants who were almost visibly cowering against the far wall, away from the machine and their lord and master. Terror was a common emotion amongst those who had to come into contact with the Lord of Helix, the man who had the power of life and death over everyone in the City.

Zirpola looked away from the machine abruptly and turned to Sarnoff, snapping out:

'How does it go? Can you start it for me?'

Sarnoff bowed low.

'Certainly, My Lord.'

He flicked his fingers and, in spite of their fear, the two assistants came forward at the run.

'Lower it. Be careful.'

The two men went over to where the assembly-line chain was tied off. They unwound it and lowered the cycle slowly so that the wheels came into contact with the floor of the assembly room, before they tied it off again, still holding the machine up but making it look as if it was balanced only on its wheels.

A moment later, Zirpola lifted his robe out of the way and bravely swung his thin leg over the wide saddle until he was straddling the machine. Ankar Moor took a pace forward as if suddenly alarmed.

'Take care, My Lord.'

Zirpola looked at him.

'It is only a machine, Ankar Moor. There is nothing that I should fear from it.'

He looked pleased that the other man had shown caution and Ankar Moor stood back again, satisfied at the reaction that his apparent concern had produced. There was no better way to flatter the old fool and keep him sweet than this. At his side, Polna kept a straight face with a great effort. He took some joy in seeing his superior snubbed from time to time. He knew Ankar Moor better than most and was mortally afraid of him.

Sarnoff now stepped forward, kneading his hands nervously, like a salesman whose product is being tested. Zirpola said to him, 'Now you may start it for me.'

Sarnoff minced slowly round the rear of the machine until he was leaning in from the right-hand side. His assistants had backed away again, one of them to one side, one against the wall directly in front of the machine. Sarnoff pointed at the left-hand grip.

'My Lord, you will find an extension in the left handle. Please pull it out as far as it will go.'

As the Lord of Helix obeyed this instruction from his servant, Sarnoff reached forward and pressed down a little red button that was on the top of the right handle of the machine. There was a cough, a moment of silence while Sarnoff's blood froze in fear. A second later he relaxed again and even Ankar Moor involuntarily stepped back a pace as the engine caught and screamed into life.

Sarnoff screwed up his face at the noise, then reached across and pushed the left extension in a short way, reducing the roar of the motor which was echoing and re-echoing round the enclosed space with an almost unbearable noise, making even Ankar Moor fight to stop putting his hands to his ears. He knew that he must fight against the impulse as he saw that the Lord Zirpola was sitting calmly in the middle of the whirlwind of sound.

As for Zirpola himself, he could hardly hear the noise, but was revelling in the throb of sheer physical power as it coursed up through him from the engine of the machine.

Another few moments passed as the cycle revved again and Sarnoff leaned over once more to push the choke in a little further, thus taking pressure off the engine of the machine, which was screeching at almost full power. Zirpola waved him contemptuously aside, then shouted:

'Now show me how it fires.'

Sarnoff hesitated for only a fraction of a second, but the look in his master's eye told him that the hesitation had not gone unnoticed and would be long remembered. It had been a mistake, the wrong thing to do. Reluctantly he pointed to two buttons that were also set in the right handle of the machine, just forward from the grip. Each had an arrow on, one pointing forward, the other to the rear.

'Those are the buttons. Just there by the grip – My Lord!'

But the warning stuck in his throat, too late. Zirpola was laughing as he pressed the button that activated the forward pod firing mechanism.

At once the assembly room was filled with an almighty and unexpected roar, followed by a flash of brilliant green light, like those that came from the anti-matter blasters that all the Enforcers carried, but a hundred times more intense. This flash resolved itself into a pair of twin beams that seemed to come out of the machine itself.

The hapless Peterson, the larger and older of Sarnoff's two assistants, was the man standing directly in front of the machine. He was caught in the beams, thrown back against the wall of the shop and, almost in the instant that his body smacked against the wall, his blood-curdling scream was cut off in mid-flow as he abruptly disintegrated in the air, leaving no trace of his presence, his atoms scattered through time and space for all eternity. At the same time, the end wall showed a blackened scorch mark where the beam had hit it after dissolving the ill-fated man.

Zirpola took his finger off the button and the green beam disappeared.

For a moment, none of the other occupants of the assembly shop moved, so stunned were they by the power, as well as the cruel waste, of what they had just witnessed. In the end, the effete Sarnoff was the first to come to his senses and make a move. He sprang forward and abruptly switched off the machine. The roaring noise was replaced by a deathly silence as he glared at the Lord Zirpola, who ignored the hatred in his stare. Remorse was for lesser mortals, not for the Lord of Helix. He merely threw back his head and laughed with a joyous laughter such as no man present could remember hearing from him for many years. Recovering himself at last, he dismounted, clearly still overjoyed by the demonstration he had activated and drunk with the feeling of power that the wanton destruction of another human being had given him. The power of life and death is a heady wine to a man of ambition and ruthless cast of mind.

Now, the hand that had so recently dealt out this destruction to another human being rose to smite Sarnoff on the back, a hearty blow of congratulation that made the scientist cough in pain.

'Well done indeed. That is a wonderful and incredible machine, the Death Machine is well named.'

He strode over and stood in front of Ankar Moor, whose dark eyes blazed through the slits in the mask that gave away no trace of the reactions of the man beneath it.

'You were right, Ankar Moor. You serve me well and faithfully.'

The Enforcer leader bowed low.

'Is it not as it was told to you, My Lord?'

'It is, it is indeed.'

'And if this is the power of one machine, think what will be the power of one hundred.'

Zirpola rubbed his hands together.

'What indeed? We will be truly invincible. Our plans will work, Triton will surely fall to us.'

Behind them Sarnoff almost gasped out loud in surprise. Up until that moment he had no inkling of the reason why he had been asked to put the machine together, along with an inventory as to how many more could be built and sustained. He had merely assumed it to be a plan for making the annual Death Sport even more complicated than usual this year. He cried out, unable to do anything but protest.

'But, My Lord, that would mean war.'

Ankar Moor's eyes blazed hatred and Polna's face looked grim, but Sarnoff was too alarmed to care. Zirpola turned calmly to face him.

'So? What if it does?'

Sarnoff quailed before his stare but tried to ignore it. He felt it was important that he protest.

'But Triton is in the Federation, My Lord, and they have outlawed war.'

Zirpola was quiet, almost conciliatory.

'And we, my dear Sarnoff, are not within the Federation. And why not? Because Triton and the other Cities have kept us out. They mean to deprive us of fuel and let us die so that we may be overrun by the Mutants. That is why I need the Death Machines, that is why I must fight. Do you understand?'

Sarnoff did not understand. He knew that Zirpola had deliberately kept the City outside the Federation, but good sense was beginning to reassert itself and he realised that it would be unwise for him to argue further – perhaps he had gone too far already.

'I understand, Lord.'

Zirpola nodded, apparently satisfied.

'You should be very proud, Sarnoff, you have served us by doing a magnificent job. Believe me, your contribution will not go unrewarded when we have triumphed. I expect you to start work assembling the other machines right away and that they will be as successful as the first.'

He bowed in a necessary show of humility.

'Yes, My Lord. You need have no fears. It will be done as you ask.'

'Thank you.'

Zirpola turned on his heel and, pulling his cloak round him, he began to stride back to the door, beckoning to both Polna and Ankar Moor to follow him. They fell in beside him and he halted immediately as some afterthought seemed to occur to him. He turned again.

'Just one thing?'

'Yes, My Lord?' Sarnoff was thoroughly frightened now.

'In leaving to you the work of assembly, I give you authorisation to draw as many men as you will need from the security pool to carry it out. None of the civilians must know about these machines until we are ready.'

'None shall be told from these lips, My Lord.'

'Good.' Zirpola nodded, then something else seemed to occur to him.

'I am sorry to have deprived you of one of your close assistants. I will of course see that his family receive the appropriate medals and commendations. He was not crucially important, he could be spared by you, couldn't he?'

Sarnoff thrust aside his real feelings. He felt he had already made enough mistakes for one day.

'He could be spared easily enough, My Lord. As a matter of fact, he was a frightful bore.'

'Then I have done you a service. Good day.'

Zirpola turned away again. A moment later, Polna was closing the door on the three of them. The noise of it echoed and re-echoed round the chamber.

Only after a moment of silence was Sarnoff galvanised into life. He found his remaining assistant trembling at his side.

'We must get to work on our preparations right away.'

'But what about Peterson?'

Sarnoff shrugged. There was really nothing he could do. The man had been scattered into atoms. For their own good, both men should now put the memory out of their minds. Sarnoff mouthed the usual formula, which he did not believe and which he knew the other man would not.

'He died for the greater glory of the City of Helix and our Lord and Master, the Lord Zirpola. There is no greater cause in which to die. Now give me that damned inventory and get back to your work. We have been charged with a great task and time is short.'

The man hurried away and Sarnoff sat down to rest. He felt nauseous at what he had just done, but a man must survive.

The Lord Zirpola and Ankar Moor emerged into the corridor from the machine shop and waited for Polna to close and lock the outer door. Then, and only then, did they speak. It was Ankar Moor who broke the silence.

'You would reward that man – that Sarnoff – who seeks to question you and your plans. I would kill him for his impertinence.'

Zirpola chuckled.

'So you would. You are too impetuous. I told Sarnoff he would receive his just reward when the battle was over and by then we will have no further need of him.'

'So death will be his reward.'

'Precisely.'

Ankar Moor chuckled as they started their return journey along the corridor. The light once more hurt Zirpola's eyes but he was less bothered than pleased that, while they had been with Sarnoff, the main power had been switched on again.

'And when can we move?'

Ankar Moor hesitated only for a moment.

'For the first phase? In just a few days, once Sarnoff has assembled enough machines for the task.'

Zirpola gave out his humourless laugh.

'And then you hope your machines will give your men the capability of capturing some of the Guides. I must say, you have greater faith in their powers than I do. You are a vain man, Ankar Moor.'

Had it not been for the mask, the ruler of Helix could have seen the livid red marks of anger that welled up on the remains of Ankar Moor's destroyed face, but the man's voice was soft when he replied. He was practiced at masking his arrogance and anger.

'I intend that Polna and I will train and supervise a group ourselves. Also, we will supervise the capture.'

Zirpola nodded.

'That would seem a good plan. After all, it is said you know the ways of the Guides, therefore you should be able to think ahead of them in a fight.'

The big man did not reply. His ancestry was something about which he had never spoken, not even to Zirpola. Normally the latter respected his silence and never referred to it. Today seemed an exception.

If he thought that Zirpola fell silent for that reason, he was much mistaken. The Lord of Helix felt the pain coming over his head again in crashing waves and he longed to get back to his private quarters in the highest part of the City, so that he would be alone to seek relief from the torture that assailed him.

The trio reached the elevator bank in silence and travelled up in the express elevator, using the over-rider that would not allow any other official to stop it on an intermediate level while the Lord of Helix was riding in it. Only officials were allowed to use the elevators these days. It was a way of conserving power, as well as a useful way in which the Enforcers might control the civilian population of Helix to better effect than formerly.

The lift doors opened and deposited him outside the door of his office and private quarters. The two men got out of the elevator with him, but he turned to them quickly, willing himself to remain upright, his brow clear of any indication of the pain he felt.

'Both of you have much work to accomplish. I will summon you to confer later, Ankar Moor.'

A moment of hesitation at this abrupt dismissal, then the two men bowed and returned to the elevator. Dizziness was making their master's head spin, but he controlled the feeling until he had got inside his own door and it had slid shut and locked behind him.

Only then did he give way to his feelings, falling to his knees with an animal cry of pain, before lying flat and pressing his raging forehead against the cold marble floor in an effort to find relief.

In a few minutes the pain had receded and he raised himself up again to go on wobbling legs to the big chair behind his desk. There was still much to do, much planning and calculation, now that the assembly of the first of the Death Machines had placed in his hand the key he needed to accomplish his ambition: the conquest of the world.

CHAPTER TWO

Day was coming again to the devastated face of the earth. The dark and ever-changing shapes of the mountains, dunes and plateaux were slowly turned from black to a ravishing kaleidoscope of golds and browns by the first rays of the rising sun. It moved up into a pale sky that gradually darkened to a bright blue like a great fireball rising over a ravished landscape.

High above, a few wisps of cloud from some polluted sea straggled across the lightening sky, but they were soon burned away by the heat of the sun so that nothing stood between the great orb and the land it would bake hard and dusty until evening. The sun was hardly up over the horizon before the baking began.

Even so, it was not a heat that promoted stillness. Here and there little eddies of sand were thrown up by the whispers of gentle wind that passed across the surface of the barren land.

Floating too, on that wind, came the faintest of sounds, the sound of two metal objects slapping together, a sound that told of some human movement in the distance. It was a sound that would not be picked up by the normal human ear, but to the man who rode straightbacked across the plateau towards the defile that led down to the plain below, it came as loudly as if the maker of it had been in sight – and it was a sound that meant danger to him. A sound that meant, in spite of the desolation and emptiness all around him, he was not alone.

Cautiously, Kaz Oshay reined in the magnificent grey stallion on which he rode and which men said was one with its master, sitting quite still on its back for a moment as he tried to locate the direction and source of the sound. He delved into his full memory to detect where and when, if ever, he had heard it before.

Even among the Range Guides, the name of Kaz Oshay, son of Oshay, was one that was respected and revered. In this band of loners, these warriors apart, riding proud in a wild land, he seemed more apart, purer by lack of contact with even his fellow Guides. A self-reliant man, a special one even amongst the positive Mutants that made up his kind, the descendants of the brave Commando Rangers of so long ago. A dangerous man.

He located the sound very quickly. It came from ahead and out of sight. From somewhere in the ravine towards which he was making, the defile that led to the plain below.

Men were moving down there and the slap of metal against metal meant that they were armed. Perhaps they were there innocently, but perhaps they were planning to lie in wait for him. If so, then their carelessness had condemned them to death.

Now his horse too heard the sound and whinnied softly as if in alarm, worried by its strangeness. He leaned forward and put a gentle hand on the creature's muzzle to calm it and, trustful of its master, it became silent.

In the rocks above the ravine floor, the three Obedience Enforcers whom Kaz Oshay had heard moved slowly forward, seeking good and hidden positions, each of them grasping a strangely-shaped dart gun in one hand. The spare darts were enclosed in leather pouches that hung from their belts and these also held their anti-matter blasters. The darts slapping together as they moved forward was the faint sound that the Guide had heard, a noise hardly noticeable even to the men themselves. Each man was dressed in the skin-fitting dark uniform that distinguished the Enforcers, though without the flashes that were on Polna's arm. Each man also had a hood-like helmet over his head for protection both from attack and from the deepening heat of the sun.

The men reached a satisfactory position and the sounds

ceased, but Kaz Oshay remained, for the moment, quite still. He knew that he had heard the sound of weapons, but his tactics would depend a great deal on whether his ambushers were men or Mutants. His great horse reared suddenly and snorted, the scent of strange life brought suddenly to his nostrils by a change in the limpid breeze.

Kaz Oshay was wearing a garment that was usual among the Guides, similar to the old jallaba worn in the deserts in the days long before the great catastrophe. Now he pulled the hood up over his wild mane of hair so it covered his proud, lean face and, careful to look casual, as if he had no clue of the impending ambush, he scanned the bleak sandstone cliffs to his left. But there seemed to be nothing, no one waiting for him above the gully.

He spoke softly to himself in the well-remembered words from the rules of the code by which the Guides lived:

'Surprise is a double-edged sword.'

As he spoke, his hand went down to touch the handle of his Whistler, concealed under the jallaba, as if wishing himself luck in the fight for which his mind was now preparing him. That too was part of the code; never run from a fight; never hide from your enemies.

The handle of the clear diamond-bladed sword felt good to the touch. It was shaped as the ancient Samurai swords of the Japanese warriors had been in earlier days, only slightly wider and sharper, light as a feather yet harder than steel, made from the fused carbon that had been left in the wake of the nuclear holocaust that had enveloped the Earth all those centuries before.

Only the Guides had such weapons. Only the Guides had the power to learn the skills needed to wield such weapons, with the great high-pitched scream they made as they slashed through the air.

Each moment of his stillness was bringing more information to Kaz Oshay, information that could be useful to him in the fight that was to come. Now sounds that came from other directions told him that, in spite of the fact that he could not see them, the three men below him were not the only ones who were laying in wait. It was promising to be a day of great challenge.

He was strong as any three Statemen, more agile than any man could possibly be, faster of reflex, with the speed and reactions of a startled animal, able to see as far as the great eagles themselves, to smell and hear much better than any animal that had ever wandered across the face of the earth.

Very tall and almost wand-like in his slimness, he was also incredibly hard, even for a Guide, a sullen and angry member of his kind, more fiercely dedicated to his independence than any other Guide had ever been.

A rugged individual, a supreme loner amongst loners, he nevertheless lived entirely in honour of the code of the Guides; following completely their personal system of ethics and guiding mythology and philosophy, which stress, for those who have the secret, the virtues of self-control, humility, responsibility and self-reliance.

Like all the Guides, he had first learnt the philosophy and had become steeped in it at his mother's knee, and now he lived almost entirely in the wilds, having little need to come into contact with other Guides or Statemen as he travelled his nomadic lonely path.

The only time he had dealings with the outside world was in warding off attacks by wandering bands of the Mutants or when, very rarely, he agreed to act as a guard and guide for one of the caravans of traders travelling from one great domed City to another across the surface of the wilderness.

But there was something even more special and apart about Kaz Oshay, something else that separated him from the others of his kind. For them, danger was a duty to be borne, but to Kaz Oshay danger was a passion to be revelled in, a trait that was not entirely in keeping with the virtue of humility that the code had taught him.

Completely prepared to die for his faith and his teachings, he was absolutely without fear.

To his right, bluffs led to a higher plateau than the one on which he now stood and he reined in to glance as casually in that direction as he had to the left.

This time his caution was rewarded. He caught a glimpse of light from high up on the bluffs, as something metallic was reflected by the sun. A moment later it was gone but the flash had been enough to tell him that he was being watched from there.

High up on the bluffs, Ankar Moor, realising that the glass had reflected the light, lowered his special field binoculars and allowed himself the luxury of a short curse. He knew that the instant's carelessness had been enough, that the Guide below him would have spotted the signal. Over his head and mask he was wearing a helmet similar to that of his men, which, combined with the mask, made him feel hot and uncomfortable under the broiling sun. Still, he could not remove it for the moment, for, attached to it by a thin wire, were special headphones and a microphone that hung before his mouth slit. As he saw the Guide starting to move forward, he whispered into the communicator:

'Be still. Do not move. He is coming. When he enters the canyon do not go to him, let him come to you.'

He waited until he had heard the confirmation of his orders back over the headphones, then raised the field glasses again and peered down to the mouth of the ravine. As he did so, Kaz Oshay began to move forward and was soon entering his line of sight. He watched until the Guide had disappeared out of sight and was well on his way to the trap that had been laid for him. From now on, Ankar Moor would only be able to see a part of the ravine and would not be able to direct operations entirely. He could only pray that his men would be fast and proficient. If they were not, it would mean death for them.

On the plain below was hidden his trump card – four men on Death Machines. He hoped he would not need to use them, but they were there just in case.

Kaz Oshay moved with infinite slowness, deeper and deeper into the ravine, aware of what lay in wait for him and that his progress had been spied out from above. In his mind floated the words of the code:

'If there are many, put your feet on the ground. Be ever more sure and manoeuvreable.'

As he remembered this, he thought for a moment of his mother who had taught the words to him and wondered for a moment where she was now. But he put the thought out of his mind quickly. He was a man now and he was his own master.

It was not yet quite time to leave his mount, but that moment would come quite soon. He could do so only when he was not being observed by the man up on the bluffs. He had pinpointed his position and knew just when that moment would come.

Ahead of him now was an overhanging point of rock. Beyond it, he knew that he would be out of sight. If he left his horse there and let it go on he would be able to catch up with it again upon the open plain. Till then, he would be on his own. He had worked out, too, that it was men who waited for him. No Mutants would have had the power or brains to organise an ambush of this kind.

He reached the overhanging point of rock and, the instant he had passed beneath it, slipped from the back of the great grey stallion. For a moment the animal stood still, whinnying, confused and frightened by the sudden departure of his master and unsure whether to move or stand still. Kaz Oshay gave him a hard slap on the rump which made him move forward, down the defile and around a large rock slide that would lead through the narrower part of the ravine where the men would be lying in ambush.

He watched the horse move forward for a moment, then ran forward himself on soundless feet to the bottom of the slide, thence up the slide, without the displacement of a single stone, so fleet of foot was he, until he was on the edge of the cliff above the ravine itself.

His horse had now disappeared, even from his own sight, as he spotted the three men below him now, farther down the ravine in their ambush positions. He allowed himself the unwonted luxury of a small smile, knowing that he would surprise them more than they had intended to surprise him. He crouched down, coiling himself up like a human spring, then leapt forward and down, out into the space above his ambushers.

The rushing wind of his fall jerked the hood back from his face and allowed his great mane of hair and shaggy beard to fly free in the wind that his dive had created. His eyes were on fire with the light of the battle that was to come and, with his teeth bared, the cry of a Guide warrior welled up from deep within his very soul as he landed with an easy grace in the midst of the surprised men.

There was no single moment of hesitation in his smooth and fluid movements. He sprang up the moment he landed and whirled round, drawing his Whistler in one graceful ballet of movement. Before any of the three Enforcers could react enough to raise their dart guns, the great sword had done its charnel work. All that the men heard was the whistle of the great sword and then their screams of death were carried away through the hot air, up the bluff to where Ankar Moor could only wait in frustrated ignorance of the success or failure of his ambush.

Kaz Oshay swung round again, ready to leap on his horse

as it rounded the bend, but another sound made him turn and this time he saw five more men dressed in the black uniforms of the Enforcers charging up the base of the ravine, the same strange weapons in their hands, poised at the ready to fire at him.

As he took a stance to wait for them, another lesson of the code sprang into his mind:

'It is only the fool who rushes into sacrifice.'

As they ran towards him, the men raised their weapons and fired, making him weave and dodge, as the strange little darts that they fired zipped past him to embed themselves uselessly in the sandstone wall of the gully. Then, as they came close to him, he made a leap that seemed to defy gravity itself, pushing himself upwards until he landed atop one of the rocky outcrops. Two similar jumps took him into the labyrinth of crags and gullies that were in the rocks above.

Once he was assured of his safety, after the jumps had taken him out of reach of his enemies, he replaced the Whistler in its scabbard and drew the anti-matter gun he kept at his belt. This was no time for close hand-to-hand combat, not until he understood the purpose of the strange weapons with which his enemies were attacking him.

He crouched down, listening to their movements as they tried to scale the rocks after him, climbing cautiously as they searched among the outcroppings. If his ears did not deceive him, the five he had seen had been joined by more enemies. If so, he was flattered that his enemies should think of him as so hard a man to take. The odds against him were growing and he readied himself for the fray:

'Be calm, be patient. All anger is held inside you.'

He remained where he was for the moment, perfectly still, his mind repeating the same instructions over and over again. From one corner of his eye he caught the sign of a slight movement down a nearby gully in the rock. He crouched down, spinning round in that direction and levelled the anti-matter blaster as his enemy came into cautious view, his own dart weapon at the ready.

Kaz fired and the Enforcer's scream died in his throat as he was blasted up off the rock and out of existence in this world. Another sound came from behind him and he spun round again. Another shot and one more of his enemies was floating, atomised, through space for eternity.

But his defence had given away his position. The others would be able to locate him now, perhaps pin him down. He did not feel that he was in an easily defensible position. He ran down the gully that his first enemy had come up and jumped up and out into space, landing like a cat further down the ravine, all the time making towards the plain where his stallion would be waiting for him, now behind a lower crag, and, for the moment, relatively safe from his enemies.

Then he spotted a widening fissure in the rocks close to him and he ducked quickly down it and moved forward, running in parallel with the gully. In his mind there echoed more teaching from the code:

'Like the sand in the wind, keep moving, always keep moving.'

High on the ridges above, safely away from the disastrous line of battle, Ankar Moor was becoming impatient and angry. He was frustrated by being able to follow so little of the action below, but he had seen and heard enough to understand that his men were definitely on the losing side so far and he was cold with impotent rage that all his training still left them helpless against one lone man.

He was close to shrieking out his rage as he spoke into the small microphone suspended above the mouth slit in his mask:

'Now flush him out carefully. Do not charge him. If you charge in there after him, then you haven't a chance. The only way to get him there is to kill him and I want him alive.'

He put the special field glasses back to his eye slits but Kaz Oshay was not in his line of vision.

The hunted man still moved cautiously forward, his back pressed against the solid crag, moving towards a point where the fissure split into two. That junction would be his point of decision. He halted in his progress, silent, his breathing shallow so as not to give him away. Without looking he was aware that a man was moving above him, but, as he made a sudden glance upwards, gun at the ready, he saw that the man could not yet see him or he the man. For the moment he would be safe if he continued his forward progress with the same caution that he had shown before.

He started to carry out this plan, then froze again as an Enforcer appeared at the cleft in the fissure ahead of him.

There was an agonising moment of indecision, but Kaz knew that he must fire or be lost, the fight over, even though it would alert the man above him. He raised his weapon, keeping himself ready to spring. The Enforcer disappeared before he had seen the Guide, leaving just the remains of his scream of death hanging in the air.

From above, the other man cried out and leapt down towards him. Kaz Oshay swivelled round, crouched down on one knee and just managed to avoid the dart the man fired. He raised his own weapon and the man was vaporised before he hit the ground.

Now Kaz moved quickly forward to the cleft in the fissure. Ahead and below was the open ground of the plain and he was already able to see his proud grey stallion waiting for him, some distance out in the plain, on the flat away from the mouth of the canyon.

Behind him came the sounds of renewed pursuit and it took him no time at all to make his decision:

'Until a better place, a better time . . .'

With that thought from the code in his head, he ran forward and down, going out into the open and towards his waiting stallion. The men who were following him and trying to flush him out spotted him at once and he was forced to zig-zag, avoiding a hail of the deadly darts as he went swiftly towards the animal.

At last he was crossing the final piece of open ground, far ahead of them. And then tragedy struck. One of the Enforcers drew his anti-matter blaster and the proud beast suddenly reared on its hind legs, whinnied loudly, then disappeared forever from the solid world.

There was no time for sadness or regret in the mind of Kaz Oshay as he saw his only friend and trusted companion blasted into eternity. The only thought he could afford to have now was for his own safety. He continued his zig-zag run past the point where the animal had been only seconds before.

High on the crags, Ankar Moor could see the object of his hunt now. He stood up out of cover and shouted into the microphone:

'Machines, start up. Come out and take him now.'

Even at this great distance, Kaz Oshay caught the echo of the shouted words in his ear and paused for a second: Machines? It was not a word he knew in the world of freedom and movement. The word itself he had heard before, but only in connection with the running of the Cities. Out here, it was not a word that had any meaning.

And then there came a great roar of sound and out from their hiding place came the Enforcers astride the great gleaming Death Machines that Sarnoff had built. The machines roared and surged forward, great roaring iron horses that Kaz Oshay had never seen the like of before, coming straight towards him, the men aboard them holding the same guns his former adversaries had fired.

Even as he stared at them in frozen amazement, the machines roared up the brow of a small hillock close to him and took to the air for a moment before landing and roaring forward again.

Suddenly, he was galvanised into action. He made a last minute desperate leap to pass over them, a greater leap than he had ever made before under the pressure of battle. But his reactions were just too late. The men raised their guns and fired at the swiftly ascending figure of their prey. This time their darts found their target and Kaz was enveloped in immediate unconsciousness, falling back down on to the sand.

As the Enforcers who were still left alive after their encounter in the gully raced up, their weapons at the ready, the four on the Death Machines roared to a halt, surrounding the inert form of their enemy.

An Enforcer sergeant dismounted from his huge metal steed and gave a quick order. At once, two of the survivors of the foot battle picked up Kaz Oshay the Guide and, carrying him gently, for they had orders not to damage him if it could be avoided, deposited him on the rear of one of the Death Machines, tying him down like a hunted and killed animal.

Only when this was done did the sergeant pay attention to the voice that was roaring into his transceiver and spoke into his own microphone:

'Yes, Sir.'

Ankar Moor was anxiously awaiting a report of success or failure:

'You've got him?'

'Yes, Sir, strapped down now, Sir.'

Ankar Moor was satisfied by the capture but not by the manner in which it had been accomplished:

'That was a miserable performance. How many of our men are lost?'

The sergeant made a quick tally:

'Seven, Sir.'

The leader was contemptuous:

'You are useless to me.'

The sergeant was used to such talk:

'Yes, Sir.'

But Ankar Moor had already broken off the transmission. The sergeant, relieved that he was not in for a longer roasting, rapped out his orders to the survivors. Hastily the Enforcers who were on foot took up passenger positions on the Death Machines and, when they were aboard, the journey back to their base at Helix City began.

High above them, Ankar Moor mounted his own machine. He wanted to be back in the City before any of the Guides were brought in. It had been a poor morning's work and he could only hope that Polna and the other group who had gone out were going to have better luck. At least he had the satisfaction of not having lost any of the machines. They were in short supply and more valuable than men at the moment.

He had given Polna an easier assignment that his own. A trade caravan had left Helix City that morning for the lengthy journey to Triton. He knew that, just outside the area of the domes, the caravan would be joined by two Guides who had agreed to guard the traders on their journey. Perhaps Polna had already overtaken the column and captured it. He hoped and prayed so. He needed as many of the Guides as he could get for the next phase in the plan he and the Lord Zirpola had conceived.

Still, the man they had captured had been strong and good. He would make a good victim for the Death Sport games.

The column that formed the caravan en route to Triton was moving slowly down the bed of a wide canyon that went past the great cliff caves where many hundreds of the Mutants were reputed to dwell. It was a nerve-racking part of the journey. There were about twenty Statemen making the trip, each dressed in the jallaba-like robe that was the best wear for travel through the desert, offering as it did the best protection from the broiling sun. For many of the travellers, it was the first time they had ever left the confines of their home City and they were nervous of everything they saw in this vast, spacious world outside.

The column was going forward in silence, each man and woman in it watching the cave openings in the cliffs for any sign of a Mutant or a group who might attack them. Only two members of the column sat erect, proud and unafraid, on their magnificent stallions. One rode at the head of the column, the other brought up the rear. Both were Ranger Guides – and both were women. Their cloaks were white and they wore them with the hoods up.

Riding at the head of the column, tense in spite of her impression of calm as she watched the cliffs, for she knew that the Mutants were watching them, was Deneer. She was a tall, powerful, straight-backed young woman, with dark piercing eyes. Impatient that her line of vision was impaired by the hood, she let it fall back and shook out her proud cascade of blonde hair. She had a dazzling beauty.

At once there came to her a faint and strange sound that had been muffled by the folds of the cloak. It was a sound that none of the City Statemen in the party could yet hear, a far off whine, a sound that she could not remember ever having heard before.

Her first reaction was to glance up at the sky to see if she could detect any other sign of the coming of a Flash Wind, with the cloud of death it carried with it; that would mean the party would have to shelter by the cliffs, a dangerous situation with the Mutants about. There was no other sign that she could discern, but in that moment the sound became loud enough for her to be able to pinpoint its direction. Whatever threat it brought with it was coming at them from the rear of the column.

She lifted herself up in the saddle and turned to look towards the rear of the column and Adriann, the Guide who was escorting the column with her. Tall and rail-thin, Adriann locked eyes with her fellow Guide, took the message from her and shook her head imperceptibly to show that she was also unable to place the sound except in direction, but agreed that it was a sign for danger. There was little out in the wastelands that could not be explained and was for good.

Adriann was older than her fellow Guide Deneer. She was also a mother and her first thought was for the young child who rode by her side on a small pony. The child was a blonde miniature of herself, destined to become a Guide in her own right one day, but for the moment just her mother's small child, as anxious and frightened as any young girl would be when hearing a strange sound she had never heard before.

Adriann felt her fear and leaned down to smile reassuringly at her:

'Karissa, it will be all right if you stay close to me.'

The little girl looked up at her mother with trusting eyes, then patted her pony's neck as a form of self-comfort, for she had seen the troubled look on the older woman's face.

At the head of the column, Deneer was still turned in the saddle, looking back hard down the canyon in the direction from which they had come. Abruptly, a decision taken, she wheeled her horse and trotted back down the line, her face a picture of calm assurance, as she rode by, to any of the Statemen who looked upon it. None of them could yet hear the strange sound and took nothing amiss. Their nervousness was still a concern for the possible threat from the cliffs.

She joined her fellow Guide at the rear of the column, smiling down at Karissa, who returned the smile shyly. As she came alongside, she pulled the jallaba aside a fraction to touch the hilt of her Whistler, as if just for luck, and Adriann returned the signal by doing the same. Karissa saw the action and knew what it meant, but her mother had assured her that everything would be well, so she maintained her lack of concern to all outward appearances.

Now the sound was loud enough for some of the Statemen to catch and those who heard it began turning their heads, then asking their neighbours to listen for it.

Deneer said:

'You do not recognise it?'

Adriann shook her head:

'No. But it is not of nature. Perhaps it is these strange machines of which we have heard rumour.'

Deneer nodded:

'That must be it. It must be a machine.'

The noise was getting closer with every second that passed. Now it was like the insistent buzzing of a bee. Soon, whatever danger it gave portent of would be in sight. Time enough then to decide what action to take. All they could do for the moment was wait.

Others were waiting to find the source of the sound and what it might mean to them. At the entrance to one of the larger caves, high up in the cliffs that overlooked the caravan route, other beings had heard the dull hum and wondered if it was to be a danger to them. The leader of the tribe of Mutants to whom these great caves were home lay in a hollow of wind-worn rock at the entrance to the cave, watching the caravan of Statemen below. It was a small group only, but to the men who watched it, it represented food and comfort for a long time. Some of the travellers looked distinctly plump even from this distance.

The Mutant glanced round at his followers, twittering at them in a strange high-pitched tone, making the reed-like sounds that are the main form of communication between such people. Some of them have brains that are whole enough to allow them folk-memories of language, but most do not. Their lives were, as they are now, short and unpleasant and there was no need for them to assimilate anything more complicated.

The leader held his entitlement by virtue of his size and strength. He was by far the largest of those who crowded at the cave entrance, almost human in looks, in fact. The others were misshapen in one way or another, many of them with the blue broken skin of the Mutants of the North. But there was one characteristic that was common to them all, and indeed to all Mutants that were ever seen then or now – their eyes, which bulged from their sockets like great, watery eggs. They also shared another peculiarity – the double row of razor-sharp teeth from which the poisonous saliva oozed constantly.

Being in a higher position than the caravan below, the leader was able to see the centre of the cause of the noise before those below. On the horizon there had appeared a large cloud of dust, which was moving steadily forward, as if hiding the source of the noise in its centre. If he was frightened, he was enough of a leader not to show it to his followers. He had already told them that it might be something they could add to their spoils and he repeated this opinion now.

Still straggling out behind the caravan, Adriann and Deneer were now able to see the dust cloud on the edge of the horizon, and, as they could see it, so could the Statemen, who spent more time turning in their saddles than looking to the front. Eventually, they ceased to move forward at all, but stood in small groups, resting on their reins and speculating between themselves as to what it could be that was after them.

One group was engaged in urgent discussion, the result of which was that the trader Bakkar, who was one of the plumpest and most prosperous-looking members of the party, took his horse out of the line and trotted it back to the two Guides. He reined in between them as they stared back at the gathering cloud of dust:

'We want to know. Are they Mutants?'

Deneer took a moment to withdraw her concentration from the approaching threat, then turned to glare at the questioner, the glint in her eyes making him quail:

'Get back with your own people.'

The man's face was pasty grey and damp with fear. Even so, he braced himself up enough to ask:

'Shouldn't we do something, not just stop here? Shouldn't we try to outrun them?'

Deneer realised that her first reaction had been unreasonable and toned down the glare. She often forgot that these were just ordinary mortals, motivated by selfishness and fear, not by the higher philosophy of the code that sustained the Guides. Her renewed answer was couched in softer tones, though just as firm in its resolve:

'No, we will not run. It will do no good. We will tell you what to do soon. Now rejoin the others.'

She turned back and concentrated on the ever-growing dust cloud. Bakkar paused for a second, then understood that this was the last word that he was going to get out of either of them. Reluctantly, he turned his horse and trotted back to join his fellow Statemen in the caravan, but not without glancing back again and again at the growing dust cloud. The noise from within it was getting louder by the second and was stoking a deeper fear in all who listened, except for the calm Guides.

He reined in next to Marcus Karl, one of the younger members of the party. It was not Marcus's first journey out of Helix. He had been to Triton before and now he was returning to be married. He even had a pass to make his home there. He was tall with a boyish handsome face and clear blue eyes, the physique and looks of a Guide rather than a Stateman. Now he asked:

'What did the Guides say?'

The fat man shrugged:

'You know what these Guides are like, so much with themselves all the time that they give away nothing. They would not tell me – but they're as worried about that cloud as we are. It must be Mutants and they must be going to attack. I suggested that we make a run for it, but the stuck-up cow wouldn't hear of it.'

Marcus sighed. He had only been a few hours in the company of Mr Bakkar, but already he had learnt that that was a few hours too many:

'We're just to wait then?'

'Wait? How can we? I say they're wrong. I say we run.'

Marcus shook his head and put a restraining hand on the man's arm:

'My father has often told me of the Guides; you must trust them without question in the wastelands. He swore that he would always trust one of their number with his life.'

The man snorted:

'Your father. What does he know? Why, he's not even allowed to leave the City.'

The rebuke was true enough, for Marcus Karl's father was an important man in the hierarchy of Helix. He was the leading doctor in the City, both in charge of the clinic and the consultant to the Lord Zirpola himself – not that there was apparently any work for him to do in this connection, for the Lord Zirpola was said never to have had a day of illness in his life. He was a strong man, a natural leader. He was above the need of a doctor. Nevertheless, Marcus's father was on permanent stand-by. That was why he had not been allowed to travel with Marcus to the wedding – and now the Mutants might attack and overcome them and he might never see his father alive again.

The cloud had been coming closer and closer and was now finally resolved into its real form. There were eight of the strange machines, like great mechanical horses. On each sat a man, and each man wore the uniform of an Obedience Enforcer from Helix, with the special helmet that all such Enforcers wore when outside the City. As Marcus turned and saw them the only comment he could think to make was:

'Oh, God.'

Deneer and Adriann saw and recognised the uniform of the riders. To them, the Enforcers had always been enemies.

They turned their horses and spurred them up, one riding on each side of the straggling, mostly halted column, shouting their commands as they went:

'Dismount, dismount quickly. Form a circle. Jump to it.'

Hastily, the Statemen obeyed the orders of their protectors and all became confusion as they slid off their horses in varying degrees of panic and bewilderment. Some remembered to calm their horses, trying to keep them quiet and subdued; others leaped from the saddles of their beasts as if they were on fire, their minds filled only with the coming threat and the thought of how they might save themselves. Even nine hundred years of living with the results of man's cruelty to himself had done little to change the selfishness of human nature.

However, even in the midst of this confusion, with Adriann and Deneer trotting round and round the group, giving encouragement and advice where they could, they were eventually formed into a tight defensive circle, at least the best result that could be obtained.

Sitting high on the saddle of the leading Death Machine, Polna was able to see the activity in the distance as the circle was formed. In truth, the sight came as a relief to him. It was one thing to fight and try to overcome and capture one of the Guides, it was quite another to carry that fight into a group of Statemen, with the danger of killing an innocent member of one's own kind.

Since he and his troop had set out from the City in pursuit of the caravan, the thought had hung over him and he had dreaded having to make the choice. But the decision taken by the Guides to group the Statemen together meant that the fighters had decided to meet the danger head on, away from the people they were set to defend. Polna, who lacked the streak of ruthlessness shared by Ankar Moor and Lord Zirpola, but who was, nevertheless, a cruel man when the need arose, gave thanks that, in his view, it was now going to be a fair fight.

With the circle formed, the two Guides were ready to go forth to meet their enemy. They moved forward and away from the group. It was then Adriann was reminded that there was one more task to perform, as Karissa spurred her pony forward, determined to remain at her mother's side. Adriann smiled down at her calmly, then pointed back to the defensive circle:

'Go back.'

The little girl looked troubled and steadfastly refused to turn the pony round:

'I want to stay with you.'

Adriann was touched by her daughter's trust, but worried for her safety. She would be a clear target by herself; among the Statemen she might have a chance:

'Go with the Statemen. You are to stay with them until it is over and I come for you.'

The little girl was still not willing to obey. Her face screwed up as if she was close to tears, though no member of the Guides or their families had ever been known to cry, and glanced towards the oncoming column. She was obviously more afraid for her mother than for herself:

'Please, Adriann. Let me stay.'

Her mother was still gentle, even understanding, but nonetheless firm towards her offspring:

'No. When you are become a Guide, then you will be your only master, but for now you must obey me. You will stay with these people. They will protect you as one day you will be able to protect them. Have no fear, I will come for you.'

Abruptly, she turned away. There was no time left for argument. She rode away from the defensive circle to come once more alongside Deneer, who had tactfully moved away a little while Adriann had talked with her daughter. With hesitant reluctance, Karissa turned the head of her pony and walked the tiny creature across the space to the defensive circle of the Statemen.

Deneer did not take her eyes off the oncoming threat for a moment as Adriann fell in alongside her again. Her whole concentration, conscious and subconscious, was on the threat that was moving rapidly towards them, the noise coming louder and louder in the still air. She was trying to work out some strategy for battle, letting her mind enter a pool of calm and flatten out ready for the fight that she was sure lay ahead:

'There are eight of the strange metal horses. There can be no question. It is us they come for.'

Adriann nodded:

'Yes. We must flank them. We must deflect their blade.'

The two women now turned their heads to face one another, their eyes looking on to one another and becoming mirrors of each other's soul, as was the way of the Guides.

They sank down into the consciousness for the ritual that is such an essential part of their philosophy, the ritual of Union and temporary co-operation. Deneer began the ritual of the code in a flat, trance-like voice:

'Our Union is limited.'

Adriann responded with the formal nod, never for an instant taking her eyes away from the other girl's:

'I agree. We are our own masters, but are now as one.'

Deneer returned the nod and the moment of ritual was now at an end. They would fight as if they were one person within the same consciousness until the danger was over. Then the Union would be broken and each would become her own master again and go her separate way. For now they were a part of a single whole.

Each woman rejected the thought of the Whistler and instead drew from her belt the anti-matter blaster she carried. Abruptly they went into action, turning the heads of their great horses away from one another and galloping at full tilt across the canyon in opposite directions, in an effort to draw a split in the oncoming group.

Polna rasped into his communicator:

'Remember, we want them alive if we can. No blasters unless you are forced. Now go to it.'

And, as the Statemen in their circle and the Mutants at the entrances to the caves looked on helplessly, the great duel began.

Polna barked out an order for the teams to split, four charging after Adriann, his own group veering off in pursuit of Deneer. As if they were two parts of the single whole, as the ritual of the code had made them, the two women reined in at the same moment, turned their horses and began to charge towards the great machines, their blasters at the ready.

As they closed with their enemies, they uttered the blood-curdling war cry of the Guides and fired, but, owing to the speed of the approach of their enemies, a speed to which both were unused, they missed their targets and were forced to weave their horses to avoid the hail of darts fired at them by the Enforcers.

Marcus was one with the other Statesmen as they watched the attack, awed as the horses charged the machines, breathless with fear as they disappeared in a cloud of dust between them, then relieved as they emerged unscathed on the far side.

Deneer wheeled round to prepare her steed for another charge and a similar movement from Adriann came only a second later. The latter dropped beneath the level of the flank of her horse for this second charge and, as the darts winged on their futile way above the top of her head, she levelled her blaster under the neck of her mount and aimed at one of the riders who had come against her.

A squeeze on the trigger button and both the Obedience guard and his frightening Death Machine disappeared into the void, to float forever in timeless space. Even the man's strangled scream was lost amid the roar of the machines. But now, under the threat of annihilation, another of the guards who had gone against her lost his head, perhaps from excitement, perhaps from fear: such emotions are so close to each other in battle, and, as Adriann wheeled her steed again for a further charge, he pressed the button that activated the rear anti-matter blaster pods. An instant later, both Adriann and the great animal had disappeared in a green and crimson flash. She did not cry out in the moment of her death, but accepted it as the ultimate and inevitable fate of a Guide.

Little Karissa had been standing at Marcus Karl's side with her pony. Now, as he stared out into the field of battle, she disengaged her tiny hand, leapt upon her pony and spurred it forward out of the protective circle:

'Adriann!'

Deneer was riding full-tilt at the machines once more, oblivious to the annihilation of her companion, concentrating only on her part of the fight for victory and life. For the briefest of moments, Karissa's sudden charge caught her eye and distracted her as the little girl spurred the pony forward towards the cave-pocked sandstone cliffs and the spot where she had witnessed the death of her mother.

That second of distracted hesitation was time enough for Polna and his men. Deneer's mount was hit by a volley of darts and, with a whinny of fear, it fell unconscious beneath her, spilling her forward on to the sand, her anti-matter blaster falling from her hand and skidding across the ground some distance from her.

Polna saw the result and shouted exultantly into his transceiver:

'Now, get her. She is helpless.'

Deneer was at an almost hopeless disadvantage, but no Guide gave up the fight until it was lost. As the leading machine roared down on her and its rider fired his dart from the special pistol, she leapt high into the air, passing safely over the machine, landing easily behind it and close to the fallen blaster. Now she lunged desperately for it, rolled over with it in her hands, before raising herself up to fire at her next attacker. Polna screamed:

'Nail her.'

She squeezed the trigger, but the action came too late as a hail of darts caught her in the chest, knocking her backwards off-balance. The blaster shot passed harmlessly over the heads of the riders as she fell back unconscious on the sand.

The men turned and slowed their machines to a halt before dismounting and surrounding their fallen enemy. Polna looked down on her and admired her for both her looks and ability to give battle:

'Good work, men. Now load her up quickly and let's get out of here.'

As two of the Enforcers lifted Deneer on to the back of one of the machines and tied her down, Polna turned to another of his men and pointed towards the huddle of the defensive circle:

'Form the caravan into a single column. Get them turned and moving back to the City. Tell them we will protect them – move!'

The man joined with two of his fellows and they remounted their Death Machines and moved over to the column, stopping in an impressive cloud of dust and revving their engines to induce the right level of fear and respect in their captives.

The leadman then dismounted and produced a small bullhorn. Marcus Karl turned to Bakkar and frowned.

'I do not understand. They are Obedience Enforcers from the City. Why would they attack us?'

Bakkar shrugged. He had no answer to the question and was filled with a terror for his own life which precluded him from trying to think of one.

The orders of the Enforcer boomed out at them, magnified by the power of the bullhorn.

'We have been sent to rescue you. You were to be led into

a trap. The Guides were in league with the Mutants. You must return to Helix. Form yourselves in a single file – quickly!'

Marcus strode forward, angry and confused, but not afraid.

'I am supposed to get married in three days – in Triton. I demand to be allowed to go on.'

As the others remounted their horses, afraid and anxious to obey the Enforcer, the man with the bullhorn walked up to where Marcus was holding his ground.

'You feel that is good reason to query our instructions?'

Marcus felt more nervous than he showed on the surface. But he was no coward and was not going to give up without some show of resistance.

'But I must get to Triton. Why have you overcome our Guides?'

'I told you. They were in league with the Mutants.'

'That is a lie. No Guide has ever been in league with them. They are the enemies of the Guides, just as they are ours.'

The man smiled grimly.

'We take our authority from the Lord Zirpola. They are his enemies and would lead anyone from Helix into danger and death. Another caravan will be going in a few days. You will be able to get your permit renewed then. But now you must return to the City. Do you want us to arrest you or will you be peaceful and co-operate?'

The threat of arrest hung in the air. Once arrested a Stateman seldom got clear of his captors. Reluctantly, Marcus turned back to his horse and mounted up. The guard went back to his machine.

In the confusion of the end of the battle, neither Stateman nor guard had taken any further notice of what had happened to young Karissa. She had trotted forward to where her Mother had disappeared, the tears streaming down blinding both her vision and her judgement. At the cliff face she had dismounted from her pony and the leader of the Mutants had looked down upon her, checking that there was no guard or Guide following her, before making the moves to effect her capture.

By the time Karissa became aware of her danger, it was too late. She found that she was surrounded by the Mutants with their misshapen, deformed bodies, their peculiar skin colours, their salivating mouths with the two rows of razor-sharp teeth and their bulging watery eyes. She was snatched up by clammy hands as she almost fainted from the strong pungent smells put out by the Mutants and pulled into the caves where the stench became so unbearable that she could hardly breathe.

As the column moved off, it was Marcus who noticed that Karissa was no longer with them. He glanced round and saw her pony, alone and deserted, trotting in a series of circles away from the cliffs. The Mutants who had gone after the little animal had become alarmed as it moved away from them and had not wanted to expose themselves to these new roaring enemies. They had therefore retreated and allowed the creature to escape them for the moment.

Marcus reined his horse out of the line and approached one of the Enforcer guards who was riding slowly alongside them. He kept a tight rein on his horse so that it would not shy at the sound of the machine.

'We have lost a little girl. She is the young daughter of the Guide you killed. I fear she may have been taken by the Mutants. We must go back and try to rescue her.'

The Enforcer glared.

'Get back in line. We have no time.'

Marcus pressed the question:

'But she is just a little girl. Please speak to your leader. We should try to rescue her.'

The Enforcer, who was, in his private life, a happily married man with a large family of his own, dropped the glare as unproductive and nodded.

'I can promise nothing, but I will speak to our leader.'

With that, Marcus had to be satisfied and he went back into the line as the guard revved up his machine and moved forward to come alongside Polna, riding ahead of the column. Polna snapped:

'Report.'

'One of the Statemen. He says that a little girl has been taken by the Mutants.'

'A Stateman girl?'

'No, he says she is the daughter of the dead Guide.'

Polna frowned, not entirely hard-hearted. But his orders had been clear. He had been out to capture Guides, not to put men and machines in danger by a battle with the Mutants. He shook his head.

'We have no time. The girl will be already dead and we

must get back to the City before dusk.'

The Enforcer saluted and dropped back. He had done his best. Polna squinted up at the sun. It was already beginning its descent. Another few hours and the wastelands would be in darkness, a darkness that made the Mutants the masters outside the Cities.

Already Ankar Moor would be angry. He had lost a man and a machine, all for the capture of one Guide. He could only hope that his captive was enough to quiet the man's anger – or the uncontrolled anger that he had witnessed in the Lord Zirpola in recent months. He was not returning to Helix a happy man.

CHAPTER THREE

As the sun slowly dropped like a great burning coal in the sky, the domes of Helix City gleamed as they clutched the towns like a great mother turtle with her little ones grouped around her. They were like silvered warts on the face of the landscape.

Ankar Moor and his depleted team had already arrived back in the City, and, after he had supervised the delivery of his unconscious Guide prisoner to the prison level of the City in the depths of the building, the leader of the Obedience Enforcers had gone straightway to make a personal report to his master, the Lord Zirpola.

He found the ruler of Helix City in his office, seated behind his huge, ornate desk. The waves of pain in his head had receded somewhat and he was in a comparatively relaxed mood.

As the door closed on Ankar Moor and the latter bowed gravely before coming forward to the desk, he asked:

'Well?'

Ankar Moor rasped:

'We have a prisoner.'

Zirpola inclined his head.

'And the other teams?'

Ankar Moor replied:

'They have not yet returned, but I have radio reports. Team Three has captured two of the Guides. Polna is now returning with the Triton caravan and one prisoner.'

Zirpola rubbed his hands together and nodded, not entirely displeased. He had hoped for more and faster results, but it was a start.

'Were there any losses?'

Ankar Moor hesitated for a moment, then:

'Eleven casualties, all annihilated.'

Zirpola grimaced, impatient.

'Not the men. They are not important. We have enough. The machines, Ankar Moor – they are safe?'

This was the moment of greatest danger. Ankar Moor was afraid of no man as a general rule, but, with his plans so close to fruition, he did not want to fall foul of Zirpola.

'We lost two machines.'

As he had feared, Zirpola reddened before exploding in a blind rage, his voice rising:

'Two machines for four prisoners. The men are worth nothing, but the machines are everything. We cannot afford to have any losses. You have failed me, Ankar Moor.'

The other man controlled his proud anger. The leather mask that covered his ravaged face helped him to hide his true feelings for the man who sat before him and he averted his head so that Zirpola could not see the anger that blazed up in his eyes. For the moment the other man was the master, but one day soon he would have to bend his knee to Ankar Moor or die. That was one promise to himself that the leader of the Enforcers was determined to bring true.

'I am sorry, Lord.'

Zirpola was satisfied that his message had got through, he took the averting of the other man's head as a sign of shame, and his anger subsided as quickly as it had come. In truth the rush of blood that had come into his head with his temper had brought back dizziness and the beginnings of a wave of pain.

'It is fortunate for us all that Sarnoff is working so well and that the hundred machines are built. I will see if he can make good the loss. You may go now. I have plans to make and may need you later.'

A minor hesitation, then Ankar Moor bowed and retreated to the door. Zirpola reached out a talon-like hand and pressed the button on his desk that allowed the door to slide open so that Ankar Moor could back out of his presence without turning.

As soon as the man was beyond the door, Zirpola pressed again and the door slid shut on him. He cried out and lay back, clutching his head. The pain was back, worse than before and it made the Lord Zirpola, master of all he surveyed, the all-powerful Lord of the City of Helix, begin to be mortally afraid for his life and the completion of his plans, the fulfilment of his ambitions.

The prison level of Helix City was in a self-contained level of its own, with a cells area, kitchens and all the refinements of a cruel society, such as the most modern disorientation chambers as well as the most ancient of torture devices. There are some skills that mankind never forgets, however great the tragedies that overcome the world.

In the main entrance to the cells area, the huge sadistic jailer who was in charge for the day leant over his television console, his completely bald head gleaming in the light, and checked the cells on the videos. His desk was placed just inside the huge main security doors, of solid steel, that were the only entrance to the cells area.

From where he sat the man could see the corridors radiating off to the cells, with their steel doors and tiny observation slits. On the monitoring console, he could see the interior of each cell and he checked them constantly. Many of the cells were empty, ready for the prisoners that it was hoped the Obedience Enforcers would bring in.

The Enforcer paid particular attention to the screen that showed the interior of the cell in which Ankar Moor's unconscious Guide prisoner had been placed. He was beginning to stir into life and the man allowed himself a cruel, thin-lipped grin. Soon he would be able to make a start at teaching this stranger the meaning of the words 'obedience' and 'discipline'. Punishment and training were pleasures that the chief jailer never failed to enjoy.

Inside the cell, Kaz Oshay blinked his eyes open and stared up at the blank white ceiling of the tiny cell. The steady lights kept it overlit and the brightness hurt his eyes in this first moment of re-awakening, but he had soon acclimatised himself to it. It was little different from the burning sun of midday. After a moment, he sat up on the cold metal floor and glanced round, his keen eyes and brain absorbing every detail of the situation in which he found himself.

The cell was a small, box-like room, all in white, measuring some ten feet by twelve. The only broken spot was that of the steel door and this too was painted white. It was the smallest enclosed space in which the Range Guide had ever found himself and he was forced to sublimate the feeling of fear that flitted through his mind. Fear was an enemy, for it clouded his judgement.

He overcame it by slowly allowing a rage to build within him, giving him renewed strength and courage. The code taught him that rage had its uses, as did calm. He rose to his feet, waited a moment until his head was clear and steady, with the blood pounding through his temples, then, with a sudden savagery, he gave the scream of challenge and launched himself into the air, his feet thudding against the locked steel door of the cell, the smash of impact reverberating down the corridor before he fell back on to the floor like a cat that had made some huge leap to safety.

The bald jailer watched this action on the console and smiled even more widely. He adjusted the discipline lever that was on another console, readying it for his first message to the cell.

To his annoyance he was interrupted in these preparations by the lighting of the wall lock by the main doors and the blipping sound of the opening code being pressed out. A moment later, the great door swung open and a group of Enforcers entered, carrying the bodies of two male Guides, both as unconscious as Kaz Oshay had been when he was brought in. Their leader reported to the jailer:

'Two more for you. They can go in the same cell.'

The man nodded. The scope for his use of discipline was widening and he no longer resented the interruption.

'Put them in cell fourteen. Next to the Guide we already have.'

The Enforcers moved forward with their dead weights and walked down the corridor past Kaz Oshay's cell to the one the jailer's console had opened for them beyond.

Kaz heard them coming and pressed his eyes to the observation slit in his cell door. He recognised both of the Guides who were being carried in. In the past Kaz Oshay had been in temporary Union with both Varros and Ikar. They were older, more experienced than himself, both much scarred by battle and the dangers of the wastelands and Kaz knew them to be amongst the best fighters in the Guides.

His fists beat against the door and he raged:

'I am Kaz Oshay, the Range Guide. I am my only master. Who dared to put me in this place?'

The Enforcers ignored him, not even bothering to glance in his direction. They dumped their load, then returned along the corridor as the cell door was rolled shut automatically.

He shouted after them:

'I am Kaz Oshay of the Guides. I demand an answer.'

He jerked his eyes upwards as a voice seemed to boom out above him. It was the loudspeaker system that operated throughout the cells and the jailer had turned it on:

'The next time you touch that door, Range Guide, I will scramble your brains for you.'

As if to show the imprisoned man that this was no empty threat, he pressed down the lever for a second. At once a violent shock of electricity was released both through the metal of the cell door and of the floor, a shock that was violent enough to knock Kaz off his feet and bring him crashing to the ground, disorientated and almost unconscious again.

So shocked was he by this mysterious attack from a direction that he could not comprehend, that he lay where he had fallen, not wanting to move until he was sure that the pain would not come again, for he knew that he was helpless to resist it.

It was close to the coming of darkness when Polna and his men escorted the caravan of Statemen back into the City. The shadows of mountain and bluff were already long over the parched earth.

Once inside, the Statemen were left to disperse and it was Polna himself who accompanied the two Guards who were carrying the unconscious Deneer down to the prison level of the City.

Left to themselves, the Statemen dispersed quickly, no complaints coming from them, as they started back to their quarters, leaving Marcus, a hot anger welling up inside him at the docility of other members of his party. For himself, he made straight for the transportation offices to complain. He had paid the fees for his journey and was determined that at least he would not lose the chance to go on the next caravan. His other complaints could wait.

The effete Stateman who was in charge of the transportation passes looked up placidly as Marcus stomped over to his desk, his eyes blazing.

'Our caravan has been forced back to the City. When is the next one due to go?'

The man shrugged amiably.

'I have no information.'

'But there must be one soon?'

The official sighed.

'There are no plans for the moment. The Lord Zirpola has told us there is trouble in Triton, civil disturbance or some such danger. All travel is cancelled and those wishing to go must wait until we have information about an all-clear.'

Marcus absorbed this. He still had no reason to believe that Zirpola's pronouncements did not carry the ring of truth. The action of the Enforcers had been puzzling, but perhaps the Guides *had* become the enemies of Helix. They were a strange people, difficult to understand.

'But I have paid for my trip.'

Inwardly, the man sighed. Ever since the order barring travel had been sent to him that morning, he had been dealing with more complaints than he could stand. He was sure that his superiors would think twice about making decisions like this if they had to deal with the results. Outwardly, he gave the stock answer:

'The amount of your payment will be credited for your next journey after the ban has been lifted.'

'But –'

The man held up a manicured hand.

'Those are the rules. If you wish to appeal, you can ask for an appointment with the Lord Zirpola.'

That should stop that angry young man in his tracks. No one would be able to obtain an interview with the Lord of Helix on a matter so trivial as that, he was sure.

But Marcus Karl was determined not to be put off as easily as all that. His father would be able to speak to the Lord Zirpola on the matter. He knew that he saw him regularly, was treating him for some small malady.

He left the transportation office and braced himself to start the long journey across the City to his father's quarters. Since the coming of the fuel shortages only the officials of the administration were permitted to use the complicated system of elevators, walkways and travel tubes that could carry a person quickly from one part of the City to another. For a civilian like Marcus a long walk was indicated.

This time, Kaz Oshay did not rise as he heard the sound of the Enforcers bringing in the new prisoner, though he was aware that the cell door that opened and closed was immediately opposite his own. There would be time enough to assuage his curiosity when he had formulated some plan that would help him to escape from these alien and threatening surroundings in which he found himself.

The closing of the cell door on the newly arrived prisoner was followed by a lengthy silence which gave Kaz some more time to recover himself from the electric shock treatment he had received and to allow his mind to go into a limbo of consciousness from which earthly manifestations of such pain would not be able to jolt him. It was a trick of suspension peculiar to the Range Guides, a manifestation that was central to their philosophy, and of which only they were the masters.

It was later, much later, when he had been in this state for long enough to find renewal, that the voice of the jailer again boomed out through his microphone link-up:

'Range Guides. You will stand by your cell doors now that you have all returned to consciousness. You will stay quiet – move!'

Kaz Oshay returned abruptly to a worldly level of consciousness. Still seething and defiant, he remained lying on the floor, determined not to obey the order. After a moment and the sound of movement in the cells next to and opposite him, Kaz once more heard the voice of the jailer booming out:

'My orders include you, Kaz Oshay, if that is truly your name. Or do you want me to hurt you again.'

Every fibre of Kaz Oshay's being cried out that he was his own master and should obey no other, but his mind told him that this was not the time for such disobedience. That time would come if he would only wait. Meanwhile the man's powers were strong and he knew that he could not fight them face to face.

He rose slowly and went to the door of his cell, peering out into the corridor. Then, having his eye caught by a glint of light in the slit of the door opposite his own, his eyes locked on to those of the prisoner watching him across the way, the Guide who had been placed in the empty cell opposite him while he was trying to recover from the electric shock treatment on the floor of his cell.

Once their eyes were together, both Guides turned them into the mirrors of each other's soul. Deneer, for that was the prisoner, transmitted to her fellow-prisoner the story of her capture. With his mind's eye, Kaz Oshay saw the caravan making its slow way down the canyon; then the fear from the strange sound and cloud of dust behind them, with the caravan halting and the Statemen milling round in panic. He saw, recognised and understood the reason for the fear, machines similar to the ones that had finally effected his capture. He saw the battle laid out, the annihilation of Adriann and, most especially, the taking of the child Karissa by the Mutants. He saw Deneer's last desperate leap, then the winging darts and the blackness of her capture.

When her story was finished he transmitted his own, together with all the information he had about conditions in the place they found themselves, particularly a warning with regard to the strange strength of the door and floors that could lay them out, an attack against which there was no defence that he had worked out.

His story told, he whispered in a low tone that could be heard only by another Guide:

'Our Union is limited.'

The eyes in the cell opposite were lowered for a fraction to denote agreement:

'I agree.' The sound of her voice told him of a soft caressing quality in her.

The ritual was done. They were joined as one for any attempt they might make to free themselves from this terrible place. Now, Kaz Oshay could talk of other things. He whispered:

'We must take care of our own. The child. I will help you to find her when we are gone from this place.'

Deneer's eyes flashed their message of gratitude. They shone as if a burden of worry had been taken from her mind by his reassurance. Such words from one Guide to another were as good as the ancient oaths made to the gods – a vow to the death.

Once more silence reigned between them as their eyes explored each other before Kaz Oshay asked:

'Do you have knowledge of why we have been brought here?'

Deneer began a reply:

'All Guides –'

After this time, the chief jailer, inspecting his video machines, had come to the conclusion that the two prisoners were communicating with each other, though he had not been able to hear a word that they had said. Still, he enjoyed being safe rather than sorry and he had sent a bolt of electricity through the door and floors of both cells. Kaz Oshay and Deneer fell to the ground, knocked almost unconscious by the force of the blows. At his console, the jailer chuckled at the results of his little surprise.

As the two Guides struggled, dazed, to their feet, his voice boomed out over the loudspeakers:

'If you disobey me and open your mouths again, I will make sure that the pain gets worse. Now stand by your doors in silence as you were ordered.'

Doctor Karl had left his office and his work at the clinic as soon as the summons came through. A summons to go to the chambers of the Lord Zirpola deserved no lesser response. As a man, the doctor had little time for the ruler of Helix, regarding him as something of a strutting, ridiculous figure, but, as a patient, he would not have dreamt of not treating him at once. In addition, as the ruler's personal doctor, he knew the man's wild changes of mood and had a great sense of self-preservation.

He was still dressed in the white, zip-on one-piece jump suit that he wore to go about his work in the Helix Clinic and he merely snatched up his treatment bag and made for the elevator complex that would take him up to Zirpola's quarters. The only delay was the moment he spent fumbling for the special pass that he could slip into the slot at the side of the elevator that proved his official status and would allow him to ride up.

Karl strode out of the elevator on to the thick pile carpet that was on the corridor floor in front of the entrance to the ruler's quarters. He was a trim, neat man in his early fifties, still retaining a good head of dark hair, though here and there there was a hint of grey streaking it. His face still retained a trace of the youthful good looks that could be seen to better effect in the face of his son, Marcus. A widower for many years, he lived only for two things; the widening of his knowledge in his craft and the future of his son.

He crossed the short space between the elevator doors and the entrance to the ruler's apartments and stopped, glancing at the bored-looking Obedience Enforcer who stood on guard outside and who nodded vaguely at him. Doctor Karl was a well-known, even distinguished member of the hierarchy and recently his treatment visits had been becoming more and more frequent. He was never summoned when Ankar Moor was around, but then the guard on duty reported all the Lord Zirpola's visitors, so there was no chance, as the ruler hoped, that the doctor's coming and going would be secret.

The guard turned to the inter-communicator console and announced that the doctor had arrived. A moment later, the main door slid open and Zirpola himself stood in the doorway, leaning against the lintel to support his shaking frame. The sweat was pouring out of his pallid, oily skin and his watery blue eyes flickered with an unbearable pain.

He took a pace forward, wobbled, then thrust out a talon-like hand to cling to Doctor Karl's arm:

'Doctor Karl, you must help me, you must. The pain. It is getting worse and my head may burst.'

Karl was somewhat taken aback by this public show of weakness. He had seen Zirpola in one of these attacks before but had never seen him give way to one in front of any other witness. He glanced at the guard, but the man was staring with an exaggerated studied boredom at the closed elevator doors as if he was unaware that anyone else was present. He knew that his life was in danger if he gave any indication that he had noticed such weakness in his lord and master.

Doctor Karl helped the Lord of Helix into his chambers and the door slid shut on them. Many times in the past, the doctor had tried to persuade Zirpola to come to the diagnostic centre at the clinic and each time he had refused the suggestion. Now, bracing himself for the tirade he felt sure would come, he tried again:

'You must come to the clinic. It is imperative. You must give me the chance to treat the causes of your pain, not just remedy the results.'

If he had expected another argument, he was pleasantly surprised. Zirpola was in too much pain to argue:

'Take me. Do what you like. But stop this pain.'

Doctor Karl took no chance that Zirpola would change his mind. He half dragged him back to the door, opened it, pulled him through to the elevator bank and opened the doors, hustling him inside and pressing the button for the clinic level before another word had been spoken. Only when they were travelling down did Zirpola say:

'None other must see me.'

Doctor Karl gave him his professionally reassuring smile:

'Trust me.'

Three levels down there was an elevator changing station, from which he could take another elevator that would land them in the hallways of the clinic itself.

He opened the doors at this level, glanced out and, seeing that no one was in evidence, he half-walked, half-carried the stricken man across and they were moving down again. By the time the elevator doors opened in the hallway of the clinic, the pain had receded enough to allow the Lord of Helix to stride out on his own. Even so, he still made no argument against going into diagnosis, but, as Karl led him to his private office, he said urgently:

'You must help me, Doctor.'

'Be patient,' soothed Karl. 'It will take only a little time and then we will know what must be done.'

They entered Doctor Karl's private consulting rooms and Zirpola sank down in a chair. But he was not going to get away as easily as that. The doctor crossed the room and opened the door that led to his examination and diagnosis room:

'Come in here.'

Zirpola, feeling a new wave of pain, tried to rise, fell back and the doctor was forced to support him into the other room, propping him up on the side of the examination table. He went back for his bag, opening it as he re-entered the room. The first essential, before making his diagnostic tests, was to stop the pain for the moment and soothe down his patient.

In recent weeks he had always kept a syringe of painkiller ready in his bag and he took one out now and turned to set about his work. Zirpola held up a shaky hand. His voice was thin and reedy with pain:

'What is that? I will not be made helpless.'

Karl had been through the same question before and he answered with his usual formula:

'It is just a drug that will soothe the pain, that is all.'

Zirpola lowered his head. In the last few years, the ruler of Helix had trusted fewer and fewer of the men around him, knowing that they all secretly hated him, knowing that they were just waiting for some sign of weakness in him so that they could depose him and seize his power, for he had no natural heir, no issue to follow him. Many of them he had had destroyed, others had been imprisoned before they had died in the Death Sport. Now there was a mere handful of men he trusted. The most powerful of these was Ankar Moor, but the closest was Doctor Karl.

An added argument for trust came with a further wave of blinding pain that almost made him fall. He nodded feebly:

'Help me, Doctor, please.'

Karl reached up with his free hand and undid the throat clasp that held up the great emerald cloak which was Zirpola's clothing of office, so that it slipped off his thin, rounded shoulders, on to the floor. The Ruler of Helix stood revealed as a rail-thin, shaky old man. He knew the routine and rolled up the sleeve of the blouse he wore, after which Doctor Karl found a spot on the oily skin where the needle had not entered before and, after rubbing it with his special disinfectant, he rammed the needle home and gave the injection.

Zirpola gave no sign of pain at this pin-prick. It was nothing compared with what was happening in his head. Karl withdrew the needle, then:

'You will feel relief in just a moment. Now lie on this table and I will prepare you for your tests.

Slowly, the Lord Zirpola obeyed Doctor Karl's instructions and swung his legs up on the examination table, lying back, resting his head on the pillow at the end. Karl could see that the injection was beginning to take effect, beating back the waves of pain inside his patient, so that he subsided from his rigid shaking tension into a sort of relaxation, his eyes wide open, the lines smoothing out of his face.

Now that his patient was more relaxed, the doctor turned his attention to his diagnostic machines, wheeling them forward along the far side of the couch, ready to make a thorough examination. He checked out the screens, making sure that everything was in working order.

It was only after he had made checks that the doctor turned his attention back to Zirpola:

'I am going to fit these electrodes on you. The machines will be able to diagnose what is wrong with you better than any human examination could. That way, we will be able to treat the cause of the pain.'

Zirpola sighed. He was relaxing now, his nervousness disappearing with the racking pain which had been threatening to explode his head:

'Very well, Doctor. Do what you have to do. I must know what is wrong. I must be cured before it is too late.'

Something in the stricken man's tone told Doctor Karl that he was referring to something more than just stopping a disease in time. Outside, he maintained his neutral, placid manner, inside, he was asking himself the question: 'Too late for what?' Later there would be time enough to follow the train of speculation that had been opened up. Lord Zirpola was a sick, perhaps even a dying man; his unhealthy pallor, the sweating, the constant bouts of pain, all these things were indications of a deep-laid malady. Diagnosis might be the only way of saving him, so that should come before curiosity. As he started to fit on the electrodes, Doctor Karl speculated on the irony of the fact that death came to great and humble alike, not sparing one at the expense of the other. Whatever progress man had made, either before or after the great devastation, he had never been able to change that.

Carefully, the doctor taped the electrodes to the man's forehead and temples, then, as the first machine started to function and absorb the transmitted information and commence its read-out of the results of sensory measurement of the patient's brain waves, he taped similar electrodes from a second machine to the man's chest and arms. A few more such attachments and all the machines were humming away at their task, correlating their information for the read-outs that would give him his answers – if he was lucky.

Slowly, Doctor Karl had been reaching out towards the moment of his greatest danger in the examination. In order to let the machines do their work with the best efficiency, the patient would have to be put to sleep for a short time, a state that would put him entirely under Karl's control. Karl knew, even had Zirpola not stated it, that the man on the table would not normally allow this to happen, so he had to make the actions that led up to it look casual, in order that Zirpola would not realise what had been done to him.

He readied a syringe and laid it out on the little table by his bag. Next, he got a length of surgical rubber hose and only then did he say to his patient:

'Now give me your arm. There's still one test I have to do by hand. We don't have a machine for it.'

Zirpola feebly raised his emaciated right arm, Karl took it and tightly wrapped the surgical hose just above the elbow, so that the veins bulged out. He reached behind him, caught up the syringe and made his injection in a smooth neat movement, watching as the fluid passed into the man's bloodstream, his face wincing momentarily at the prick of the needle:

'Now, my Lord, if you will count from ten to one very slowly, please.'

Zirpola might not have liked the injection but he had no inkling that he was being put under. His brow contracted and he began:

'Ten . . . Nine . . . Eight . . . Seven . . . Six . . .'

He got no further, his voice drifting away into silence as his senses fled from him and he was carried to a lower level of consciousness; asleep within himself, but still able to respond to the stimuli around him.

Karl breathed a sigh of relief that it had been so easy. He removed the syringe, destroying it and mixing it with other debris in the trash can in the corner of his consulting-room. He could only pray that, should Zirpola realise what had happened to him when he came round, he would believe that he had fainted away and would not be able to find any evidence that he had been doctored. To be safer still, he pressed a button by the trash can and the whole contents slid away down into the great disintegrators that dealt with the City's rubbish. Now he was able to turn his full attention to his patient. On the level of dream-filled consciousness where his mind was balanced, Zirpola groaned and licked his lips in a repellent reflexive action, like some great lizard basking in the sun.

Doctor Karl checked the dials on his machines and the pulsing scan graph that hummed quietly away in one corner. Then he was ready to begin the questioning that was so vital to the diagnostic process:

'My Lord, how long have you suffered from this pain?'

He had guessed that it had been many months before Zirpola had succumbed to the pain and had first come to him for help. There was a momentary pause as some final defence mechanism in his patient's brain fought against the free answering of any question asked by another, then the fight was over and he began to respond, his voice floating softly out of him as if he had no control over it:

'Some months . . .'

'How many months?'

'I do not remember; many months. Since I learnt of the Death Machines and their power.'

Karl had been preparing to write sensible answers on a little pad. Now he stopped, frozen by the answer. No one in the City of Helix had yet been told about the existence of the Death Machines, though there had been rumours circulating:

'I'm sorry. Would you repeat? Since when?'

'The machines. Since the Death Machines came to light.'

He was on to something that frightened him. Just to be sure that Zirpola was not at a level of consciousness where he was hallucinating, he leant forward and checked the screens. The read-out on the man's brainwaves and general metabolism seemed level enough:

'The Death Machines? Explain to me about the Death Machines.'

The drugged man immediately became agitated. His brow wrinkled, smoothed and wrinkled again. He groaned, his head moving from side to side, and the tongue flickered out to lick his lips over and over again. The machine that measured brainwaves now began to show a marked agitation, and an intensification of brain activity. Karl decided that his only choice was to press his questioning, to capitalise on this:

'The Death Machines. You must explain what they are. It is important to my understanding.'

The patient sucked in his breath:

'They are very powerful, invincible.'

'But what are they?'

Zirpola hardly seemed to hear the repeated question but pressed on down his own track of thought:

'Now that we have them, there is no one who will be able to stand in our way.'

Karl frowned:

'Stand in our way? Why would they want to? What would they want to block us for?'

The voice of the man on the table got louder, rising almost to a screech that made Doctor Karl step back a pace:

'From war.'

The use of the word and the intensity with which his patient had spoken it gave the doctor an almost physical pain. He was suddenly as frightened by the sight of the man before him as that man had been by his pain. War was to all intents and purposes a forbidden word, as it had become an impossible concept, diametrically opposed to the survival of what remained of humanity on the face of the earth. It had led to the degree of destruction that humanity now faced and, in effect, it had been unthinkable for nine hundred years, though it had only been formally banned by the members of the City Federation from a much later date. Ever since the Statemen had found it possible to journey beyond the confines of their own City, they had never conceived of renewing rivalry with the citizens of other Cities in this old-fashioned and outmoded way. War had been forgotten and forbidden, never to enter the range of human understanding again. And now this man, this sick, enraged, twisted mind, was pronouncing the word with a force and conviction that seemed to give it new life.

Karl thought for a minute, looking down on his patient with disgust. It would be so easy to end it all now – an accident with the machines – a reversed power surge and Zirpola would be dead. But Karl was above all things a doctor, and a doctor never takes human life:

'War? What makes you talk of war? We are not at war. There is no one who would fight us.'

The man on the table shook his head and chuckled evilly:

'War will come, for I have need of it. We must take it from them if we are to triumph.'

'Take what?'

'Their fuel. We need their fuel. They have it in plenty and we must take it from them.'

That answered one question, now Doctor Karl pressed the other:

'And from whom is the fuel to come?'

Zirpola became even more excited than previously. It was as if these questions, triggering off, as they were, his secret plans, gave him access to an internal power that was not always available to him. To Karl, it was a frightening sight to witness.

'From Triton. Triton has all the fuel we need.'

'But have we not asked Triton? Surely Triton would help us, would give us what we need?'

The man laughed harshly.

'Only a fool would show his own weakness by asking. They would then have a weapon to hold over us. They would withhold it in order to destroy us. We must attack without warning and snatch it from them, destroying them so that they cannot fight back. We must, we must. The machines will do the job for us, we will be invincible.'

Karl glanced down, the man's fists were clenching and unclenching and the sweat was pouring off his oily pale skin in his rage. Recovering from his own shock at the answers his questions had provoked, Karl moved to quiet the man. Such a spasm as this could not be anything but dangerous to the general health of a man under anaesthetic, and, whatever Karl felt he must add to his knowledge, his first duty was to the ease of Zirpola.

The man went into a total body spasm and Karl leapt forward as his back arched and threatened to throw him off the examination table. After that, it was mainly a question of holding him down in place until the spasm slowly subsided. Then the doctor knew that he would sleep for a few minutes, and would wake with, normally, no memory that he had been put under.

When the man was calm and sleeping, his breathing coming easily, Doctor Karl allowed himself a few moments to recover from his own shock, letting the mechanics of checking out the read-outs from the machines help calm him down, and starting to correlate the information on the read-outs from each machine.

By the time the Lord Zirpola's eyes flickered open, he was ready to remove the electrodes. He said quietly:

'There. It has only taken a few moments.'

The watery eyes watched him as he unfastened the electrodes.

'You can sit up and get dressed now, if you like.'

The man tried to sit up, lost the fight, then tried again and this time succeeded enough to swing his legs off the bed and sit upright. He was gradually becoming less weak and shaking all the time. The small period of sleep had at least done him that much good, even if, at the same time, it had completely destroyed Doctor Karl's peace of mind and confidence in the future. For the moment he could not even look at his patient, so disgusted was he. He covered this feeling by turning his back and walking over to his desk, apparently absorbed in his calculations. Zirpola picked up his robe and dressed himself.

By the time Zirpola was prepared to ask the inevitable question, Karl was ready for it.

'Well. If your machines are cleverer than you, have they found out what is afflicting me?'

Karl could do nothing but look grim.

'Do you want the truth?'

This response, at least, had the effect of riveting Zirpola's full attention – giving a signal as to just how serious his condition might be.

'Is there any other answer?'

Karl felt strangely petulant and it made him brave, giving him a courage that he did not know he possessed.

'I could lie to you, as others do.'

'That is the grossest impertinence,' snarled the Lord of Helix. 'Just how serious is it?'

Karl hesitated and the man began to perspire again, his skin pallid and shining in the light. He was obviously frightened and no longer able to fight off his fear, no longer able to convince himself that his headaches, the waves of pain and dizziness, were just a temporary phenomenon. The doctor decided to go the whole way, in spite of the possible consequences to himself.

'You are a dying man.'

If it was possible for the dull, oily skin of the Lord of Helix to become paler, it did so then. He concentrated on doing up the robe at his throat, his breath loud in the silence of the room about him, but, by the time he spoke again, his voice was calm and steady:

'Are you certain?'

Karl nodded sadly.

'As certain as any man may be, My Lord.'

This confirmation produced another silence as the information sank into Zirpola's ice-cold brain.

'I see.'

A lengthy silence fell between the two men. Doctor Karl would not have been happy to go on unless the man pressed him for more details. At last Zirpola strode forward and banged the desk.

'You must tell me what is wrong with me.'

Karl sighed.

'It is outside my previous knowledge. There is no certain name for it. I am not sure what it may be called. Its cause is most likely related to long-term exposure to radiation.'

Zirpola lifted his hand as a physical signal to cut off the doctor's speculations on cause.

'The cause is not important. It has happened. What is going to happen to me?'

Now Doctor Karl was brought to the nub of the problem. He took a deep breath, coming, as he was, to the edge of the precipice that was his own moment of greatest danger.

'You have a sort of degenerative brain disease. The neurons in your brain, the thought-transference tissues, are rupturing. Your brain cells seem to be tearing apart and are dying in their millions as every moment passes, thus producing the pain and dizziness, My Lord.'

Shocked by the stark matter-of-factness of the doctor's revelations, Zirpola groped for the chair that was behind him and sat down heavily. For a moment he was too beside himself with fear to speak. Doctor Karl was anxious to press his advantage now that he had been able to say this much, but not anxious to be the one to break the silence first. With the other man's mercurial changes of mood, it might prove fatal to him. Already he felt that he was in the greatest of dangers. It was a situation that might even cost him his life – especially if the Lord Zirpola had any suspicion of what he had revealed under the anaesthetic.

Zirpola saved the situation, deflating the silent tension that was growing between the two men. His watery blue eyes fastened on the doctor's face.

'How long do you think I have?'

Karl shook his head.

'I don't know. A disease like this is beyond my experience. It could be a while, it could be . . . '

His voice trailed away. If the man survived for any length of time and he was proved a liar, temporarily at least, he had signed his own death warrant.

Zirpolà struck the desk angrily.

'How long? I demand to know.'

The doctor could only plunge ahead with suggestions.

'I believe that you are slowly losing control over your faculties of reasoning. I am afraid you must face up to the question of turning the leadership of Helix over to someone else, before it becomes impossible for you to take such a decision for yourself.'

Again, a terrible silence fell across the room. Doctor Karl knew that the least he had done was to utter a basic treason against the person of his lord, but Zirpola did not reply violently as might have been expected, but sat quiet, as if weighing the doctor's words one at a time and carefully. When he spoke, his voice was controlled and steady:

'What you are trying to tell me, Doctor, is that you believe I am going mad?'

As far as Doctor Karl was concerned, it was a situation that had already arrived. But it would not be helpful to either of them to say so. He could only nod in partial agreement.

'As your brain cells die and decay, so madness will overtake you, my Lord.'

Zirpola's unattractive mouth hardened into a firm, thin line. He had heard more than enough from this man whom he had trusted for so long. Still, for the moment he did not show his true feelings. To tell the truth, he felt a little afraid in this clinical, closed office. So he nodded and sat in his chair, frowning. The doctor finally added:

'I will alleviate your symptoms as much as I can and then make your end as peaceful and as quiet as possible.'

Zirpola nodded. His voice was quiet, even grateful:

'Thank you, Doctor. I appreciate your offer. I think I will go back to my own quarters now, will you help me at least a part of the way?'

As he rose from his chair, he looked weak and shaky again. The doctor was relieved. It had all been much easier than he had thought it would be. The man put out an arm for his support and he rose quickly to give it. He walked him out of the office and back to the bank of elevators that went up from the deserted interior of the clinic.

To his surprise, Zirpola shook his head.

'It may seem a silly request, but I would like to go among my own people on my way back. You have given me much to think about and they are a part of my decision.'

Karl relaxed more; he had no suspicion of any treachery. It seemed to him that Zirpola was accepting his verdict gracefully and proving himself more human than he had thought possible. Even the memory of what the Lord of Helix had said under the anaesthetic was pushed to the back of Karl's mind.

This false sense of security was just the effect that Zirpola wished to produce. It would make his revenge all the sweeter when it came. For he had a particular surprise in mind for the unsuspecting doctor. No man would ever tell him that he was close to madness and get away with it.

They left the main doors of the clinic and walked down the steps. A few of the civilian citizens of Helix were around and they were surprised and frightened to see their lord walking amongst them, without guards and in the company of their doctor. It did not seem natural to them and they shied away. The Lord Zirpola was not that sort of person.

It was a while before Zirpola saw a pair of Obedience Enforcers coming towards them. Only when they came level did he suddenly push the doctor away from him and shriek out:

'Arrest this man. He is a liar and a traitor. I demand that you seize him.'

Startled by this sudden move, Doctor Karl made no attempt to resist. As the two men grabbed him roughly, he could only regret that he had not obeyed his original instinct of fear and self-preservation. If he had only lied, there would have been no punishment. The other man would have been dead before he could have nailed the lie. The two Enforcers held his arms and Zirpola strode forward to slap him around the face.

'I will teach you to try and frighten me with your stupid lies. I know that there is nothing the matter with me. I am the Lord Zirpola, ruler of Helix.'

He hit his prisoner again, even more viciously, then turned to the guards and gave his orders:

'Take him to the cells. Beat him but not too badly. He must be held for the Death Sport.'

With that, he turned on his heel and hurried towards the elevators. He did not feel secure abroad and alone in the City. There were so few of its citizens he could still trust – and they were getting fewer every day.

CHAPTER FOUR

Night had come and had spread its blanket of darkness over the great empty wastelands and the metallic domes of the surviving Cities of the Statemen. Deep in the bowels of the City of Helix, Kaz Oshay knew that the darkness had come, for a Guide always knew such things even if cut off from them, in spite of the brightness of the lights that burned down on him, constant and unwinking. He strained anxiously to keep at least some mental contact with the freedom of the land outside his prison.

Several times during the period of the coming of night outside, the sadistic jailer who was in charge of the cell area had called all the prisoners to stand by their doors in silence, then allowed them to return to the floors of their cells, to sit or squat, waiting and watching, but for what they did not know.

The slightest sign of disobedience from any of them had resulted in his own particular form of punishment to them all. The electric shocks had rammed through the floors and doors of their cells with a monotonous regularity. He was having an unusually good day.

These Guides proved a great deal less submissive than the broken prisoners who were brought to him from the City. He would enjoy the sight hugely if they were ever to be placed in the disorientation chambers.

Now he called them again:

'Stand by the doors of your cells.'

Once more, Kaz Oshay rose and obeyed the booming

voice. He hoped that the others were doing the same. He wanted an unbroken space of time to exchange more messages and information with Deneer and each time up till now some infringement of the orders by one of them had snatched the chance away.

He waited at the door, holding his breath in anticipation of a new shock, but nothing happened. This time, the jailer must have been very disappointed. Doubtless he would finally suspect the two of them of passing messages, then the shocks would come. But he hoped that he would have a little time before that.

He stared out through the narrow slit in the cell door and once more the eyes of the two Guides locked together as the waves of their power passed between them. Kaz waited for a moment before braving communication. Then he said in his softest tones, below the hearing of the normal human car, but with enough sound for a felow Guide to pick up:

'I know you.'

'From where?'

'We travelled once.'

Deneer's brow furrowed in thought and memory for a moment, then she remembered:

'Yes. It was a long time ago. I know you too. We journeyed together to Triton with a caravan. You are Kaz Oshay.'

Kaz smiled that she had remembered his name. They had both been very young Guides then:

'And you are the Lady Deneer.'

Even as he spoke her eyes clouded over with a great sadness. She had remembered something and wondered whether Kaz knew of it. The only way to find out was to tell him, however cruel it might be:

'I knew Oshay, your mother.'

'She is well?'

So he did not know. Her brow furrowed again as she knew that she must tell him, however much it would hurt. For no Guide ever lies to another of his kind, however troubled the circumstances that have brought them together:

'I was with her, close to her, last year, when she died. She fought well, she was truly powerful.'

On the surface of his face and eyes, Kaz Oshay showed no sign of emotion as the news of his mother's death was relayed to him. A Guide is his own master, but the ties of mother love are never completely broken, even under the rigid rules of the code. Inside, he seethed with an emotional pain at the bereavement, and anger welled up in him again. He wished to rove across the wastelands and find and avenge himself against whomsoever or whatsoever had killed her, and his confinement seemed unjust and ill-timed. Now it would be impossible.

With a supreme effort, he controlled himself. To show emotion was to succumb to weakness and a Guide should never do that, particularly to another of his kind. His voice came flat, without inflection:

'I had no knowledge of her passing – each of us is alone when death comes for us.'

Deneer's eyes flickered with a message of sympathy. She had seen with ease through the mask he had created to cover his true feelings. He spoke again, this time his voice a shade louder, as if wiping out of his mind the news she had brought to him:

'If you have knowledge of it, Deneer, can you tell me why we have been brought here?'

The girl raised an eyebrow. She had heard the guards talking but had not entirely understood what they had said:

'We are to fight in the Death Sport. I have no knowledge of what this is to be.'

Kaz frowned in surprise. He had heard of this barbaric ritual of the Statemen. It was a game that only they played, only the Statemen of Helix City. It was a strange ritual, but then many of the ways of the Statemen were strange.

They lived their protected lives in their enclosed Cities, hardly ever even seeking out the open plain and the burning natural light of the sun. Kaz was unable to fathom them. Of course there were dangers on the outside of the great domes. Dangers from the plain itself with the tremendous heat that sometimes built up, danger from the marauding bands of the Mutants and from the great Flash Winds with their rolling clouds of atomic death, but they were just natural hazards that had to be accepted and overcome. They took nothing away from the delights of freedom. For people who were totally protected from such things to bring the possibility of death amongst themselves, or to get pleasure from watching it come to others of their number, these were things that could not be understood.

Aloud, he said:

'The Death Sport, but that is a Stateman game. Why do they want us for it?'

'I do not know.'

Kaz uttered one of the formalities of the code:

'We have Union. We will break together.'

'Yes, Kaz Oshay.'

She made the formal nod that is the answer to the ritual and this time there was enough movement in her for the jailer to pick it up on the video screen and know that two of his prisoners were once more engaging in forbidden communication.

His hand, which had been hovering over the punishment levers, flashed down and a bolt of electricity knocked all the confined Guides from their feet, half-conscious on the floor of their cells.

His sadistic laugh came over the loudspeakers:

'I warned you to keep quiet in there. You know that any communication between the cells is forbidden. You had better listen to me and learn your lesson – unless you are enjoying this treatment and would like some more of the same.'

In spite of the pain that Kaz Oshay knew another shock would bring to him, he felt his impotent anger rising to snapping point. In a sudden movement, he threw himself up from the floor, leaping high enough for his arms to reach the ceiling as he tore the video eye from it.

At once, one of the video screens on the main console flashed bright, then went blank. The jailer stared at it, then, realising what had happened, he roared angrily:

'You bastard. Now you're really going to know what punishment is.'

He adjusted the lever, then pulled it down. The bolt of electricity that was released knocked Kaz Oshay to the floor and put a greater level of pain through him than he had felt before. It hardly had time to recede from him before the treatment was repeated, and, even with the rules of the code to support him, he could not help but cry out. The sound was as manna to the ears of the jailer and he pressed the lever down yet again. So concentrated was he on the pleasure he got from this procedure that he was oblivious to the blipping sound and the light pattern playing out in the door panel that signalled the imminent opening of the main door to the cell area.

A moment later, the code played through, the great steel door swung open and the newcomer entered.

It was Polna and, taking in what was happening at once, he strode over to the console and knocked the man's hand aside before he could press down the lever yet again:

'Stop that!'

He looked down as the man rubbed his wrist and whimpered in pain, more hurt in his dignity than physically:

'But he required it. I must have my orders obeyed. I must have order in the cells.'

Polna leant forward so that his face was thrust into the other man's, threateningly close:

'We do not want him too hurt. He must be kept in good condition. He's got to be able to fight. Why the hell do you think we went to the trouble of knocking out and capturing the bastard, instead of just killing him out in the desert?'

'But he has destroyed the video.' The jailer's protesting voice was a squeal.

'But nothing.' Polna reached past him and switched off the controls of the punishment console altogether:

'That is enough.'

The jailer was sweating, afraid of his superior:

'It was just for discipline, Sir.'

Polna grabbed the man by the throat, half-lifting him, in spite of his bulk, from his seat.

'Don't you let me catch you doing that again without my permission, unless you would like to join the other prisoners – and perhaps take part in the Death Sport yourself?'

He let go and allowed the man to sink back down into his chair. He had the satisfaction of seeing him go grey with fear:

'Yes, Sir. I mean, no, Sir.'

'Just remember then.'

It dawned on the jailer that no senior Obedience Enforcer would come to the cell without good reason. He asked timidly:

'You wanted something. May I be of assistance?'

Polna nodded.

'In a moment. The guards are coming down with an important prisoner. We will have to place him with one of the Guides. We are saving him for a special death in the Sports. He is not to be hurt any more than he is already, is that understood?'

'Yes, Sir.'

There was a silence, then the man asked timidly:

'May I ask who the prisoner is to be?'

Polna shrugged.

'Why not give yourself a surprise. You will recognise him soon enough. He is a Stateman, a traitor.'

A moment later there came the sound of Enforcer guards coming towards the open door. They were moving slowly, as if dragging a heavy weight. The jailer's question was answered as Doctor Karl was dragged through the doorway into the central hall of the cells. He was battered and bleeding from the beating he had taken at the hands of the guards, who had obeyed Zirpola's instructions to the letter, but he was struggling to walk by himself, though incapable of doing so, most of his weight being supported by the accompanying guards.

The jailer gasped and his mouth hung open in surprise.

'But that is Doctor Karl; who will run the clinic?'

Polna shrugged:

'That is not your problem, jailer. The Lord Zirpola will see that it is taken care of. This man has betrayed him. He will not be so difficult to replace.'

Privately, his inner question was the same as the other man's; there was no other doctor in the whole city as qualified or as expert as Karl.

'What was his crime?'

Polna again turned to glare at him.

'That is not your concern. Suffice it to say, he was a traitor. Now you must keep him fit and safe for the Death Sport – understand?'

The threatened man could only nod dumbly. He directed the guards to the cell that they were to put Doctor Karl in, the cell that contained Kaz Oshay.

They went down the corridor with their burden and he worked the mechanism that would unlock the door without the occupant of the cell being aware that it had been done.

Kaz would not have noticed anyway. He was still rocking back and forth in pain on the floor, trying to bring all his faculties back into focus to help him recover from the pain the punishment had brought to him, and had no time to notice what went on around him. He hardly even looked in the direction of the door as it opened and the body of his intended cellmate was thrown to the floor at his side. The door clanged shut again and was secured from the central console.

The doctor lay face down where he had fallen and the sound of the guards' feet on the metal floor of the corridor slowly retreated. After a pause, this was followed by the echoing clang of the great steel door that led to the prison shutting and being made secure.

Kaz Oshay continued to concentrate on bringing himself out of shock and back to a state where he might stand and flex his aching muscles. Only when this exercise was completed and he felt himself again did he turn his attention to helping the man who had been so unceremoniously dumped on him. The new prisoner was lying, shaking his head as if to clear it, his face still streaked with the blood of his beating. Very gently, Kaz, having seen that he was a Stateman and therefore not so well able to bear pain, lifted him up and seated him with his back to the wall, before squatting in front of him and looking into his dazed eyes:

'Who are you?'

The man cleared his throat before speaking painfully through cracked lips. He had been hit in the mouth and dried blood ran down his chin.

'I am Karl, Doctor Adam Karl.'

Kaz Oshay had heard of this man. He was known to be a man of great accomplishment, a true scholar among the Statemen:

'You are a doctor?'

'Yes, I run the clinic of Helix City.'

Kaz nodded, though surprised that such a man, a Stateman, was capable of the work that Doctor Karl was reputed to have done. To the Guides, such medicine was foreign; they had their own means of cure in the great wastelands and needed not the medical magic of the Statemen. He waited for the man to be a little more recovered, then:

'Why have you been brought here?'

Doctor Karl shrugged:

'The Lord Zirpola ordered it. He is mad. I made the mistake of telling him so.'

There was a silence, then Doctor Karl got enough strength to lean forward and grasp Kaz Oshay's arm.

'His madness is dangerous to the whole world. He intends to make war on Triton, for their fuel.'

Kaz looked at the other man in silence, digesting this

snippet of information. He understood what was being said, but was not quite sure how he should respond. He knew, of course, what war had been, and how it had become an unthinkable concept. Yet if that was the wish of the Statemen, how could he, who would have nothing to do with them if he could help it, do anything about it – or wish to, even if he were not imprisoned? The result would be that the Statemen would destroy each other, leaving the world free for the Guides and the Mutants. Doctor Karl's grip on his arm became firmer.

'We must find some way to stop him. We cannot have war. It would kill us all.'

Kaz Oshay shrugged:

'You Statemen, who do not know how to live by your words, can never have the knowledge to know the ultimate truth that is peace.'

Doctor Karl, who was becoming more aware of his surroundings with every moment that passed, said:

'Good heavens. You are a Range Guide, aren't you?'

Kaz stared hard at him, but seemed to be going to ignore the question. He was very still for a moment, then rose and went over to the door of his cell, moving on silent feet. With the video ripped out, the all-seeing jailer would not be aware of his movements. But he knew that Deneer would be able to hear him and would respond.

Her eyes appeared at the slit in the door of her cell almost as soon as he looked. When he spoke, it was in a firm, loud voice, as if he had no fear of any other punishment this defiance of orders would incur:

'We must break – or die.'

Deneer nodded and answered him with equal determination and courage:

'Yes. I am my only master. It is my choice.'

They braced themselves for the shocks that must inevitably come. But the jailer had been thoroughly intimidated by Polna's threats. He had too high a regard for his own skin and could only sit impotently and curse the breakdown of discipline under his command. Perhaps the Lord Ankar Moor would come. Then he would be able to appeal against Polna's decision. Ankar Moor was less fastidious in his attitude to the punishment of prisoners, however close the day of the Death Sport might be.

At that moment, the leader of the Obedience Enforcers was just re-entering the City. It was the first time that he had taken any of his men out for a night run on the Death Machines. It was something they would have to get used to, for the journey to Triton would take more than one calendar day. They had been afraid of the strange landscape that had been presented to them, the dark shapes and shadows of the moonlight making frightening ghosts of the rocks and the plains, a landscape entirely foreign to them. Even the bright lights on the front of their machines had done little to alleviate their nervousness.

They could only follow their leader, who was not afraid. Ankar Moor had known the wastelands both by night and by day, until his ambition and his betrayal of the code had brought him to work for his own greater glory, through his attachment to the Lord of Helix and his own, longer term, plans for conquest and power.

He had ridden out, far ahead of the men he was training, to be alone with his own thoughts. His use of the Lord Zirpola to further his own ambitions was rapidly coming to an end. Until the conquest of Triton, the Stateman would remain useful. After that there would be time enough to eliminate him and be declared the lord and ruler of both Triton and Helix in his place. By then, there would be none who would dare to oppose him and his ambitions.

He looked up at the dull moon, hanging hugely in the sky, which provided what little natural light there was. He felt a whole person under its wan glow. He glanced round. In one direction stretched the open plain which was the first step on the six-hundred-mile ride to Triton, in the other, the shadows of the domes of Helix City.

He let the time come into his brain and gave orders for the men strung out behind him on their machines to follow him on the turn that would take them back to the City. He followed his path, leading them in a wide circle, then glanced back to watch the pools of light that came from their machines as they moved cautiously forward. The moon was at his back now and he could almost feel the power that flowed in from it to him, as if it was taken from the whole universe, just to make him stronger.

As they approached the domes of the City, he slowed down to allow the men to come up with him in close formation, but still in single file. Now he went past the domes, taking the riders round the edge of the City until they came to an outcropping of rock beside which stood a small, semi-circular, bunker-like concrete structure, disguised, but paler than the surrounding rock in the moonlight.

It contained the entrance to the ramp that would take the machines back down to their storage area, without anyone in the City who did not already know of them being aware of their existence.

The men waited on their throbbing machines of death as Ankar Moor dismounted from his machine and went silently forward. There was a small slit by the metal door and he placed a special card in it, a card that activated the machinery which would open the door and reveal the artificially-lit ramp to the depths below. He then waited by the door and watched as each of his men descended the ramp, secretly disgusted by the pallid fear he saw in their faces and the relief that showed as they entered the familiar well-lit environment, out of the dangers of the dark wastelands.

Only when they had all entered and the sounds of their machines were fading into the depths below, did Ankar Moor remount and drive his cycle inside. He did not have to dismount this time, just stop his machine and reach out to press the button that re-closed the camouflaged door at the head of the ramp, Then, gunning his machine, he roared down as fast as he could. Woe betide any hapless guard who had been too slow in his descent.

He dismounted in the store and ordered his men to service their machines before being dismissed. The door to the assembly shop swung open and Sarnoff hurried through, mincing towards him. Ankar Moor was surprised. At this time, the scientist was normally getting what he coyly referred to as his 'beauty sleep'.

He snorted.

'What keeps you up at this time, Sarnoff?'

The scientist puffed to a halt and bowed.

'The Lord Zirpola said I was to wait for you. He wants to see you the moment you return.'

Ankar Moor shrugged.

'It is late. He will be sleeping now. The morning will be soon enough. I will see him then.'

But Sarnoff shook his head.

'I would hate to argue with you. After all, I am merely the carrier of the message and the great Ankar Moor is bound to know better than I. But I think that now would be a better time. He has stated his intention to wait for you. He seemed very angry.'

He accompanied this information with a small moan and Ankar Moor's eyes glared out disdain. Unable to bear the hatred that he saw, the scientist turned and scuttled away, back to his assembly shop and comparative safety.

Ankar Moor shrugged and went to set an example by going to service his own machine with infinite pains and slowness. After a while, his anger at the summons subsided and he thought more rationally. Perhaps it would be better if he went to the Lord Zirpola now. The longer the delay, the greater the man's anger would be, and Ankar Moor had enough to deal with without having to put up with that as well.

Zirpola, the Lord of Helix, sat alone in the innermost room of his private chamber, waiting for the chief of his Obedience Enforcers. Spread out before him was the detailed map that showed the main features of the terrain between Helix and Triton. He was studying it intently, making sure that he remembered every detail, an important facet of his conquest of Triton. From the history computer he had heard again and again about an early fighter called Napoleon, who had led a warlike state of people called the French and who had fought his battles in the most primitive of fashions and yet had managed to get a whole continent under his sway. Planning had been his secret, careful planning and preparation. Only the perfidy and treachery of the greedy men who had surrounded him had eventually brought him down and delivered him to the mercy of his enemies. It was something that the Lord Zirpola had taken to heart and learnt well. It was not something that was going to happen to him. Once he had conquered Triton and had made himself irresistibly powerful by the fuel he would then control, he would deal with any problem of that kind.

Recently, he had seen signs of treachery even in Ankar Moor. The man was becoming less and less respectful to him, more independent in his decisions and advice. Zirpola knew the signs. His servant was gaining in greed and ambition. But for the moment he was needed. Once Triton had succumbed to him, he would be able to pick and choose a good General to replace him.

He pored over the maps, remembering each detail and storing away the memory in his decaying brain. The room was in darkness apart from a spotlight above and behind him. This was the easiest way he could read his maps these days. The light hurt his eyes more and more, but by hiding its scource he obtained some relief.

So concentrated was he on his task that he almost jumped as there came a firm knock on the door. The guards had allowed his visitor to come that far and it was only Ankar Moor who was allowed such freedom. He reached forward and pressed the button on the huge desk that would release the door mechanism:

'Enter.'

Ankar Moor marched inside and the door slid shut behind him. He walked straight to the far side of the desk over which the map was spread, and stood waiting with as great a show of patience as he could muster. The Lord Zirpola had returned to his study of the maps and looked down at them in silence. Slowly the patience slipped away from the leader of the Obedience Enforcers and he became more irritable and uncomfortable, not even being invited to sit. He cleared his throat:

'You wanted to see me?'

'In a moment.'

The Lord of Helix did not look up and there was another silence as he continued with his studies. At last he sat back and surveyed the standing man through his watery, blue eyes:

'You have been out on night training?'

'Yes, My Lord.'

'You are not wasting too much of our precious fuel, I hope?'

Ankar Moor swallowed his anger:

'The training is necessary. They will have to travel by night.'

Zirpola nodded:

'True. The men, they are coming along well?'

Ankar Moor drew himself up proudly:

'They are becoming better and more competent with every day that passes, My Lord.'

The Lord of Helix snorted:

'But not competent enough. Not with the disasters of

yesterday. How can you face me and make such a boast?'

Ankar Moor was puzzled.

'But we achieved our aim, My Lord. We captured four of the Range Guides for the Death Sport.'

Zirpola glared and slammed his hand palm down on the surface of the desk with a loud crack.

'And at what cost?'

Beneath the mask, the Enforcer's mangled flesh reddened.

'Well, as I told you yesterday, the combat cost us some eleven men altogether. But there are plenty more. Men are always expendable.'

Zirpola came to the point he was making. He screamed:

'But my precious machines are not.'

'But Sarnoff has more spare parts.'

'Parts, yes. But he reported to me this evening. There are not enough parts to put together any more complete machines.'

This information was stunning even to Ankar Moor, leaving him bereft of speech for a moment.

'But it has only cost us two of them.'

'That is two machines too many. Damn it, do you think that such a loss is an accomplishment? And how many more machines do we risk losing in the Death Sport?'

Ankar Moor shrugged:

'We will still have more than enough to take Triton. In the depths of their City we know they will have the same storage rooms as we uncovered, and our spies tell us they have remained sealed and have never been opened. We can make more machines when we have captured the City.'

Zirpola brushed this truth aside:

'But if too many of the machines get destroyed in the Death Sport, the result could be catastrophic. None must be destroyed, do you understand that? They must be seen to vanquish all comers.'

Ankar Moor tried to temporise:

'But we cannot account for accidents that will happen. Anyway, what is the Death Sport if there is no edge to it?'

The man was genuinely puzzled by Zirpola's attitude. Every gamble carries the seeds of some risks within it. He had always made the assumption that even someone as blinded by ambition as the Lord of Helix could see that.

His master disillusioned him further now.

'But the object is that the people must be made to believe

that riding a Death Machine will make them as powerful as any of the Guides. We have to use the Death Sport to build that confidence. It is crucial to our war effort.'

In spite of his disdain for the weak, ageing man before him, Ankar Moor understood his reservations and fears. But there seemed to be no way to get through to him the risks that were involved. He leaned forward across the table, resting his huge palms face down on the surface of the map, blotting out the features on it. When he spoke, his voice was as hard as granite:

'I understand you perfectly, My Lord. Believe me, the way I have planned it, the Death Sport has been carefully structured this year and although I cannot guarantee one hundred per cent that no machine will risk being lost in combat, I can absolutely guarantee that none of the Guides will survive the day's sport.'

Zirpola was leaning right back in his chair as if the other man posed an immediate physical threat. But his watery blue eyes showed no fear and his anger at the other man's attitude was building up within him, preparing to erupt.

'Your life is my guarantee of that, Ankar Moor. Never forget it for an instant.'

As Ankar Moor backed away a little, Zirpola came abruptly forward, clutching his head in his hands. To the other men it looked merely like frustration and anger at work, but in fact the pain was returning to him as the doctor's injection was beginning to wear off.

For the first time he felt a weakness in his resolve, regretting the way in which he had had the doctor arrested and locked up, beaten and condemned. Who would relieve him of the pain he felt? There were no other good doctors in the City, certainly not one who could be trusted to the extent that Doctor Karl had been. True, Karl had trained the people in his clinic so that they were able to carry out the routine work of treatment, but Zirpola would not like any of these bunglers to know about the pain from which he suffered.

More than just the fuel of Helix City was running out now for the Lord Zirpola. Perhaps time was as well; perhaps Karl had been speaking the truth; perhaps he was going mad from the pain, even dying.

The wave of pain receded a little but it still showed in his eyes as he looked up. His voice was filled with despair:

'The Death Sport must bring me volunteers from among the people. We must have enough men for every eventuality, or the conquest of Triton may still not be sure.'

He stood up, not waiting for an answer and began to pace up and down, more to take his mind off the pain than for any effect. Ankar Moor felt the time had come to soothe him. He was getting tired of the interview and had much business of his own to take care of:

'The volunteers will come, My Lord.'

'Are you guaranteeing that too?'

Ankar Moor nodded.

'They will come forward after they have seen the Death Sport. They will fall over themselves to be part of the conquest of Triton, for the glory and the rewards.'

'How can we be sure that that ambition still burns amongst the ordinary people. There has been no war for nine hundred years, not since the great holocaust that came close to destroying us all. The people, perhaps they do not understand what is at stake. They are fearful, they do not have the vision to see ahead as you and I do.'

Those last words told the masked man that he was back in favour.

'But you will give them that vision, My Lord. You and the demonstration of the power of your machines.'

Zirpola stepped back into the pool of light and banged his fist down on the desk.

'I must wage war with a solid front, my people must be made to believe that they are invincible, that they cannot suffer harm in the war that is to come or I will not just lose the chance for an army, I will have an insurrection to deal with and then what will we do?'

For this, Ankar Moor had no reply. After a moment, Zirpola wiped a shaking hand over his brow and collapsed back into his chair as if the tirade had exhausted him. The pain in his head was getting stronger by the minute and he knew that he must soon terminate his discussion or Ankar Moor would find out what was the matter with him. The two men eyed each other in silence for a moment and at last the Lord of Helix leant forward again. Now his voice was soft, as if the anger had been washed out of him.

'Now do you understand my fears, the burden that is placed upon me as a leader?'

Ankar Moor modulated his own rasping voice to bring reassurance to his leader.

'You have no need of fear, My Lord. Normally, one Guide might destroy an incalculable number of Statemen in the Death Sport. But this year we are going to pit two Guides against a number of men mounted on their machines. They will only have their own weapons and the people will see them quickly destroyed.'

'Yes, I am sorry to have doubted. They will be convinced. I am sure of it. My fears are only the fears of one who must lead.'

Ankar Moor could have reached over at that moment and squeezed the life from the man's scrawny neck. But he held his rage in check, the time was not right, as he had to keep reminding himself.

'Yes, My Lord.'

Zirpola rose with difficulty.

'I am tired, I must rest now. You should do the same. You have worked hard and well for my cause and there is more to do on the morrow.'

He pressed the button on his desk and the door slid open again, a signal that the interview was at an end. The two men walked to the door together and Ankar Moor said:

'There will be no rest for me yet, My Lord. I must go and see how the prisoners are faring – and perhaps make the arrangements for the Guides to enjoy the pleasures of the disorientation chambers. That will underline my guarantees.'

'Go then. We will meet again on the morrow, before the Death Sport is due to commence.'

Ankar Moor bowed again and walked forward. A moment later, the door slid to, blocking out Zirpola's view of the back of the huge Enforcer leader.

The stricken man turned and almost raced across the open space, only just making it to his chair before he collapsed, giving in to the waves of pain that were washing over him. He was able to scream aloud for relief now that there was no other person within earshot.

After a while, the pain receded a little, and the curtain of redness lifted partially from in front of his eyes. There was one thing keeping him going, keeping him from giving in. His plans for his conquest of Triton. Perhaps when they had taken that City he would find a doctor who would not only stop the pain, but would cure him for ever. Karl had been no good. Karl had been a traitor. He could not be going mad, he could not be dying. He was the Lord Zirpola, ruler of Helix and, soon, conqueror of the world.

He leant back against the rest of the huge chair and slipped into a fitful doze. He would stay here for the night, if the pain would let him alone for so long.

Marcus Karl was tired too. He seemed to have walked for hours, but at last he had reached the level on which were housed the privileged technicians, in quarters larger than those of most of the workers in the City.

It was here that he had grown up, looked after by his father after his mother's death. In spite of the lateness of the hour, people were still wandering, apparently aimlessly, in the corridors, pausing in small groups to look up at the Public Service Television screens that were set at intervals in the walls and were giving out the usual formula of bland, banal programming.

At the moment, Carol Rabids and Howard Koslow, the two commentators who specialised in outside broadcasts of events in the City, were showing a programme of clips from Death Sport – 'Great Kills of the Past' – in preparation for the annual Death Sport the following afternoon. They were a popular couple for most televideo viewers, but Marcus had never understood why and did not even glance up at them as he hurried along.

He turned one last corner and found himself in the almost deserted corridor that contained the entrance-way to his father's privileged living quarters. He was so preoccupied in the triumph of completing the journey without rest that he failed to notice the printed announcement that was pasted across the door below the seal that had been put on it. His hand went to the automatic palm plate that would open the door and he glanced up at it only when nothing happened. Then he paled.

PUBLIC NOTICE. THESE QUARTERS ARE SEALED BY THE SPECIAL EXECUTIVE ORDER OF THE LORD ZIRPOLA, LORD OF HELIX. THE OCCUPANT HAS BEEN IMPRISONED FOR CRIMES AGAINST THE PERSON OF THE RULER.

Below this was a list of crimes, of which treason to the person of the Lord Zirpola was the first. Marcus could not believe his eyes, and, as he read down the list, his hatred for Zirpola hardened and a bitter anger began to well up within him. No man should have such arbitrary power over his people. Even now, he did not question Zirpola's right to rule, only the manner in which he carried out his duties.

He turned, almost blinded by his rage, and walked the short distance to the entrance to the clinic, which was maintained on the same level as his father's home. It was late and there would be few people on duty at this hour.

The duty nurse on the entrance desk looked up as he blundered in.

'Marcus – '

As she rose he pushed past her and half-walked, half-ran down the corridor to his father's office. He opened the door and blundered in on the occupant.

His father's personal nurse was sitting by the desk, her face buried in her hands as she sobbed. There were files piled everywhere and she had obviously been overcome by her emotions as she cleared his office. Zirpola and his men did not waste a moment once a man had been thrown into the Helix prison.

The nurse, Embra, was a middle-aged comfortable-looking Statewoman who had been with his father for as long as Marcus could remember. He had even been under the impression that her devotion had been motivated by more than just a desire to serve. Her tears stopped at once as she looked him up and down.

'Marcus! What are you doing here?'

'Trying to find my father. A notice on his door says he has been arrested.'

'But you were on your way to Triton – to be married. What has happened? You couldn't possibly have heard.'

The Enforcers followed us on strange machines. They killed one of our Range Guides and captured another, then they turned us all back with some story that the Range Guides were in league with the Mutants.'

She was surprised.

'That cannot be. The Range Guides would never do that. It would be a breaking of their code.'

He frowned.

'Strange things are abroad in Helix. Why has my father been taken?'

This was enough to set Embra bawling again and Marcus

put a comforting arm around her shoulder, soothing her.

'Tell me, I must know.'

She managed to hold back the tears for long enough to respond.

'They say he was a traitor to the Lord Zirpola, working against him, and that is fatal for any man.'

'My father would never dream of involving himself in politics. He is an honourable man, serving all mankind within the City. And any who would come to him from beyond its confines.'

'Nevertheless, he was taken. There must be something behind it.' The woman was unable to believe that Zirpola was anything but the purest of fair men. Marcus snapped:

'Has he been taken to the prison?'

'Yes. There was no trial. An arrest on Lord Zirpola's orders is a statement of guilt.'

'You mean he is already condemned without a hearing?'

The woman nodded.

'The next time we shall see him will be in the arena for the Death Sport games tomorrow.'

If that was what she thought, Marcus Karl was determined to change that outcome. He was not going to await the death of his father with tranquillity. He sat down, his brows heavy with thought. After a while, the crying of the woman became more subdued, then died away altogether. She recovered herself enough to ask:

'What will you do now – wait for the next caravan that is going to Triton? You can stay with us until you go.'

Marcus managed to smile his thanks at Embra for her generous offer, but shook his head. A plan was beginning to take shape in his mind.

'No, I intend to be gone from this City long before that – and not alone, either.'

A shocked gasp came from the woman.

'What are you saying? No Stateman has ever made the journey across the wastelands alone and survived.'

Marcus stood, his mind made up.

'With God's help, my father and I will. Also one of the captured Guides if I can free her too. Embra, your husband, he was once a guard in the prison?'

The woman was frightened for the young man she had loved as much as she would have loved a son of her own.

'He was once, but he has been dead for nigh on five years.'

He seized her by the shoulders, as if prepared to shake the information from her if she did not answer him freely.

'Where are the kitchens from which the prisoners are fed?'

Her answer was speedy enough:

'They are on the same level as the cells. But Marcus, no one can get on to that level without the proper identification. Only the Enforcers may go freely to that level.'

He looked grim.

'Then, Embra, I am about to become an Enforcer and you will aid me. Get on the video and put out a call for a guard.'

'Please, no, Marcus, I beg you.'

'You will do it for my father, Embra.'

She ceased to protest and he went on:

'Tell him that you have found something strange among Doctor Karl's files – some evidence of treachery that Zirpola will want to see, something important.'

'But . . .'

'Do it now.'

Reluctantly, the woman went over to the desk and pressed down the emergency button that would put the nearest Enforcer guard in contact with her immediately as he hurried to the source of the emergency. Lord Zirpola had introduced an extremely efficient policing system to the City with the help of Ankar Moor.

A man was in contact almost at once and Embra blurted:

'Doctor Karl's office at the clinic. Come quickly. There is evidence of treachery.'

Marcus smiled his thanks. That should bring the man on the double. He glanced round for a suitable weapon and found it in a large paperweight of fused carbon. He picked it up, before placing himself out of sight to one side of the sliding door.

He did not have long to wait. The guard entered, his weapon at the ready and, seeing only a sobbing woman by the desk, strode forward into the room, reholstering it. Marcus stepped forward and the paperweight smashed down on the guard's head. He lay very still on the floor and when Marcus bent over him, he felt sick. The force of the blow had crushed the man's skull and he was dead.

Marcus had already steeled himself to divest the guard of his uniform and weapon when Embra recovered herself enough to speak.

'Marcus. You will be condemned yourself for this.'

The light of battle shone in Marcus Karl's eyes.

'Not if they do not find out – and I know that they will not from you. Get anyone else you can trust and have his body taken to the morgue. It will seem to be just an accident.'

As he spoke, he hustled her to the door, knowing that if she stopped for a moment he would have a woman in a state of complete collapse on his hands.

'Perhaps we will see each other again, one day, Embra.'

'I hope so, Marcus. I will pray that it is not in the Death Sport arena.'

The door slid shut behind her and he turned back to make a hasty finish to his grisly job, putting the guard's clothes over his own. The anti-matter blaster he picked up and held gingerly in both hands. He had never used such a weapon before. Now a new idea occurred to him. He aimed the deadly weapon and fired. At once the dead body disappeared as if it had never been on the office floor. He was ashamed not only at killing a man, but at the thought of destroying the man's body. When that happened, he had been taught, the soul can never find peace, but goes to live among the Mutants. However, it might help to save his father's life and any step was justified if that was to be the result.

Another moment and he was out into the corridor and down to the front of the clinic. He was at first surprised to see that people moved out of his way as he went forward in the direction of the elevator banks and it took him a little while to realise that it was the uniform they feared. Morale had sunk to a low ebb amongst the population of Helix. He walked into an open elevator and, using the over-rider that he found in the pocket of his new, official outfit, he set it to move down into the bowels of the earth, to the prison level.

The next part of his plan was not entirely clear in his mind, but if it involved killing, then so be it. He had to get to his father and get him out alive.

CHAPTER FIVE

On those occasions when Ankar Moor went in person to visit the prison level of Helix City, a warning was always flashed to the men in charge of each section well in advance, so that all could be ready for his visit. Such warnings were usually inclined to put fear into the hearts of the men who ran the level, for Ankar Moor was a cruel task master. But on this occasion, the man in charge of the prison area was pleased by the warning; with any luck, the head of the Obedience Enforcers would overturn Polna's orders with regard to punishment. Someone, anyway, would be worse off for his visit. That was always the case when Ankar Moor called on the prisoners.

Meanwhile, the flashed warning told him that the man was coming on a visit to inspect the new intake and the jailer switched on the loudspeakers to get them prepared.

'Attention. Stand by your cell doors, quiet and ready for immediate inspection.'

In the cell that he now shared with Doctor Karl, Kaz Oshay at first took no notice of the order. He had had enough of this enemy who hid behind a booming electronic voice machine, such a coward that he did not dare to come and challenge the Guide in the open, even though the latter was unarmed.

Doctor Karl had fallen into a fitful sleep but now he awoke with a jerk and at once got wearily to his feet, still battered by the beating he had taken. He swayed over to the door and used one hand to prop himself up from the wall as he waited.

Now Kaz rose as well, realising that by disobeying the order he would be inflicting the same punishment on the Stateman as he would on himself, and realising, too, that the other man probably did not have the strength to take it. Such treachery to weaker brethren was contrary to the teachings of the code.

They stood next to each other in silence for a while, waiting to learn if there was any reason for this latest drill. The doctor wearily broke the silence, at last:

'What do you know of the Death Sport?'

Kaz shrugged.

'I have heard of the game, of course. It is played by Statemen so they can live through the deaths of others. We Guides have no need of such odd behaviour.'

Somehow, his flat tone took all offence out of any insult to Doctor Karl as a Stateman that might have been implied by the answer. The doctor managed a painful smile. He had always admired the Guides for their quiet skills and boundless courage and he seemed to be faced with a very special man, even of their calling. He tried, haltingly, to explain about the games and the reasons for the Death Sport.

'It is not just a sport in itself, it is a ruse that allows the Family of Zirpola to maintain their power over the Statemen of Helix: a trick as old as the rule of one man over the other.'

Kaz frowned.

'But it is still just a game, is it not?'

Doctor Karl tried to make his explanation clearer:

'No, that is only the surface of it. Have you ever heard of it being played in any of the other Statemen Cities – in Triton, for example? There at least I know it is not played.'

Kaz Oshay frowned in thought. The man spoke words of truth. He had travelled far and wide across the wastelands and the deserts and had come into contact with the citizens of many Cities, but he had never heard of the Death Sport, except from the citizens of Helix.

'What you say is truth, but then there is much about the City of Helix that is different from the homes of the other Statemen.'

The doctor could not restrain his curiosity.

'Different?'

Kaz hesitated. He was groping for the right words to use to describe what he had seen and heard.

'Well, their leaders. In the other Cities there is usually a council of wise men or one wise man. He is proclaimed by the other citizens for a period of time, then makes way to be proclaimed again or to let another take his place. Only in Helix does the power pass through one family, from father to son for as long as they live.'

Karl nodded. He had heard about what other Statemen

called 'elections' from travellers passing through the City who had come for medical help. Most citizens of Helix were not allowed to mix with temporary visitors, but the doctor had occupied a privileged position, as he now realised, bitterly.

'Do you know of differences other than that?'

Kaz nodded. 'The guards. They have them too in the other Cities, but they are helpful men, charged with helping the citizens and protecting them. Only here do they have the strange name of Obedience Enforcers and answer only to the whim of the master of the City – and then there are the trees and the flowers . . .'

Karl frowned. He seemed to have memory of such things from books and tapes in his youth. 'What are those?'

Kaz smiled. 'They are things that grow. They are green mainly, but some have leaves and blossoms that are all colours. I have been told that they have grown inside the Cities for many centuries. Now, Statemen from some of the Cities are trying to make them grow in the deserts that surround them. A few have succeeded.'

Doctor Karl sighed. He remembered now. They were things that had grown all across the earth before the land had been poisoned by the terrible war that had ended all wars. Truly, this night was teaching him hard and fast that he had always lived in an oppressive place. He spoke at last:

'Yes, Helix is a City apart and the Death Sport is central to what makes it so. The power of the Lord Zirpola would be lost without it, for while it brings excitement to those who watch it, it also brings fear into their hearts as well as providing entertainment to Zirpola's followers and cronies.'

Kaz Oshay eyed his cellmate with a growing respect. Why, the man even thought in the manner of the Guides. To Kaz's mind that was the highest compliment that he could pay. He had before him a man who would honour the teaching of the code itself, a valuable man.

His attention was diverted back to the door as the blips sounded and the light code lit up on the inner panel of the huge metal door at the entrance to the prison area. For the jailer, this augured the arrival of Ankar Moor at last and he stood smartly by his console, waiting for the door to open and the mighty leader of the Obedience Enforcers to stride in. He suppressed the sudden fear he felt, the fear all men felt when Ankar Moor came to them.

As Ankar Moor entered, the jailer was irritated to see that Polna was at his side and he let his words about the use of punishment die on his lips, unspoken.

Ankar Moor glared at him through the slits in his frightening mask and snapped:

'I will see the new prisoners at once.'

The jailer bowed low, aware that, behind his master's back, Polna was giving him a malevolent grin, and pointed out the corridor down which the giant would have to go.

The two men moved quickly forward at a military pace, their hobnails ringing on the metal floor, sending up a shower of sparks as they went down the corridor. Ankar Moor came to an abrupt halt as he reached the door of Deneer's cell. He turned to Polna.

'Is this the cell of the woman you found for me?'

'Yes, Lord.'

Ankar Moor nodded brusquely and squinted into Deneer's eyes through the slit in the door. His voice rasped out:

'Who are you?'

She made no reply, but her eyes stared bravely, challengingly into his own. He felt a sudden stab of unaccustomed fear and covered it over by snarling: 'I demand to know.'

The hatred and defiance that sparked from her eyes grew in intensity. She recognised him and his covered face from long ago, but she reserved part of her hatred for the leader of the men who had captured her.

'I am Deneer – and you are the damned Ankar Moor, the destroyer of the code.' She had spat out his name as if even the sound of it on her lips was poisonous.

He was amused by the intensity of her answer. On balance again, his first fear gone, his voice became low, but still hard:

'Yes, I am Ankar Moor himself. There is perhaps some reason why you do not approve of my name?'

Her eyes turned to mirrors and he saw himself, the dark side of the code, reflected back at him, but he was unable to tear his own eyes away for the moment. Her reply seemed oblique to Polna, but struck straight at the heart of his companion.

'Everything is within the self. Nothing is outside. It is known to all who abide by the code that you have lost yourself. Ankar Moor is a man who is without a soul. A name to be despised.'

On the surface the chief of the Enforcers was accepting the challenge of her eyes and her words, but deep within him he felt a terrible cold fear, all the more frightening for being unassuageable. He used his own hatred and contempt for her teachings to try to stare her down, but with no success. Each word he used was rasped out with a deliberation that was supposed to burn into her brain, but made no apparent impression on her.

'Ankar Moor, you say, has no soul. But Ankar Moor stands free. You stand where you are now, enslaved by him. Your self is not your own, it belongs to me. Show me your humility or I will break you.'

Deneer did not show whether she had heard by so much as the movement of a muscle, but continued her level stare until it was the big man who was forced to lower his eyes. Then she spoke:

'You have not the power to break me, empty man. I am my only master. Take away my body and my soul will still be mine, forever.'

For a long moment Polna watched with real fear in his heart as he wondered what his master might do. Ankar Moor had pulled himself up close to the door as if he was about to try to tear it out bodily to confront his prisoner, at the same time remaining as if he had been carved out of stone.

Behind the mask, his brain was seething with anger at the insult she had offered to him in the terms of the code he so despised. He could have her killed now, at once. Just one bolt of electricity at the right intensity would do the job. But the anger died in him as he thought of witnessing her death in the arena the following day. When he spoke his final words to her, his voice was flat, hiding his inner emotions.

'You are lucky, Guide. Today you may continue with both soul and body; today, I still have need of you.'

He turned abruptly on his heel and walked across the corridor to face another door where a pair of eyes blazed out at him, filled with hatred. The look of them was as dreadful as those of the woman he had just torn himself away from.

'And what is your name, Guide?'

Kaz Oshay did not give him a direct answer. His voice was as soft and as devoid of emotion as if he was in a trance:

'It is a name that I can carry with pride.'

The anger that was burning inside Ankar Moor welled

up once more as the implication of the answer sank in. 'You must answer me. I demand to know.'

Kaz let his eyes blaze in disdain at the querulous tone of his interrogator.

'I am called Kaz Oshay. I am the son of Oshay.'

The effect of this information was immediate and startling to Polna as he watched his master closely. Ankar Moor's hands came up as if to protect himself from some blow and he took an involuntary pace backwards in the corridor, as if the man in the cell had threatened him. Inside the cell his reaction was matched by the intake of Doctor Karl's breath. So this was the son of the legendary Oshay of the Guides.

Ankar Moor recovered himself in an instant, aware that his reaction had been seen and anxious to cover it up.

'Kaz Oshay, you say. I knew your mother.'

Kaz nodded calmly.

'Yes. She often told me of you, Ankar Moor. It was she who gave you your disgrace. It was you who betrayed the consciousness. Your dishonour is a legend among the free Guides.'

Inwardly, Ankar Moor shuddered as he remembered his fight with the woman who had destroyed his face and had banished him forever from the Guides for his betrayal of the code. She had him at her mercy and could have killed him. That he could have stood. But the deformities she had stricken him with would remain forever, keeping him apart from normal men. The stigma was upon both his body and his soul.

He shrugged away the painful memory with the thought that the code held no magic for him now, no place in his plans and ambitions. They were foolish and outmoded in this world which he would so rapidly change. When the time came, he would destroy all the free Guides and the stigma would be lifted from him.

His voice was harsh and he made no attempt to hide contemptuous hatred for the man who faced him from behind the locked door of the cell.

'My dishonour is now your fantasy, Kaz Oshay, son of Oshay. But what is reality is that I can now return to you a better gift than ever your mother gave to me – your death, Guide. I would give it to you now, but am happy that you will receive it in the Death Sport.'

Kaz Oshay was not frightened by such threats, his eyes

remained level as he repeated the formula of the code that Deneer had used:

'If you take away my body, my soul will still be mine, forever.'

This was the second time this answer had been given to him and it acted on the chief of the Enforcers like a slap in the face. He could only take comfort in the knowledge that before another night had fallen, their bodies would have died and their souls would be wandering away from the Earth for eternity. They would be no further threat to him then. He turned on his heel, pushed past Polna, who hurried to get back alongside him, and marched away from the cells.

Only when he was in the main hall, and was sure that he was out of their sight, did he pause to try to relax the tension that had grown in him, the fear that had gripped his heart. He turned to Polna and the sadistic jailer smiled as he heard the order given:

'Starting at dawn, you will put them in separate chambers and feed them disorientation.'

Polna nodded, keeping his face as devoid of expression as Ankar Moor's mask made the latter. If he had seen and recognised the fear in Ankar Moor he was wise enough to give no indication of it.

'It has already been arranged.'

The two men approached the great door and, with a show of impatience, Ankar Moor waited while Polna tapped out the appropriate code on the light panel that would break the security circuits and allow the door to open. A moment later they strode through the space and were gone, the sound of the closing door booming through the cells.

But Ankar Moor and Polna had not been out of Kaz Oshay's sight for a moment. Pushing the doctor to one side, Kaz had moved round so that by putting his eye to an oblique angle in the slit, he had been able to squint into the main area. The light panel by the door had been fully in his view and he had committed the tapped-out code to memory, should the opportunity to make a break for it arise. He had no plan in his mind, but a Guide stores away any information he can acquire in a given situation, in case it should assume some importance in the scheme of things. Nothing is too insignificant to be overlooked. If he could, he was determined to be far away from the City of Helix before the Death Sport was due to begin.

In the silence that followed the closing of the main door, the doctor did his best to contain his curiosity, but at last could do so no longer. His voice was awed as he asked:

'Your mother, she was truly Oshay?'

Kaz nodded. 'Truly.'

There was no hint of boasting in his voice, just the flat statement. Now that he knew she was dead, his mother belonged to the closed book of the past. The future was all that was ever important to a Guide, the promise of the future and the dangers of the present.

He turned away from the doctor and back to the slit in the door, his eyes once more locking on those of the girl in the cell opposite. Karl, however, was still going to let curiosity override good manners.

'I had always believed that Oshay was a myth.'

Kaz did not break the gaze. 'She lived. I am her offspring, her proof.'

He was not really inclined to talk about her, but he respected and admired this Stateman and would not dismiss his questions as he would have done those of other men.

Karl pressed on:

'The powers that she is said to have possessed. They never seemed quite believable to me. Not even for a Range Guide.'

'But they were true. She had such powers.'

'But it is said that she just had to feel the open air and then knew, even days in advance, that a deadly Flash Wind was going to come off the wastelands. Could she really do that? It does not seem possible.'

The locked-on stare between the two Guides in their separate cells remained unbroken.

'It was possible. She could do it.'

'And all her faculties were equally in tune with the elements – her smell, her hearing, everything?'

Kaz sighed.

'All that men have heard about her was true.'

The doctor was now so deeply involved in his own thought processes that he could not cease the questions. As a medical man he was profoundly interested that the human race could have mutated to such an extent as that. 'And do you have these powers?'

This time, Kaz Oshay withdrew from the gaze and he turned to look deep into the doctor's eyes as he replied:

'It is sometimes true.'

'Why not always?'

'My life is not yet over. I do not know if I will retain them.'

An answer like that, so simple, so primitive, underlined the truth of all that Kaz had ascribed to his mother. The doctor fell silent, locked in his own mind for a moment. What a waste a quick death on the morrow would be.

As for Kaz Oshay, he returned to gaze into the eyes of Deneer, while the doctor began to pace up and down the tiny cell. At length, realising once more the extent of his exhaustion, he leaned against the back wall and allowed himself slowly to slide down into a sitting position, with his back pressed hard against the metal. His arrest and beating had exhausted him more than he wished to admit, even to himself. He was amazed that he had been able to stay active this long and ascribed it in some measure to the latent vitality of the man with whom he was incarcerated.

Had he not drifted again into sleep, he could have watched for one long hour as Kaz Oshay stood at the door of the cell, his eyes locked on Deneer's. During that time he would have been unable to detect a single movement in the other man.

It was at the end of this hour that the blips came again on the light screen at the side of the main door and Kaz withdrew his gaze from Deneer to squint again along the line of sight he had found for himself as he watched the light pattern coded out.

The great door swung open and one of the Enforcers entered. Behind him came another of his kind, pushing a large trolley of stainless steel, which carried food bowls for the prisoners. Bringing up the rear was a third man, who, like the first, had his anti-matter blaster at the ready. All three were wearing their protective helmets and had their visors down, so their faces could not be seen. It was the man pushing the trolley, who had taken the shift to allow Levron some time off, who had told the men to don all this equipment. He had already been wearing his own and said that the orders came directly from Ankar Moor, so they had not been questioned.

Marcus Karl pushed the trolley forward into the main area, his heart pounding in his ears as if it – and they – would burst. For the second time in his life, he had killed a man.

In his uniform, it had been easy to gain entry to the prison level. No one had asked for a pass. His uniform had been enough to get him through. He had gone directly to the kitchens and here he had struck up a conversation with a guard who seemed to be hanging around with little to do.

Marcus had quickly learnt that the man's name was Levron and it was his duty, in company with the guards Haddash and Methro, to push the food trolley in and serve the prisoners, once the meal had been prepared. He was waiting now while the preparations were made.

Marcus had been able to persuade the man out into the corridor on the promise that he would show him something very special on a portable video unit out there and, once they were alone, he had used the blaster he had stolen to deadly effect.

He had then re-entered the kitchens, quickly located Haddash and Methro, and had informed them that Levron was unwell and had gone to lie down, after asking him to take his place for the night's detail. It had been almost too easy. So, also, had the order from Ankar Moor regarding the helmets.

Accepted as a replacement with ease, he was now facing what he knew would be the most dangerous moment of his life in his attempt to rescue his father.

A moment of danger came at once. The men's faces may have been hidden, but the jailer was good at his job and recognised a stranger immediately. He held up his hand for the guards to halt:

'You are not the usual guard.'

Behind his mask, Marcus froze, unable even to breathe, much less to answer. It was Haddish who unwittingly saved him:

'He's standing in for Levron. Lazy bugger says he isn't well again, wanted to lie down.'

The jailer nodded, satisfied:

'That bloody Levron, always skiving. You'd think he'd be able to make it on a soft detail like this.'

He signalled the trolley forward and Haddash said to Marcus, 'I know the routine. You just follow me and you won't go wrong.' Both men now went ahead of him, which allowed him to unsnap the holster on his own anti-matter blaster as he went forward. He pushed the trolley down the corridor and came to the first cell on the right. There were two men in the cell and the guard used the special code to unlock the door. At once both guns were trained on the interior against any movement, but the occupants were both Statemen, already cowed and just waiting for the day of their death.

With the cell secure, thanks to the pointed guns, Marcus took the first two bowls and placed them inside the door. As he stepped back, the door closed and locked again.

The same routine was followed at the next cell in the line – the cell that contained Kaz Oshay and Doctor Karl. As soon as the door slid back, Marcus saw his father and his heart leapt.

Now was the moment of greatest danger. He stepped back from the trolley and drew his blaster as the two men stuck the muzzles of their weapons inside the cell. A second later, he shouted:

'Freeze.'

Marcus's order to the guards came just a split second too late. Kaz Oshay was both unaware of his identity and his intentions. To the Guide, the man who had drawn his gun behind the trolley was but another of the hated guards.

Kaz had taken up a position against the back wall. Now he launched himself in the air across the tiny cell with every ounce of pent-up ferocity that was in him.

He was too quick for the guards, one foot smashing each of them to the ground with their necks broken. His flight carried him on so that he crashed into Marcus, whose head made contact with the far wall and who slid to the floor, unconscious.

He landed lightly and, with no delay, snatched up the blaster that the youth had dropped. He spun round and his eyes caught those of Deneer, staring out from her cell door.

'I will be back.'

He ran as fast as he could down the corridor to the main area. But the head jailer had already heard the sounds of the deadly scuffle. At once, almost by a reflex action, he had hurled himself forward over the console and had tripped off the alarms which now exploded into sound, not only in the prison itself but at key points throughout the City. He then tried to duck down, but he was too late. The anti-matter blaster that Kaz Oshay carried pushed him into the oblivion of space.

Kaz spun to the main door, but he was too late. The anti-blaster shield, that electric field with its green glow, which affords such perfect protection, came down between him and the door, effectively sealing him into the main compound and the cells. While it was down no one would be able to either enter or leave.

Kaz crashed into it and spun back. He fired the blaster at it, but there was no apparent effect. He quickly realised that he had come up against something that would not respond to attack. In such circumstances brains must replace speed and physical skill.

He went to the console and pressed down all the buttons he could find. They did nothing for the shield. That could now only be turned off from outside the compound. The result of his groping was that all the cell doors were opened and the prisoners, Statemen and Guides alike, came pouring into the main hall.

With a scream of animal rage, Kaz Oshay shouted:

'We are sealed in!'

Deneer hurried over to him. He could not help but admire her beauty and grace of movement which so matched her perfect eyes into which he had looked so steadily and for so long.

Varros and Ikar, the two older Guides who had been captured, followed her. All four looked at one another, ignoring the Statemen who were milling around, still bewildered over what had happened:

'Our Union is limited.'

'I agree.' The words of the ritual echoed four times round the group.

'What is the situation?' asked Varros. 'Why can we not move from here?'

Kaz answered quickly:

'The jailer threw up the blaster shield inside the entrance before I could get to him. I have tried to blast it out, but I have failed. There is no hope that way.'

Deneer glanced round.

'The shield is only in that direction – perhaps we can blast our way through one of the walls.'

Kaz Oshay nodded. It was worth a try. He glanced round for Doctor Karl but could not see him amongst the milling, bewildered men. He hurried down the corridor back to the cell. The doctor was a man worth rescuing, worth protecting.

Doctor Karl had managed to get to the cell door and was gazing down in amazement. The blow from Kaz Oshay had knocked Marcus's helmet off as he fell. Deneer and Varros pushed past him, snatched up the guns dropped from the hands of the two dead men and blasted them into eternity. Kaz raised his weapon to do the same to the third man, but Doctor Karl leapt forward, blocking his line of fire:

'For God's sake, no!'

Kaz lowered the weapon and frowned.

'Why not, Stateman?'

'That is my son.' As he spoke, he knelt anxiously at the youth's side. A moment later, he smiled. The boy was alive and coming round.

Kaz could not understand.

'You mean your son is one of the hated guards?'

Doctor Karl managed to smile.

'No. He must have been trying to rescue me.'

'He is a brave man then. Truly, like you, he has the outlook of a Guide. I am sorry, I did not know. It is lucky that those other two slowed me up or he would be dead as well.'

Deneer re-emerged from the cell. She pointed her blaster at the ceiling:

'Perhaps that is the way.'

Once again, Doctor Karl leapt forward to knock the gun aside.

'The main fuel lines for the whole City run directly over us. It will explode and we will all die.'

Deneer lowered her gun. Kaz stepped forward. In the short time they had been together he had learned to trust this man. Now it seemed he was familiar enough with the layout of the prison area to be able, perhaps, to show them a way out.

'What lies below us?'

Doctor Karl frowned.

'It's solid rock. We are on the lowest level of the central City.'

'And around us?'

The doctor shook his head:

'Solid rock again.' He hesitated, then: 'Wait a moment, there is one spot with a shared wall, if I can only remember just where. Give me a moment to think.'

Even Kaz's voice was urgent:

'Please, be as quick as you can. We must hurry. They will be moving against us and we must get free.'

Lord Zirpola had managed to slip into a fitful sleep in the

huge chair behind his desk in spite of the oncoming tide of pain that threatened to engulf his reason. Now, as the alarm bells started to sound in his quarters, telling him that there had been a break in security at the prison, he snapped into complete wakefulness.

As he rose, he realised that there was an emergency and pushed the pain away from him. He leapt up and refastened his cloak of office. He put his ornate belt round himself and slipped a blaster into the holster it carried, his mind and body co-ordinating in a way that it had not done for a long time.

He was already out in the corridor by the main bank of elevators when Ankar Moor came striding towards him, strapping on his own blaster.

'What is the alarm?'

Ankar Moor reported quickly. He had already had a status report from Polna and had come prepared.

'The Guides have led a break of all the men in the prison area; all the cells are open, My Lord.'

'Have they broken out of the prison area?'

'No, they are sealed in the compound. That stupid jailer managed to activate the anti-blaster shield before he was annihilated.'

Lord Zirpola felt a rising irritation with Ankar Moor. So the situation was being contained, but why did he have to be so calm about it? He should not have allowed it to happen in the first place.

'And just how do you plan to right the situation?'

The chief of the Obedience Enforcers felt the steel in Zirpola's tone and realised that, come what may, the blame for the escape and any botch in its handling would be placed squarely on his shoulders.

'We will use the gas.'

Zirpola nodded, pleased with the idea. While he held the lives of the Enforcers as cheaply as did Ankar Moor himself, a major slaughter in the City itself was bound to be heard of by the civilians. They knew something was wrong after all, having heard the alarms, and this would be bad for morale, and what Zirpola liked to call his credibility.

'Are the canisters ready?'

The other man bowed.

'I have given the orders. They are being prepared for release at this moment.'

Zirpola nodded. He had calmed down a little since the

first alarm and the pain was coming back. He wanted to be on his own again to fight it. It had not been such a good idea to come out like this, after all.

'Then I think you have things well under control. You will have no need of my assistance. I would like a report on the loss and damage when you have righted the situation.'

With that, he turned on his heel and retreated to the door of his private quarters. As it closed on him, he would have been less calm, had he seen the unnerving look of hatred in Ankar Moor's eyes.

As it was, he was able to undo the weapon belt and unfasten his cloak before settling down once more in the chair. This time, sleep reached him before the pain got too bad to bear.

The doctor took a great deal more than a minute to come up with the answer. Kaz was beginning to lose faith in his knowledge when he looked up abruptly and pointed to the blank wall at the end of the cells:

'I know it. It's down there at the end.'

He led the way to the blank wall at the end of the corridor between the two rows of cells. Hot on his heels were Kaz, Deneer, Varros and Ikar, then a still dizzy Marcus. The other prisoners began to move down the corridor after them, jamming themselves into the corridor to do so.

The doctor pointed to the wall:

'That's the only shared wall-space.'

'What is on the other side?'

'Another corridor as far as I can remember. But I don't think a hand blaster will be able to cut through it. The wall is at least five foot thick and has steel bars in it.'

Kaz nodded.

'This other corridor – does it lead anywhere or will the alarms have cut it off like this one?'

The doctor frowned:

'No. It will not be isolated. It is somewhere in the headquarters of the Obedience forces. I'm not sure exactly where. I was only in there once to deal with an accident case.'

Kaz nodded, before turning to Deneer, Varros and Ikar:

'We will have to fire in sequence. That is the only way. We have a big job, even for the blasters.'

It was then that he noticed the bewildered Statemen crowding in, some of them like the doctor himself, others tough, hardened criminals who really belonged in these cells.

'We must clear these people out if they are not to be hurt by the blasters.'

Most of the Statemen began to back away, but one of their number stood his ground. This was Durc, a massive man, powerful of arm and scarred of face, a picture of evil. He was a murderer and had been rightly convicted of the charge. He was determined that he would not die in the Death Sport, but was pleased of a chance to avoid the test.

'I'll move for no other man. What do you think you are going to do? It will be impossible to blast your way out of here. The wall is far too thick for the hand-guns.'

It was Deneer who turned on him, her eyes blazing so that even he was forced to back away from her. He was a brave man but he had never faced the anger and authority of one of the Guides.

'Stand back, or I will blast you now.'

Durc backed away, but he was not prepared to surrender his self-esteem in the process.

'You're crazy! What do you think you're going to do? You'll just get us all killed.'

Another prisoner gave the answer:

'They do not care about their lives, only their freedom. They are Range Guides.'

'That is right, nodded Deneer. 'We are the free, even in a prison cell we are our own masters. Now we have a chance to make you all free again. Get back in your cells. Move quickly. You will be safe there.'

Even Durc was prepared to back down in the face of this conviction. Still grumbling to his fellow-prisoners as he went, he hurried back into one of the nearby cells, so that Doctor Karl and Marcus were the only Statemen prisoners left standing with the Guides.

Kaz turned to them.

'You two go to the main hall – let us know if the anti-blaster shield is lifted. They could be getting ready to attack us.'

The two men nodded. With no argument, they trotted down the corridor until they found themselves in the main hall, where the shield was still holding firm.

Back at the end of the corridor, the Guides suddenly realised that there were only three blasters between the four of them. Ikar stood back while the others got in line. Kaz said:

'We will go in sequence. I will give the first blast at the aiming spot. Are we ready to act in Union?'

'We are,' replied Deneer and Varros.

With that, Kaz raised his blaster and fired, the other two following in quick succession. Again and again, the firing sequence was repeated. At first the wall only showed scorch marks, but after a while a gouge mark began to appear in the wall as the blasters bit deeper and deeper. The next halt came as the iron bars that were half-way through appeared, gleaming in the light.

Kaz and the others paused in their task to adjust the aiming angle of their blasters, then aimed them at the bars, half-melting and half cutting through them with every shot they took. It was a lengthy labour, but at last the bars were gone and they were dealing with concrete again. The sweat was pouring off them, but they kept on in regular sequence, with the concentration that only the Range Guides have.

It was as they started their attack on the second thickness of concrete that the gas began to come. It eddied down out of the vents in grey clouds, unnoticeable at first, but falling thicker and thicker.

The prisoners in the cells noticed it first and began to cough and rub their watering eyes. They did not realise the significance until it was too late, thinking in the early stages that it was merely a dust cloud set up by the blasting.

In the main area, Doctor Karl glanced up at the ceiling at the same moment as the gas began to attack his lungs and skin. A moment later and the prisoners who had not yet succumbed began to shout in pain as it attacked their nervous systems.

As much as he could, Doctor Karl held his breath, and, beckoning Marcus to follow him, he ran down the corridor to the Guides. They arrived just at the moment when Deneer's shot finally cut a hole through to the corridor on the far side and they were able to see the lighted area beyond. They were too close to be beaten. It was a triumph of endurance and patience, for the wall was nearer seven feet than five.

Doctor Karl shouted: 'The gas. Look out for the gas.'

But his warning was too late. A great cloud of it now billowed round them, filling the hallway. The Guides, with their greater endurance, held their breath and began to blast away, making the hole bigger and bigger, but their precautions did them no good. For this was nerve gas that Ankar Moor had ordered to be released; it attacked through the skin as virulently as through the lungs.

Even so, the endurance of the Guides was greater than that of the Statemen and they were still widening the hole as the doctor and his son slumped to the ground.

The sound of the prisoners had died away, telling that they too had been rendered unconscious. Varros and Ikar fell first, leaving Kaz and Deneer still working away with renewed determination. But in the end, they too were overcome. Kaz succumbed first, slumping to the ground, the gun falling away from him. Deneer turned as he fell, ready to help him up if she could in spite of the great pain she was feeling in her chest. But as she bent, she too slumped into unconsciousness, her head falling on to his chest, her hair covering his face.

Ankar Moor and Polna had already collected their team and stood now on the outside of the main door to the cell area, their blasters at the ready. They were dressed in all-encasing black rubber body suits, with matching masks, the whole picture making them look like the old archive video pictures of men exploring under the sea. They were able to communicate through microphones in their masks. They waited patiently, then Ankar Moor said at last:

'The gas will have done its work. We will enter, Polna, switch off the shield.'

Polna moved over to the outer control board and obeyed the order.

'Blaster shield removed.'

Ankar Moor nodded and moved forward to the door-locking panel. Any emergency within automatically changed the combination and he tapped out the new one now. After a moment the huge door swung open. Already the vents had gone into reverse and were sucking out the gas to release it through ducts to wilderness areas far away from the City. The atmosphere outside was polluted enough by the Flash Winds and if any Mutants were nearby when it reached the outside air, so much the better. They were particularly vulnerable to this kind of gassing. Even with this efficient service, great clouds of the gas still hung in the air in the main area, corridor and cells.

Ankar Moor entered at the head of his men, a position, Polna reflected, that might have been given to him had there been a danger of anyone waiting for them. He knew Ankar Moor would not have done this out of cowardice – only because he regarded himself as too valuable to lose.

The only sound inside the area came from the slap of the rubber against the metal floor and the strange sound of the masked men's breathing, like a man sucking water through a straw.

Leaving Polna to relock the men who were already in the cells, Ankar Moor strode down to the end of the corridor. He came back quickly and beckoned Polna to follow him.

'I have found them.'

He led his assistant to the end of the corridor where the Guides lay with Doctor Karl and Marcus. They looked with admiration at the determined job the Guides had made of the end wall, then turned their attention back to the bodies. Ankar Moor pointed down to where Kaz lay on his back, Deneer sprawled across him.

'He's the one. He was the leader. I am sure.'

Polna looked at him.

'Do you want him killed?'

Ankar Moor was still for a moment, then shook his head. He was obviously uncomfortable with his leather mask under the mask of the body suit.

'No, he is the one for punishment.'

'Just him.'

Ankar Moor shrugged:

'I would like to do the same for the girl, but she might not survive. He will still be in the Death Sport tomorrow. Just him for punishment.'

Polna beckoned two of the guards forward to take Kaz pulling him out from under Deneer and taking him through the main hall and out of the cell area to the punishment block of the prison level.

Ankar Moor pointed at the wall.

'They nearly got through.'

'But it was you who stopped them.' Polna always knew the right thing to say. He had been with Ankar Moor for a long time.

Ankar Moor pointed at Deneer and the Karls:

'Put them in the empty cell. We will let the man join them when he has been punished.' He began to move away, then pointed at Ikar and Varros almost as an afterthought.

'Those two can be destroyed. We will not need them now.'

He walked back down the corridor, leaving Polna and his men to get on with their grisly work. Behind him two shots from the anti-blaster gun told him that his orders were being carried out. A moment later the last cell door was shut and locked. Deneer and the Karls were safely locked away.

He smiled inside his mask. The attempted escape had been a futile one. His pre-planning and precautions had proved too much, even for the Guides. His power was proven, theirs was vanquished. Now he would enjoy the punishment of Kaz Oshay – the first part of his revenge for the destruction of his face by the Guide's mother.

On the way out, he stopped at the console to enter his report for the Lord Zirpola, then he walked through towards the punishment section.

CHAPTER SIX

The punishment block of the prison level of the City of Helix had been specially designed by the Lord Zirpola and Ankar Moor to suit their own special tastes. It would better have been described as a torture chamber. When the Lord Zirpola had become the ruler of Helix, there had been no such place. His forebears might, in their way, have been cruel hard tyrants, but they were men who held a certain balance of fairness in their cruelty and were not much given to the more sadistic amusements of punishment. The Death Sport each year had provided them with the sight of quite enough death and maiming.

Both Zirpola and Ankar Moor had particular tastes in this respect and they had set about creating a torture chamber that would strike terror into any Stateman who fell foul of them. To help them do so, they had dived into the video bank archives on such matters before the great devastation and, as a result, they had come up with a design plan that was a cross between a mediaeval dungeon and space-age sophistication. While it boasted the latest electronic equipment, it also had a wall hung with chains, and employed Enforcers who were stripped to the waists and wore black masks, to add to the authenticity when they prepared their long whips for a beating.

After the others had been locked in their cells, Polna and two men had carried the still-unconscious Kaz Oshay through to the torture chamber where Ankar Moor, already divested of his anti-gas costume, was waiting.

The masked man said: 'Leave him to me.'

Polna was only too happy to go off and change. He did not find such torture displays to his taste. He preferred the disorientation chambers, with their torture of the mind, any day.

As soon as Polna was gone, Ankar Moor turned to the torturers:

'Strip him.'

Hastily, the guards stripped Kaz of his clothing, revealing the smooth skin, with a singular lack of scarring and the tight musculature of his torso.

Ankar Moor bent close to inspect the helpless body. He chuckled cruelly. It would be a pleasure to put a body like this to the whip.

'I want him chained so that he cannot move.'

The torturers lifted the inert form of the naked Guide and quickly and expertly chained him to the wall. Ankar Moor gave them a lot of practice at this task. His wrists and ankles were spread-eagled against the hard, cold metal and clamped into place, holding him rigid, his back muscles stretched as far as they would go, ready for the lash, his body completely helpless, unable to twist or resist the coming lash.

Ankar Moor inspected the job and expressed himself pleased:

'Now bring him round.'

One of the men hurried away to a medical chest that stood in the corner of the room. For torture it is necessary that the subject be conscious and all specialised equipment for this purpose was kept there. The man got the tiny pot of salve that was the antidote to the nerve gas and went over to the chained man, rubbing a little over his lips and the ends of the nostrils. As his shallow breathing took the substance into his system, he slowly swam back into a consciousness in which he was as helpless as the gas had made him – and also aware of a greater danger. He was shamed as much by his helplessness as by his nakedness.

Ankar Moor stepped forward, close to Kaz Oshay. His huge hand grabbed a handful of the mane of hair and he jerked the imprisoned man's head back so that he almost choked and felt that his neck would break.

'Now, Guide, Kaz Oshay, son of Oshay, you will feel my wrath and my vengeance. I will have you beaten to within an inch of your life. I will flay your flesh and destroy it as your mother destroyed mine.'

He pushed the man's head forward so it hit the wall and let go of the hair. He was only sorry that he could not mark the Guide's face the way his had been marked. But it was important that he look a perfect and complete Guide in the arena the next day.

In spite of the blow, Kaz managed to turn his head and his eyes looked into those of his captor for a moment, blazing with a hatred that put new fear into the other man, in spite of his position of advantage.

Ankar Moor stood back and one of the swarthy torturers stepped forward, a long whip in his hand. Ankar Moor barked:

'Wait.'

He snatched the whip from the man's hand and inspected the end of the lash. What he saw did not please him:

'Get me a knife.'

His order was obeyed with alacrity and he split the end of the leather with the sharp knife he was handed, before tying two small, tight knots in it. They would inflict as much damage as the lash itself, bringing out that extra flash of pain with each cut that would make Ankar Moor's enjoyment of the occasion all the deeper. Only when he had finished these preparations did he hand the whip back and step aside, giving a nod that was an order for the punishment to commence.

The man stepped forward and pulled back his arm, before bringing it forward in a wide sweep. The end of the whip lashed out, making a singing noise through the air as it went, as if boasting of its power to hurt and maim, before finding its mark and making the first red bruise across the pure, unmarked skin of the helpless Guide.

Kaz Oshay felt the pain rush through him and gritted his teeth, determined that he would make no sound that would show his torturer he was having an effect. Again and again, as the lash fell on his unprotected back and buttocks, each searing pain became more difficult to fight than the last, the end of the lash burning through his body like fire, almost forcing the sound out of him. Even through his clenched teeth he was forced at last to give out a scream of pain.

Behind his leather mask, Ankar Moor smiled as he heard the sound. It was a sign that he was winning, that he was humiliating the Range Guide and beginning to feel the sweetness of the revenge he was taking for Oshay's deeds.

It was not long before the whipping began to draw blood and, as stroke after stroke fell, the flesh underneath the ruined skin was exposed and mangled by its touch.

By this time even the comforts of the code had fled from Kaz Oshay's brain and he was crying out in sheer pain, not hearing the sound of his own screams in his ears as his heart seemed pounding in them towards bursting point.

The blood ran in rivulets over his buttocks and down his legs to the floor. For a while the torturer rested and the only sounds were the steady drip of the blood and the strange bubbling in Kaz Oshay's throat, as he gasped for breath, fighting against a feeling that death would soon overcome him.

Ankar Moor had watched all this in silence and, as the torturer got into position again and curled the lash back, he grabbed at the end of it, still wet with Kaz Oshay's blood and jerked it out of the man's hand.

'Enough. I do not want him dead just yet.'

He let the whip fall to the ground and moved forward to inspect the helpless prisoner. Once more his huge hand grasped a handful of Kaz Oshay's hair, now matted with the sweat of his struggle against pain, and yanked his head back as far as the bonds would allow, causing the Guide to choke and cough in his blinding pain. But the eyes of Kaz Oshay were still clear enough to see, still blazing with a concentrated anger that he projected at the man who had ordered this humiliation and torment on him. He opened his cracked lips and managed to gasp:

'Ankar Moor. You are an animal.'

The Chief of the Obedience Enforcers threw back his head and laughed aloud.

'You call me an animal – after all I have done to try to make you feel at peace, Kaz Oshay?'

Kaz kept together all the determination that he could muster in his battered, torn body, calling upon all the strength of the consciousness to make him firm in his hatred and resolve.

'You must fight me.'

This amused Ankar Moor even more:

'I fight you? But I have already won. You belong to me, both your body and your soul.'

He emphasised this by jerking Kaz's head back still further until the chained man thought his neck might snap like a dry twig. Nevertheless, his resolve was firm.

'You must fight me, and you must fight me alone. I call on the backing of the code. You must fight.'

Ankar Moor was contemptuous of the ravings and bleatings of his torn prisoner. Didn't the man before him realise that he was beaten? All he gasped now were merely words, formulae, outmoded symbols of an age that the plans he had with Zirpola were sweeping aside:

'You call upon your code. What code? Not mine. I live by my own, which is to have no code at all. You are nothing more than a broken reed, a helpless prisoner. By your code, truly, I am my only master.'

Kaz Oshay tried to ignore the sneering with which Ankar Moor was attempting to discredit the code of the consciousness.

'Fight me, you animal.'

Ankar Moor found that his sense of triumph was draining away. His patience with this man, who refused to break, was wearing thin. He glared at the prisoner and his tone was filled with venom.

'No, Kaz Oshay, son of Oshay. I will not fight you. I will not allow you to die in privilege. I could kill you now and I would enjoy the act. I will enjoy the morrow even more, for then I can just watch as you are destroyed in the Death Sport.'

All the time they spoke, Kaz found that hatred was helping his strength to return. He desperately wanted to keep Ankar Moor talking, talk would undermine his feeling of superiority. He feigned ignorance:

'The Death Sport?'

'Yes, in Helix, as they will throughout the world, the laws of the Death Sport have replaced the laws of the code. You cannot win, you must break. If you do not believe me, just remember the words of your own code: Every tear of patience builds the value.'

This time, even Kaz Oshay could find no reply. Talking was finished. He felt an infinite weariness in which pain was the blanket of peace that would comfort him. He allowed himself to slip slowly into the pain, so that his eyes glazed over and he slipped into a trance-like state of unconsciousness that freed a Guide from the pain of his earthly body.

Ankar Moor held the head back for another moment, rage building as he realised the way in which Kaz Oshay had withdrawn from him. Then he pushed the man's head forward against the cold metal of the wall to which he was chained and turned away to walk abruptly from the torture chamber, his triumph evaporated.

Polna was hurrying down the corridor outside to join his master, having changed back into his normal uniform, the three flashes of silver on the black sleeve. Ankar Moor walked past him, pausing only to snap:

'Return him to the cell with his fellow Guide.'

'Yes, Lord,' But Ankar Moor had already charged on.

Polna beckoned the two guards who stood at the entrance to the torture chamber to holster their weapons and follow him. As he entered the torture chamber, he had to use all his control to stop from gagging at the sight of the destroyed back of the chained prisoner, raw and bleeding in the light. He had the opportunity to turn his head away to give the order to the guards:

'Take him down and return him to the cell that contains the other Guide, the woman.'

He went back to the door, to glance down the corridor as if waiting for somebody, as the men went about their business. It would not do any good, either for him or for them, if they were to see how close to sickness he had been brought by the sight of the injured, chained man.

He felt a deep, black fear in his heart. He was too close to Ankar Moor. Too many times he had deflected the heat of his superior's anger when it fell on him, knowing that one day the other man's patience would be exhausted and he, just an ordinary Stateman, would feel more than the lash of his tongue and the burning contempt of his eyes. One day, perhaps, he would give mortal offence, and then it would be his turn for the torture chamber, his skin lacerated, his spirit broken.

Deneer had been locked with Doctor Karl and his son in an otherwise unoccupied cell. While the two Statemen lay slumped on the floor, trying to recover not only from the nerve gas attack, but also from the unaccustomed ordeals that they had faced during the day, they found that they were filled with a burning anger that would not allow sleep to come to them, but sent a debilitating nervous energy coursing through their veins.

On her own recovery from the gas attack, Deneer had risen and now stared out through the slit in the cell door, her eyes mirrors, unseeing, as she prayed to the consciousness for the soul and body of Kaz Oshay and begged that he might return to her in safety. Even in close confinement, her mind could not be so imprisoned and she allowed it to relax and expand, to roam free over the wasteland that had been her home for all her life. She remembered the feel of the wind in her hair as she had galloped her beloved steed forward across open plains and through narrow gullies. That was the only life for a Guide, free and alone. And yet there was now one corner of her mind that doubted this proposition, a corner that saw her not alone, but with Kaz Oshay. True, it was still connected with the roaming of the wastelands, but she was not alone any more, felt that she no longer wished to be just her own master. In these thoughts she felt a strange guilt of betrayal of her adherence to the code, as her mind fought with thoughts of tasting freedom just once more, but with Kaz Oshay as her companion, always by her side.

It was in this strange conflict of thought that love came to Deneer, the way it had come to many of the Guides before.

Marcus sat silent, fighting off his anger and frustration, trying to calm himself down so that he might slip into a healing sleep. But it was not yet to be. He turned to his father:

'I am shamed by failure. But why are you here, what happened?'

Doctor Karl gave him a smile of reassurance.

'Your attempt was compliment enough for me. As for myself, I ran a diagnostic test on Lord Zirpola and was foolish enough to give him the true results.'

His son smiled.

'I know you, you could have done no less. Is he really ill, then?'

The doctor opened his mouth to speak, then hesitated. He had his own battle of conscience to fight. The vows he had taken were similar to those of the medicine men of earlier ages and it went against the grain for him to reveal the secrets of the consulting rooms.

But then, the Lord Zirpola had not respected the word of his doctor. The latter's conscience was clear. Lord Zirpola's action in stripping him of his office and imprisoning him had released him from any vows he had in regard to the ruler of Helix.

To the Statemen of the City he was no longer their chief doctor, merely a condemned criminal. His answers should be guided by that.

'He is in great pain. I have been treating him for months, but he had only allowed me to treat the symptoms, had never let me inspect the source of the trouble to see if I could effect a cure. Until today, then he allowed me to diagnose . . .'

'And?'

Again Doctor Karl hesitated for a moment, then shrugged. What harm could it do now.

'He is a dying man. The tissues of his brain are rupturing. That is the cause of the pain.'

Marcus nodded and thought for a moment. You cannot live all your life as a doctor's son, with a love and respect for your father, without absorbing a little of his teachings, even if you are not interested in taking up his profession for yourself. He realised that he understood the meaning of what his father was saying.

'That explains his strange moods and rages anyway. He must be going mad both from the pain and from the damage?'

The doctor nodded:

'Not *going* mad. He is mad already. I advised him that he must give up his power and hand over the reins of government to another before he is too far gone to take the decision for himself . . .'

His voice trailed away and he was silent as he remembered the other things he had learned when he had had the Lord Zirpola on the examination table. Marcus waited for a moment. He knew his father, knew that there was more to be said:

'What is troubling you? You have told me some of it only. You must tell me the rest. It may be important.'

Doctor Karl sighed.

'He is determined on his plans for war.'

Marcus frowned, it was unbelievable.

'But that is an outlawed concept throughout the world. No man lives by that code any more.'

The doctor shook his head sadly. His son was still young, still an idealist. He had much to learn yet about human nature.

'It is not true, my son. He told me of his plans.'

'No man, even he, can be so mad as to do such a thing!'

The doctor frowned.

'No normal man, perhaps, but the Lord Zirpola is not a normal man. It was my own fault that I learned such things. I wish I had not succumbed to the temptation.'

'What temptation?'

'I wanted to learn more than the diagnostic machines were able to tell me, so I gave him a hypnotic drug and questioned his subconscious. It was then that I learned the distance down the path of madness he has already gone. We are running short of fuel in the City. That is why the power is cut and the lights go off now and again. He believes that Triton is deliberately withholding fuel supplies from us and he means to conquer that City and take them.'

Marcus gasped, hardly able to comprehend what his father was saying:

'But it is unbelievable that he should wage war in such a cause; no man will follow him.'

'Believe me, his plans are far advanced. He will find a way to make them follow.'

Marcus balled one hand into a fist and brought it down on his open palm so hard that it made a loud cracking sound that echoed around the cell like a gunshot.

'We must get out of here and find some way to tell the people. If they knew about his insane plans for war, if they knew that they were led by a madman, they would rise up against him and make sure he was replaced before any more damage could be done.'

His father shook his head:

'He is supported by Ankar Moor and the Obedience Enforcers. That man is walking evil. It would not be possible.'

'But father, the Federation of the other Cities would welcome it and allow them in. Zirpola has kept them outside the Federation, but he cannot fight the world. All that needs to happen is for the people to be told the truth.'

There was a silence between father and son and, into this silence, Deneer spoke for the first time, giving an indication that, while the main part of her mind and concentration had been far away across the wastelands with Kaz Oshay, she had still listened and absorbed the conversation between the two men.

'All that your people will need is faith in themselves, faith in their own power.'

Marcus glanced up at her, surprised at her sudden contribution, but stunned at the truth of her words. All the time, his thoughts were ranging over his remembered experiences of Triton on the previous visits he had made there in pursuit of the hand of the beautiful Stategirl with whom he had fallen in love.

At once he felt a tightness in his chest, a sadness. She would not yet be aware that anything was wrong, that he would not be arriving in time for their wedding. Only a few days more, however and she would know the worst, perhaps realise in the non-arrival of the caravan that he was lost to her forever and she to him. Such thoughts merely strengthened his anger at what had happened.

But there were other things he remembered. The calm and peace of the City and of its people in contrast to the tension that was always present in the day-to-day lives of the citizens of Helix, thanks to the rules of the Lord Zirpola. Triton had been a place of advance, not stagnation. Both in culture and science, new discoveries were being made daily, raising the level of hope of society for the future of Statekind.

It was then that he remembered and blurted:

'But if we overthrow Zirpola and join the Federation, there will be no problem over fuel.'

'What do you mean?'

'They are working at this moment on a way to produce all the fuel they need artificially. There have been exciting breakthroughs and it is now only a matter of time before it can be produced in large enough quantities to satisfy all needs and prolong the survival of the Cities forever, even if the wastelands are never habitable.'

His father frowned again and then nodded:

'I have heard rumours of such things from travellers who have come to the clinic. I can believe that such things should be possible, but most of the people will not.'

'If they do not believe, then they are lost men.'

His father sighed:

'But the system of Zirpola is very efficient. They are used to believing everything he tells them – and what he will tell them tomorrow will tip the balance and make the war inevitable.'

Without turning, Deneer said quickly:

'And what is it that your mad lord will tell them tomorrow?'

Now it was time for the doctor to drop his biggest bombshell and he hesitated before doing so.

'He will tell them that the Death Machines, which he claims his scientists have created, will make the people invincible and that they must go to war on them to get the fuel that will help Helix to survive.'

Marcus interrupted.

'Deneer and I have seen the machines. They brought about her capture. They are truly frightening.'

Deneer nodded.

'They are different, not frightening, but the people will not be familiar with them and what is not familiar is often frightening.'

Marcus rose and began to walk up and down the tiny cell.

'It is a lie, though. They will make no one invincible, just better able to kill and maim. We have to get out of here and get to Triton to warn them of what is threatened. If we cannot stop Zirpola now, we can at least make sure that all attempts are made to avert war.'

The doctor sighed.

'I cannot argue against you on that, Marcus, but it is easier to say such things than to do them.'

Deneer had turned back to the door, but now she felt the moment had come to break her concentration. Some wave from the consciousness had told her that Kaz Oshay's punishment was over and that he still lived, albeit his powers of preservation were stretched to the limit. But the powers would hold and he would survive his present ordeal.

Her eyes were soft as she locked them on to those of the brave young Stateman.

'Maintain calm.'

Marcus almost shouted:

'Maintain calm. That's easy for you to say. It is not the problem of the Guides, but only of the continued life of the Cities of Statemen. Their tragedy will mean nothing to you.'

Her rebuke was still gentle.

'If war is to come again then it will surely destroy what little there is left of the world, which will mean the end of the Guides just as surely as it will wipe out the Statemen Cities and the Mutants. But for now, be calm. This is not the time or place for anger. It will accomplish nothing in this place, but feed upon itself producing more anger. For the moment, you must use your mind, not your emotions.'

The doctor smiled up at her. Her words were wise.

'What you say is true enough, Guide, but for a young man it is not easy. Youth is the time of ideals and anger.'

Realising that his father was using Deneer in order to tease him out of his mood, Marcus exploded.

'Do nothing. Be calm. It is just that attitude that has allowed Zirpola to get as far as he has already. Now is the time for action, not for contemplation.'

Deneer looked momentarily affronted, but the doctor said quickly:

'My son is hasty. Our talk has made him angry. Forgive him.' He beckoned his son. 'Sit by me.'

With a reluctant glower at the other occupants of the cell, Marcus eventually subsided, sliding down the wall to sit next to his father. The doctor tried to pour oil on the troubled waters that conversation had brought about.

'All that Deneer is trying to remind us is that we should conserve our energies for the dangers that tomorrow holds. We need to rest, not spend ourselves in anger. Tomorrow is the day of the Death Sport. If we can win, survive the games, perhaps we will be rewarded with freedom and can then seize a chance to get to Triton and warn them.'

Marcus shrugged.

'You know that a man has to serve in the Enforcers if he is rewarded with his life after the Death Sport – and death is the only escape from their ranks.'

'But it will give us time, and time is the most valuable thing we need.'

Deneer spoke flatly.

'The code teaches us that while life remains, then hope will remain alive.'

Marcus was about to make a comment to the effect that the code need not necessarily be right, when he was saved from offering her real insult by the sound of the door-opening code being played on the console. Perhaps Kaz Oshay was going to be brought back to his confinement. Deneer turned her attention back to the slit in the cell door while the others sat and waited.

After a moment there came the sound of the main door opening, then the slow footsteps of several people entering the prison area. Their slowness made it seem likely that they were carrying a heavy load.

The loudspeaker system crackled into life and the voice of a new jailer, which contained no less threat than his now annihilated predecessor, boomed out at them.

'Cell twelve. You will rise and stand against the rear wall of your cell.'

With weary resignation, the Karls, father and son, heaved themselves to their feet, but Deneer stayed in her place, squinting along the sightlines of the door slit towards the main hall.

With the video ripped out of the ceiling, there was no easy way for the jailer to check that his orders had been obeyed and she was willing to take the risk of disobedience. Now she could see Kaz Oshay. He was being carried by four guards, still naked, his beaten, bloody back visible. Another guard came alongside them, carrying the stricken man's clothing – Polna, his gaze averted from the bloody wreck his men carried.

Her hopes for Kaz Oshay's return realised, Deneer went swiftly and joined the others at the far wall. There was a moment of silent waiting, then the door of the cell slid open and she allowed herself to relax.

While Polna stood in the doorway, his blaster at the ready, the four men dragged the broken body of Kaz Oshay into the cell and dumped him face-down on the metal floor. He moved slightly, groaning as he came back to consciousness and the reality of the pain seeped back into his system.

The men turned to leave and Polna threw the clothes into the cell just before the door slid shut and was automatically re-locked. The footsteps of the guards retreated and then there was a silence, followed by the echoing closing of the main door.

As the echo died away, Deneer darted forward and knelt by the side of her stricken fellow Guide. After the lecture that she had given Marcus, she could still understand why her own anger grew as she saw the mess that had been made of Kaz Oshay's back. It was too painful for anyone to look upon and remain calm.

Kaz Oshay's eyes flickered open as he groaned again and shifted on the hard surface of the metal floor. He looked round, then struggled to bring himself upright. She helped him, holding him up so that his back would not have to make contact with floor or wall as he rolled over into a sitting position. Neither of them seemed to take any notice of his nakedness. Deneer spoke softly:

'Who did this thing to you? Was it Ankar Moor?'

He gasped, 'It was he.'

'But why this? Would he not fight you?'

Kaz Oshay winced in pain.

'No. I called upon him. I called him out against me in the name of the code, but he refused.'

She was surprised.

'But he was once of the Guides, he followed the code. He could not refuse.'

Kaz Oshay shook his head:

'He is long banished from the code and lives and fights by his own code now. He felt no pull to accept.'

Deneer was harsh:

'He who has no code is an animal.'

Amazingly, considering the pain he was suffering, a fleeting smile played on Kaz Oshay's lips as he looked up at the girl:

'You speak the truth. I told him so.'

He shifted again, obviously in great pain. Deneer became at once absorbed in his condition.

'Are your bones broken?'

'I think not. Only my flesh.'

Still holding him up so his back would not fall against the wall, Deneer knelt down so that she could look into his eyes. The girl used all her power to lock his eyes into hers, forcing the strength of the concentration of the consciousness into him, to dull and smoothe away the pain he was feeling and to move her strength to join with what was left of his and combat his suffering. After a while, she withdrew her gaze and whispered:

'Together we will turn you over.'

He tried, but could hardly move, from stiffness and suffering. Most of the effort had to be hers.

'I will help you.'

Their eyes locked on one another again, oblivious of Doctor Karl and his son sitting watching them. They went into a trance for the special ritual that joined the strength of the Guides under such circumstances. They were already awed at the sight of Kaz Oshay. The doctor knew that the wounds Kaz Oshay had received would have killed a Stateman.

Deneer spoke:

'Trust me, Kaz Oshay, son of Oshay. I am Deneer of the Guides. Our Union is real.'

He nodded in desperate, pain-wracked agreement:

'Yes . . . Yes . . . I need you.'

She nodded in return, then took his face in her delicate, soft hands. It was a miracle that the hands of a warrior should become so gentle and soft. She reached forward and closed the lid over his left eye before planting a soft kiss on it, then performed the same ritual with his right eye.

As the doctor watched, the man's breathing gradually became more regular, the pain of his wounds vanishing from him, thanks to her magic. With this calming process completed, Deneer was able, alone, to turn Kaz Oshay over on his stomach, his eyelids still shut. He made no sign as he lay flat on the cold metal floor.

Doctor Karl finally realised what was going on, and he felt a professional interest in what was about to happen. He had heard of the legends of the healing power of the Guides, but he had never seen them in action. Now he was about to have that privilege, which few Statemen had ever seen. He turned to his son and, holding a finger to his lips, he whispered:

'Watch this carefully. You are about to see something that few Statemen ever witness.'

Marcus frowned but kept his voice at a whisper:

'What is she going to do?'

'Just watch.'

The two men leant forward in silence as Deneer, still oblivious to their presence, went about her work. First she bent over Kaz's head, stroking his hair and the side of his cheek with tenderness. This was a formula that anaesthetised him for the medication that was to follow. She stopped when he appeared to have dropped into a deep sleep.

Only then did she turn her attention to the hideous torn mess that had been Kaz Oshay's back. Gently, oh so gently, she began to trace her fingers through the blood and over the outlines of each deep wound.

Marcus gasped at the sight and would have turned away, wanting to vomit at the sight of her hands playing with the torn, bleeding flesh, but a glare from his father was enough to keep him silenced and under an effort-filled control.

Deneer went on with her work, performing the healing magic of her fingers before their eyes. It was as if the touch of her fingertips alone was slowly kneading his broken flesh together. The body of the Guide beneath her remained absolutely still in a trance-like state, the sleep that she had induced in him.

As she worked, she recited the ancient poem of healing of the code:

'You come to me and you need me.
I go to you and I join you,
For now, our Union is real.
I become you now,
And you become me,
And I heal you,
And I heal myself.'

All this was said in a sing-song high voice, like the chanting of the ancients, the magicians of the time before there was learning and the enlightenment of today.

With infinite patience and gentleness, she completed her job and, when she was finished, the last of the great wounds on Kaz Oshay's back was closed. His skin gleamed in the bright light of the cell, healed, with no trace that torture or punishment had ever taken place.

Kaz Oshay remained in his deep sleep and Deneer slid down to lie beside him, totally exhausted by her efforts of healing. She too slipped into a sleep as deep as Kaz's own.

Now Marcus turned to his father:

'What I have seen is like a miracle. Tell me it is real, not a dream I have had.'

His father smiled at him:

'It is real enough, my son, and it is our best hope for what is left of the world.'

Marcus's face clouded over at this reminder of the problems that faced them.

'We will have to do something, my father.'

His father, who was equally worried himself, managed a thin smile as he pointed to the couple sleeping peacefully, close to one another on the floor of the cell.

'For now, the best we can do is follow their example. We are, after all, only Statemen, and we will need all the reserves of strength we can muster to survive tomorrow.'

With that, he lay flat on the floor and closed his eyes, preparing himself for sleep. Marcus could do nothing but follow his example, trying to empty his mind of both anger and fear and find sleep that way. A little later, the cell was silent as they all slept.

High above them, in the private quarters of the Lord of Helix, the situation was not in such good balance as the night moved inexorably onward towards a new day. True, Zirpola had achieved a rare hour of uninterrupted sleep, but the pain had rolled back into him, taking over his brain and had awakened him.

He rose from his chair, clutching himself in agony, holding on to his head as if he wished to tear it from his body and hurl it from him, anything to be free of the pulsing pain beating within it.

He staggered up and down the room, trying to control and suppress the spasm, trying to suppress a scream, a giving in to the pressure. Then, unable to control himself any longer, he crashed down to the floor, pressing his head against the cold marble and screaming:

'Stop it! Stop it! I can stand it no longer. I cannot endure.'

After a while, the pain gave him momentary surcease and he was able to drag himself to his feet once more. He staggered weakly back to the desk and snapped on the light behind it. Perhaps if he concentrated again on his plan of attack for the City of Triton, that would keep his mind enough occupied to ignore any return of pain.

He spread out the maps and began to study them closely once more, forcing all his concentration into the exercise, blotting out his constant fear that, each time the pain recurred, it would not go away again.

Eventually, he began to make a high-pitched giggling noise as he envisaged the attack he would make and the slaughter there would be. Triton would pay a hundred fold for the slights that the Lord Zirpola imagined he had received from the City.

Triton had been quick to join the Federation, but Zirpola had held Helix aloof, the truth being that one of the conditions of membership was that each City would have to elect its leader by a popular vote. To Zirpola, who knew that he was feared, not loved, by his people, it was merely a trick devised to wrest power from him. That was the secret behind his resentment of the Federation. That was the real reason why he would beat them by making war on them and showing them what a true leader was like. But he was impatient at any further delay in his plans.

Deep inside him, he had taken in the lies that the treacherous Doctor Karl had fed to him, had taken them in and absorbed them; subconsciously aware that the doctor had, in fact, spoken the truth. If he was to die, he wanted to be master of the world – to have taught them all – before that time came.

His other major problem at present was Ankar Moor. The cruel brute was useful to him – but only for the moment. Once Triton was subdued, enough strong men would come forward to join his cause to make Ankar Moor an unnecessary luxury. Only then would he be able to do away with the chief of the Obedience Enforcers.

The pain was coming back and he clutched his head again, his concentration ebbing away. The next afternoon would be the time of the Death Sport. God keep him free from pain until then.

He would have been even more worried had he been able to see Ankar Moor, sitting at his own desk, in his own chambers, and had been able to read his mind.

He too was taking advantage of the dead fastnesses of the night to review his own plans.

Once the Death Sport had stirred up the people of Helix City so that they attacked and overran Triton, then would be the time to strike. His master, the Lord Zirpola, was a weak man, filled with a sense of his own vanity which blocked out any true intelligence and cunning. It was Ankar Moor himself who had the foresight and strength that would defeat the Federation and make him master of the world, bringing even the Guides under his sway, so that he might destroy them, taking true vengeance on his tribe who had cast him out, with just the same feelings with which he would delight in the destruction of Kaz Oshay and Deneer on the morrow. With that happy thought he prepared himself for a little sleep to face the morning and the moving forward of his plans.

The great red eye of the sun heaved itself up over the horizon of the wastelands, blotting out and making unnecessary the weak reflected light of the moon that had lit the shadowy night.

In the cells in the depths of the City, the Guides had no sign to tell them that the dawn had come, but Guides require no such visual signals and they sprang into wakefulness the moment the great orb appeared on the horizon beyond the dome of the City.

They glanced over at the still-sleeping figures of Doctor Karl and his son, then rose silently and in unison, being careful not to disturb the tranquil Statemen. They would need more sleep to recover themselves than the Guides did.

Kaz slipped into his clothes,. There was only the memory of his wounds in his mind. There was neither trace of them nor feeling from them in his back. Deneer had done her work well and he was whole again, as if the entire episode had not occurred, and he was as refreshed by her spirit and touch as he had been by the sleep itself.

They faced each other and then went down in a crossed-leg pose that the ancients called the Lotus position and their eyes locked together in Union. Then each of them allowed their eyes to glaze over so they were both locked into some point of infinity at the far end of the universe, that was also mid-way between them. Slowly they raised their arms, stretching them out in front of them so that just their fingertips met and touched for an instant. Then they let their hands fall back into their laps, palms upwards.

They concentrated on sinking into the level of consciousness that would prepare them for the battles of the day ahead. From deep in their throats, they started the humming that would raise them to the plane where their souls would become as refreshed as they had made their bodies, a level where they would join the whole state of consciousness and draw their strength from it.

Only when this state had been reached did they begin to speak. Their tones were low, as they enacted the spirit of the ritual that would prepare them for battle. Kaz spoke first, his voice soft and flat as if it did not come from within himself:

'I move in rhythm with the earth. I am held steady. My true path never wavers for an instant. My purpose is clear before me as a wide road.'

Deneer echoed him:

'My purpose is clear before me as a wide road. Of no more importance to the universe than a leaf is to a tree, I am still. I share the life. I am one with it.'

Now the echo came from the man:

'I share the life. I am one with it. I Guide upon the waste. I take no advantage. I give no quarter. I defend my own. I am as strong as I need to be.'

Again Deneer took up the chant:

'I defend my own. I am as strong as I need to be. Powerful or weak, I am become whatever I would choose to make myself. I give what I can, no one owns me.'

It was left to Kaz to complete the formula:

'I give what I can, no one owns me. I am sacred to myself. No one can touch myself. I am free. I am my only master.'

Once more the hum came deeply in their throats, fading away into a heavy silence. After a while, their eyes unlocked from their glazed state and they locked onto their mutual stare once more, each checking that there was strength and renewal in the other, each knowing that their Union was one though they were not yet joined.

After that, they rose and went into each other's arms, embracing the flesh, one of the other, as they had already embraced their souls through the rituals.

Kaz now spoke in his normal voice.

'Now we are as ready as we ever will be for anything they wish on us. We will not break before them.'

Deneer nodded.

'No, we will not break.'

He sighed. 'I hear the sound of our captors, they are stirring. They will come for us soon.'

Deneer whispered, more an ordinary woman than a normal Guide:

'We have till then.'

Kaz shook his head, still smiling. He indicated the sleeping Statemen on the floor.

'We cannot be joined yet. We must respect the scruples these people have about such things.'

Deneer grinned.

'They are strange, the ways of these City dwellers, these Statemen. Have they shame about their bodies – or are you afraid of me, Kaz Oshay, son of Oshay.'

For a moment his eyes blazed at the insult, then he realised that she was teasing him only for affection, playing with the strange emotions that were welling up in him.

'I fear nothing, but I have respect for these men.'

This brought back to Deneer the thoughts of what was facing them, the threat to them all contained in the Death Sport:

'Is there any way in which we can save them?'

Kaz Oshay shook his head sadly:

'I know of nothing. I am not even sure, except in my soul, that we will be able to save ourselves. But we will see what can be done. Much will depend on their own courage.'

Deneer sighed.

'So be it . . . but, if we can . . .'

He nodded his promise. 'If we can.'

From outside they now heard the sound of the door-opening pattern being repeated on the lock of the main door. Their captors were coming for them and there was time only for another glance of reassurance to pass between them before they prepared themselves for their next ordeal.

Outside, the great door swung open and there came the sound of the steel hobnails of the guards' boots.

Deneer said softly: 'It is time.'

'Our Union is one,' murmured Kaz Oshay in return, to comfort himself as much as her, to keep them both calm, though he knew that her strength was as great as his, that she was the perfect mate for him amongst all of the tribe of Guides. She was as strong in herself as he could ever have wished a mate of his to be.

Like the men who were following him into the cell area, Polna held the tranquilliser dart pistol firmly in his fist as he strode down the corridor towards Kaz Oshay's cell. They were halfway to their destination before the loudspeaker system crackled on and the sleepy jailer roared:

'Prisoners, waken. Prisoners waken. Stand by the rear wall of your cells for an inspection.'

The time for niceties was gone. As the Karls rubbed the vestiges of sleep from their eyes and heaved themselves to their feet, the jailer sent a mild bolt of electricity zapping through the cell floors, knocking the occupants of all the cells to the ground – a very effective way, however, of waking anyone who had not already obeyed his call. From the yells and groans that came from the other cells, it had proved an effective device.

Polna halted at the door to cell twelve. Once more the electricity was zapped through that particular cell to throw the occupants off balance. A second later, Polna slid the cell door back and he and his leading guards fired their darts. All found their almost helpless targets – Kaz and Deneer – and they slumped to the floor, drugged into unconsciousness. The tranquillisers were of the mildest type and Polna knew they would not be out for long. He stepped aside and signalled his men forward:

'All right, take them away. Be quick about it.'

The Enforcers so ordered hurried in and grabbed the two inert forms that were stretched out on the floor. Doctor Karl was galvanised into action. He picked himself up and stepped forward with a sudden access of courage that he was not formerly aware he possessed.

'I demand to know what you are going to do with them!'

Polna glanced at him, even smiled at the courage of the man.

'You are hardly in a position to make any demands, Doctor. But I think it will do no harm if I tell you. They are being taken to the disorientation chambers.'

The doctor paled and gasped. That would surely be the end of them. Surely not even a Guide's mind could withstand the power of the disorientation chambers. No one was ever known to have left them with their brains intact. Polna gave him only a second to take this in, then:

'Now you two can come along with me.'

'But, if they have been through disorientation, they will stand no chance in the Death Sport.'

Polna grinned:

'I think that's the idea, Doctor.'

Marcus snapped: 'Is that where you are taking us?'

Polna chuckled again.

'Heavens, no. We want to teach you how to ride the Death Machines. It is the day of the Death Sport and you will be using them. Now hurry, you need all the practice you can get.'

As they moved outside the cell they could no longer see the unconscious forms of Kaz Oshay and Deneer, but the other prisoners were being herded from their cells for the practice riding on the Death Machines. Polna had them put with the others before he left them to hurry off and supervise the use of the disorientation chambers.

In the corridor outside the main door to the cells, the guards were strapping the two unconscious prisoners on to separate trolleys, making fast their wrists and ankles, before wheeling them down the corridor to their destination.

One of the men strapping down Deneer snarled: 'Dammit, they're coming round already.'

Polna snarled back at them as he joined them: 'Then hurry – move them.'

They wheeled the trolleys quickly down the smooth metal corridor, Polna jogging along behind, stopping only when they reached the entrance to the chambers.

'Put them inside. I will set the monitors.'

The doors to two of the chambers were opened and the trolleys were wheeled inside before the doors slammed shut. Polna hurried on to a small door set in the wall of the corridor.

Using a light code, he waited for the door to slide aside, revealing a short staircase. He stepped inside, reclosed the door, then went up the steps, which led to a small chamber whose main item of furniture was a large control console, into which were set the inevitable video screens.

He sat down in front of the console and snapped the buttons that switched on the video screens that spied into the chambers where Kaz Oshay and Deneer were now lying. Both showed blackness.

Next, he snapped on the pulsing lights that lit the two chambers, the pulsing approximating a normal heartbeat. A special piece of equipment gave him a pulse reading on each of the Guide's heartbeats – much slower than a human pulse – and he keyed the light pulse in each chamber into this.

Now all he could do was wait patiently until the two Guides came round. He sat back in his chair and started his wait, praying that it would not take too long.

In his own way, Polna was as cruel a man as his master, Ankar Moor, but he preferred this more sophisticated form of torture to the brutal physical kind that the Enforcer leader took so much pleasure in.

Kaz Oshay was the first to come round. Polna leant forward and peered into his screen as the man began to struggle against his bonds, before he realised that to struggle was useless and lay back to relax and concentrate his mind.

Polna chuckled and spoke in the empty room:

'There is no easy way out of there, Kaz Oshay. And you won't want to find one by the time I have finished with you.'

A moment later Deneer too came back to wakefulness. Now was the time. Polna turned his attention to the controls.

In his tiny prison, Kaz Oshay ignored the pulsing blue light and tried to concentrate, though it seemed to be winking even inside his brain. Faintly, he could feel Deneer's closeness, then a surge of power as she came round and did the same, so that their minds were linked, keeping their Union joined as they reached out for one another. They were trying to make an unbridgeable union of their minds to fight off whatever torture was now to be inflicted on them.

And yet Kaz was still a little afraid. He had heard of the chambers of disorientation, that may take a man's brains and turn them round in his head and leave him a raving idiot. He had never heard of such a fâte coming to one of the Guides, but that did not mean that it was only Statemen who were so affected.

Above his head, he could see the eye of the video and knew that he was being watched, so he lay still, giving no sign of his inner alarm.

The noise, when it came, flooded through his head at an intensity that almost made him scream out.

Above them, Pòlna pressed the buttons that would fill the chambers with the high intensity sound that was central to the process of disorientation. He smiled down at the video screens:

'Do what thinking you can now, Guides, for this is the last time that what you call the consciousness will be able to get through the scramble of your brains.'

He knew just how much of the torture to give them. They had to be on their feet and able to show some of their courage and fighting ability when the time of the Death Sport came. Only in that way could they be killed convincingly enough to make the civilians of Helix believe that the Death Machines made them invincible.

And all the time, as the sound became louder and higher in pitch and less easy to bear, the two prisoners reached out for one another with their minds, keeping them joined against all the odds.

Deep in the recesses of their minds, they were both chanting the ritual:

'I am one. I am one. I am one. I am powerful. I am powerful. I am powerful. I am my only master. I am. I am. I am.'

And all the while, the pulsing of the noise came louder and louder and louder and higher in pitch so that it seemed to be cutting through their heads like a knife.

Just at the point before which a Stateman brain would crumble, Polna reluctantly threw the cut-off switches and silence came flooding back in the tiny cells. He switched off the lights and all the controls and let himself out of the tiny cockpit once more.

The guards were waiting for him in the corridor.

'You may take and hold them now. They will go up the special shaft to their changing room just before the Death Sport begins.'

The two prisoners were wheeled from the disorientation chambers, apparently unconscious. But their minds were still joined and, deep in their subconscious, both of them were whispering in unison:

'I am my own master. I am the one ...'

CHAPTER SEVEN

The hours that the Statemen prisoners spent in preparation for the Death Sport were as frightening in their own way to Doctor Karl and his son Marcus as the disorientation chambers had been to Kaz Oshay and Deneer.

The arena where the games would take place was located on the edge of the City, outside the domes. It was dominated on three sides by tall towers, in which those members of the public and the officials of the administration who had been allocated tickets sat, the fourth side just being open to the wastelands plain beyond. The arena itself was as filled with small hills and dips as the plain all round, making the riding of the Death Machines a difficult feat.

At the top of the tallest tower was the special box in which Lord Zirpola and his special guests sat and from which he would make his normal speech, opening the games. The arena was made secure by an anti-blaster shield which would cover the whole area like an abstract dome and which it was impossible for anyone to get through.

There were two sets of changing-rooms with an archway, where the anti-blaster shield could be broken for a moment, leading to each. One of these changing-rooms was to be the home of the Statemen for the next few hours as they waited, first to practise, then for the Death Sport itself.

The end of this room was dominated by a huge colour screen on which those not taking part at any given moment could watch the activities outside as they were relayed on the television service of Helix City, courtesy of those ubiquitous commentators, Carol Rabids and Howard Koslow.

The Statemen had been shepherded by the guards into the changing-room area, where they waited to go out, in teams of ten, to practise and try to learn how to ride the machines. It was a tall order, but it was all the time that the Obedience Enforcer trainers had been given to train them.

Once they were seated in the changing-room area and waiting for their turn, Marcus Karl turned to his father:

'There's no sign of the two Guides anywhere. What do you think has happened to them?'

His father sighed, his face troubled:

'They have been taken to the disorientation chambers for some special treatment. We won't see them before the time of the Death Sport.'

'But that will drive them mad.'

His father nodded:

'It is part of Zirpola's plan to make them easier to kill, to tip the scales.'

'We must do something.'

'There is nothing we can do, we must just wait and hope.'

At last the time came when their group was ordered out into the arena for their introduction to the riding of the great gleaming machines of black and silver that stood in a row before them. The anti-blaster shield had not been put on, so there were plenty of guards around to make sure that none of the prisoners tried to make a break for it into the wastelands.

Both Marcus and the doctor blinked as they came out into the bright, hot sunlight. Marcus had seen the machines before, so he was not overawed by them, having even seen one of them destroyed by a Guide, but his Father gasped in horror at the hitherto unimaginable sight.

Guards helped them mount the machines, then showed the prisoners how to start them. To Doctor Karl, both the roar of them and the feeling of suppressed power under him were more frightening than all the experiences he had so far undergone.

A guard carrying a clipboard walked up, one silver flash on his black sleeve denoting that he was a sergeant.

'Right you lot. You're sitting on Death Machines. Once you've learnt a few simple tricks for riding them, you'll be invincible, able to take on even the Guides. Some of you will fight each other, some of you Guides, this afternoon, so you haven't much time.'

The murderer Durc was in the same group and he snarled:

'This afternoon. There's not enough bloody time.'

The sergeant glared him back into silence.

'Nevertheless, you'll bloody learn by then or it could be your head. Now, in case any of you have got any ideas for some smart move, you can see all the guards that are posted to stop you riding off the field, so don't try it or you'll never even see this afternoon.'

He went on to instruct them how to throttle and steer the machines before instructing them in the use of the weaponry.

'And before you lot get any bloody ideas about that, it's only fair to tell you that the blaster pods have been put out of action for the morning's practice. Now get riding.'

Marcus turned to his father, to try to give reassurance:

'I watched the Enforcers who chased after our caravan and captured the Guide. The blaster pods are only active at the front and rear. It is mainly a question of balance.'

He followed this up by starting off and immediately falling over, the machine on top of him. The sergeant and another guard helped him up. No word was spoken, but Marcus was aware of an undercurrent of ridicule on their faces.

He remounted and this time managed to keep his balance – at least until he came to one of the small hillocks in the arena. He went up fast, left the ground, then fell away from the machine when it landed. Once more he had to be picked up and helped back to the machine, which was still roaring, its wheels spinning uselessly in the air.

Meanwhile, his father was driving quietly around, getting used to the balance and controls, but making no attempt to engage in any fancy manoeuvres.

The sergeant had some words for him this time, many of which Marcus had never heard in his life before, but, from the man's angry face, he got the general drift of them.

In the whole of the hour of practice they had before it was the turn of the next group, Doctor Karl only once lost control of his machine – and that was on the occasion when Marcus careered into him, not able to control the direction in which he was travelling.

As they walked back into the changing-rooms together, his father put a reassuring arm round his shoulder.

'We'll survive somehow.'

Marcus sighed. 'I hope so, but I don't want to have to kill one of those Guides to do so. Do you think I'll have to?'

His father frowned. Along with the general question of killing for his own survival, it was a specific question that he was trying to avoid, as he saw no way out of the moral dilemma in which it placed him. He could only practise what he now preached to his son:

'We will just have to wait and see if there is a way.'

The whole City seethed with preparations for the Death Sport. It was the most important entertainment and sporting fixture of the Helix year.

In his chambers, the Lord Zirpola, the pain under control this morning, put the final touches to the important speech that he was going to make at the opening of the proceedings.

In his headquarters, Ankar Moor checked out his own plans for the organisation of the Sport and what would follow. Polna, now grittily tired from lack of sleep, ran through the arrangements with him.

On the field, Carol Rabids and Howard Koslow checked the camera points and their own commentary positions as the television units set up for their coverage of the day's events.

In the City, the Statemen either started to make their way to the stadium seats, or settled in front of the televideo screens to view.

In the changing-rooms, the Statemen prisoners tried to pretend to one another they were not nervous as they waited for the moment that would decide their fate.

And, in a small cell in the depths of the City, Kaz Oshay and Deneer lay, half-conscious, struggling to keep control over their minds, as the moment for their ordeal drew closer.

In the changing-rooms, the huge video screen sprang into colourful life, with the test card of the City television station – a huge multi-coloured pattern dominated in the centre by the symbol of the Lord Zirpola, a symbol that he had derived from the archives. The symbol was called a Swastika, the ancient eastern symbol of luck from the times before the great disaster. There was a moment of music, then the symbol faded and the face of Carol Rabids filled the screen, a hand microphone hovering just in front of her.

She was on a clear hill-top position overlooking the empty arena. A skinny woman in her forties, with a shock of unattractively-cut blonde hair and an expression of professional detachment, she, as usual, talked down to her public from a great height of intelligence.

As the doctor looked at the screen, he thought that it was no wonder she had never married. Any man who went with her would have to be suffering from an outsize inferiority complex. She began her introductions over his thoughts.

'Good afternoon, ladies and gentlemen of Helix City. This is Carol Rabids reporting.'

As would occur again and again throughout the day, the cameras cut abruptly to her male counterpart, Howard Koslow. He was plump where she was thin, happy and smiling where she was grim and superior. They made a perfect team:

'And Howard Koslow. Welcome to our programme.'

The cameras cut back.

'Once again it is our privilege to welcome you to the Death Sport games.'

This apparently exhausted her because they were back with Howard Koslow again almost before Carol had finished.

'This year's Death Sport games promise to be the most unusual, the most exciting and the most dangerous in the one hundred and forty-five-year-history of the games.'

Back to Carol.

'As in the past, Statemen prisoners will be set against each other to fight to the death – the prize for the winners: their freedom.'

Over to you Howard.

'Heroic contests will pit man against man in a struggle to the death for the most cherished luxury that life has to offer, but this year dramatic new changes have been made in the mode of combat which will completely alter the style of the contest, though not its purpose.'

Back to Carol, her expression even grimmer than before.

'This year the prisoners will fight each other on Death Machines. You'll be seeing these marvellous new creations later, but I note that the Lord Zirpola is entering his box and he's going to have a few words to say on the subject of this year's competition when he opens the games. Ladies and gentlemen, I hand you over to our beloved leader, the Lord Zirpola, Lord of Helix.'

The shot of Zirpola's box filled the screen as he entered, his emerald cloak around him. Ankar Moor stood ready to meet him, resplendent and frightening in his silver metallic outfit, the brown leather of the mask making him look all the more frightening. Also present, and very much on camera on a couch to one side, were four nubile young ladies, who grinned up inanely at their lord and master as he came in.

Watching the screen, Doctor Karl could not resist turning to his son and whispering: 'You see those girls?'

'Yes.'

'All show. He's been impotent for years, but he thinks an image of virility helps the people to admire him.'

Marcus glanced round.

'Quiet, father, watch the guards.'

From the moment Zirpola had appeared upon the screen they had moved in closer to the prisoners and were watching for any sign that they were going to treat the appearance of the Lord of Helix with anything less than the reverence it deserved.

Ankar Moor's voice boomed out: 'The Death Sport is ready to begin, My Lord.'

Zirpola nodded graciously and stepped forward to the front of the box and also to the dominant position in the forefront of the screen. It had all been carefully rehearsed. The doctor could see the tell-tale tremor on his left eyelid that told him the Lord of Helix was fighting off his internal pain:

'Statemen of Helix, my loyal citizens. Today we face a crisis of tremendous importance and proportions. It is a crisis for which we did not ask. A crisis which none of us sought to create. Nevertheless it has come upon us and we must all rise up and overwhelm it if we are to survive into a golden future.'

As he paused dramatically, one of the braver prisoners in the changing-rooms made a loud raspberry. At once the Enforcer guards were upon him, beating him to the ground before dragging him away. One moment of courage had lost him the chance to fight for his freedom for another year.

At the same time the guards in charge of Kaz Oshay and Deneer, who still lay, apparently mindless, on the floor of their tiny cell, got the signal to bring their prisoners up to the other empty changing-room for the start of their preparation. They were pulled to their feet and forced, with the use of cruel electric prods the men held, to walk up a small ramped corridor which seemed to lead endlessly upwards but which culminated in a tiny security lift that would take them up to the arena.

The Lord Zirpola was continuing.

'As you are all aware, our forebears saw to our needs with supplies of liquid fuel for the powering of the City. They are critical of our continued existence. For all this time they have fuelled our life-support systems, a total of over nine hundred years. These precious stores are close to being entirely used up and our very lives depend upon our being able to replenish them before it is too late.'

He paused dramatically to let the significance of his words sink in and Polna entered the changing-rooms at that moment. He glanced round and selected two prisoners from the group nearest to him.

'All right, you men. If you survive, one of you will be able to watch the repeats.'

Guards handed the two men overalls and helmets – one of the helmets blue, the other yellow.

'You two will be fighting first.' His eyes wandered round the other groups. 'The rest of you can relax for the moment. I'll be back to choose six of you to fight the Guides.'

Zirpola began again and the Karls did not let their attention waver from the screen.

'The solution to our problem is at hand. For centuries the people of Triton have stood in the way of that solution. They have vast hoards of stored fuel and, while they have squandered what they can, they have repeatedly refused to share their fuel with us in a vicious and calculated plot to bring about our downfall.'

While the two prisoners dressed, guards had wheeled forward two of the Death Machines, taking them to the end of the tunnel, just to the point where the entrance to the arena was blocked by the blaster shield which was now activated over the whole arena. Here they had activated the blaster pods and the two men were marched forward and placed on the machines, which were then started up, ready for the signal for the blaster shield to be lifted so that they could roar into the view of the crowds and the cameras.

Zirpola continued his tirade.

'The choice before us is stark and clear. We can either continue to deplete our limited resources and then allow ourselves to die a cruel death at the hands of the Mutants when they overrun the City – or we can strike now while we still have the fuel to power us and take from Triton what we rightfully deserve and what our destiny demands that we take.'

In the depths of the City, the two Guides moved slowly forward, the men with the prods behind them. Deneer stumbled to her knees and was forced again to her feet by the cruel prodding of one of the guards.

'Get a move on, you bastards. You mustn't keep the Death Sport waiting.'

He felt almost ashamed of his roughness as he saw the glazed, bewildered expression on the faces of the two Guides. It was almost a shame to be feeding these two to the arena, their minds broken, and their spirits with them. It was as if they were dead already. Still, he was just a guard and had his duty to do. He prodded them again:

'Get a move on.'

In the changing-rooms, Doctor Karl was watching the screen with a mixture of disgust and fascination. So far the speech had been a perfect rabble rouser, as clever a piece of manipulative propaganda as he had ever seen. Mad or not, the Lord Zirpola knew how to capture the minds and imaginations of his audience.

The doctor had heard and had been taught of men like this in the past, men with the power to mesmerise the masses in spite of their unprepossessing physical appearance and habits. His memory told him that the end result had usually been disastrous for those who became followers, but it had never been a lesson that mankind had been prepared to learn.

Zirpola was speaking again:

'To help secure our protection and future, I have chosen this Death Sport to reveal and demonstrate to you a secret weapon, created by our scientists, that will make our conquest of Triton not only possible – but inevitable.'

Here the man's voice rose to a scream:

'Here is the key to our salvation.'

As he spoke, a portion of the blaster shield was lifted, allowing the two men in the tunnel to gun their bikes forward into the arena. As they appeared, Zirpola shouted:

'Citizens – the Death Machines.'

The cameras cut and zoomed in on the machines and their riders as they zoomed out into the arena, kicking up a tremendous cloud of dust as they went. Music blared out over the speakers, music specially chosen by Zirpola to heighten the effect that the first sight of the machines would place in the minds of the citizens of Helix.

Marcus and the doctor shuddered as they saw the results of Zirpola's manipulation. It had been a beautifully calculated effect. The crowds in the arena rose and cheered their leader to the echo and they could imagine the people in their homes leaning forward in excitement to watch the machines as they were ridden powerfully round the arena.

The prisoners made two circuits, then brought their machines to a halt, as they had been instructed, immediately below the box that contained the leader of the City. Now he stepped forward again.

'For months these men have been perfecting their skills, learning the full power and use of the Death Machines, readying themselves for the danger and excitement of this contest, this trial of power and wits – and the greater struggle beyond. Now, here in the arena, you are to be privileged to witness the power that these machines can give to ordinary Statemen. Later you will see the machines overcome even the powers of the Range Guides in deadly combat. But first a traditional gladiatorial duel between two equally matched Statemen – let the Death Sport begin.'

He took a proud pose as the camera moved in on him for these final words, his head held high to emphasise his strength and vision. Amid a poorly recorded fanfare of trumpets, his face slowly faded from the screen and was replaced by a shot of the whole arena, as the cameras waited for the contest to begin.

The crowd fell silent in expectation and the only sounds came from the low hum of the blaster shield and the roar of the enormous cycles.

Far below, still in the depths of the City, the two Guides were pushed into the tiny security elevator and the controls were set. As the elevator started to move, one of the guards communicated a signal to the empty changing-room where other guards stood ready to receive them.

Inside the little cage, the glazed look fell from the eyes of the two Guides and they looked at one another, their stares locking on to each other as they pulled themselves upright in the confined space.

Both of them were aware how much the disorientation chambers had weakened them and Kaz managed to gasp: 'Deneer, we must try to rebuild our strength.'

Deneer nodded.

'I agree. We must do it together.'

Each of them reached up, gently touching the temples of the other with their fingertips, each pulling the other's head forward so that their foreheads rested against one another, their eyes still locked on to each other's.

The deep hum started up from their throats, in key and in unison. All of their attention and the attention of the consciousness became focussed into them.

Deneer began to chant softly:

'Float with me.'

'I float with you.'

'Let your thoughts float together with mine.'

'I let my thoughts float together with yours.'

'Let all noise and torment wash from your mind.'

'All noise and torment washes from my mind.'

'Bring peace.'

'Bring peace.'

They floated in through the windows of each other's soul. Their eyes became mirrors behind which they were renewed, cut off from the reality of the small cage that ascended with them.

After a while, they floated back to reality. Deneer said:

'Feel me, feel yourself.'

Kaz echoed her:

'Feel me, feel yourself.'

There was another moment of silence between them, before Kaz intoned softly:

'I am one with you. We are together through time and space in the silence and power of the consciousness.'

Their foreheads remained together as they reached up and touched each other on the temples once more, gently, with their fingertips, feeling each other's pulse, so that the beating of their hearts slowly came together and synchronised with one another, the sound of it communicating through their foreheads, blotting out all other sound, taking them over.

Deneer intoned:

'Listen as you grow . . . Listen as you grow with every beat . . .'

'I listen as I grow . . . I listen as I grow with every beat . . .'

'You are more powerful . . . More powerful . . . More powerful . . . Now you can feel it within you . . . You are become as powerful as you need to be to overcome.'

'I am as powerful as I need to be to overcome . . .'

There came another period of inner sound and outward silence as they continued to stand together, their foreheads still touching, neither of them moving in spite of the swaying rise of the elevator cage. Both felt stronger and more sure with every second that passed. At last, Kaz Oshay said quietly:

'I am restored. I am as powerful as I need to be.'

'I too am restored.'

Once more they touched each other on the temples before their foreheads parted and the ritual of renewal of strength was at an end. They floated back out through the windows of their souls and their breathing and heartbeats separated and returned to normal in their individual bodies. They were healed in mind as well as body, themselves again.

The elevator was slowing up as if it had completed its journey. Kaz said urgently:

'We must pretend that we are still affected by our treatment in the disorientation chambers.'

Deneer nodded. 'It is vital. At least until the contest.'

They assumed the same blank, bewildered expressions that had been on their faces below. The elevator jolted to a halt and the door slid open, letting in the strong, cruel artificial light of the changing-room, bright enough to hurt even their eyes, causing them to cover them for a moment in order to adjust – which only went to underline, for the guards, the poor condition they were in.

They were pulled from the elevator and fell in a crumpled, bewildered heap on the floor. The guards looked at one another.

'Poor bastards. They won't last a minute in the arena.'

Kaz and Deneer were able to see each other's faces and they exchanged a wink; it was just the effect that they had wanted to create.

Outside, in the arena, the crowd was waiting with growing impatience for the contest to begin. The hot sun beat down through the blaster shield as they waited to see the first demonstration of the Death Machines.

The delay had occurred following the end of Zirpola's speech. While he had given the order for the whole games to begin, he was needed to signal the start of the individual contest.

The delay seemed perfectly timed, as if calculated to heighten the tension that gripped the City. But Carol Rabids and Howard Koslow knew better when the pan-out had been for the events and they were puzzled as they filled in as best they could, describing every detail they could see of the machines that idled under the Royal Box, the crowds, the excitement and the weather, that final stand-by of any commentary on an outside broadcast.

The truth was that all was not well. As the cameras faded on his visage, the Lord of Helix had staggered suddenly and grasped the front of the box to hold himself up. He was fighting off his first strong attack of pain for the day. He turned to Ankar Moor:

'You start the contest.'

The other man, puzzled by the look of pain that had crossed Zirpola's face, was more mystified. He shook his head:

'No. You must. It is important.'

Zirpola made a supreme effort and drew himself up. Over the picture of the arena, Carol Rabids interrupted Howard's dissertation on the heat of the sun.

'Thank you, Howard. Now I can see that the Lord Zirpola is coming to the front of the box to give the signal for the first contest to begin.'

Zirpola managed to hold himself upright. He raised his hand and the crowd cheered afresh. Only Doctor Karl could see what was wrong on the video. He turned to his son.

'He's in pain. He may collapse.'

Marcus shrugged. 'Not soon enough.'

Zirpola snapped:

'You fight for your freedom. Let the contest begin.'

The two men gunned their machines and turned away from each other to zoom round the arena before letting their battle of power and wits commence.

In his box, Lord Zirpola reeled backwards, unable to hide his feeling of pain any more. He collapsed into his chair and looked up at Ankar Moor, who was staring frankly at him, surprised by this sudden show of weakness.

'How did I sound?'

The other man's eyes held questions behind the leather mask. He put none of them into his voice. 'Fine, My Lord.'

Out in the field both audience and television cameras watched in a breathless hush of anticipation. The two men had reached points on the far side of the arena from each other.

Now they turned their machines and began to charge at top speed across the open space towards each other. A head-on crash seemed inevitable and if they went for the kill they would only succeed in blasting each other out of this world and into the next. But neither the blue-helmeted man nor his yellow opponent seemed willing to be the first to back down from the confrontation as they approached the central hill of the arena.

At the last possible calculated moment, when they were on the periphery of their effective blaster range, the prisoner wearing the blue helmet swerved suddenly to one side, taking a hard ninety-degree turn in a shower of sand and dirt, before halting his machine. At the same moment, the yellow-helmeted gladiator hit the hillock and took off over the brow of it, flying entirely airborne. Blue helmet fired his rear blasters, but the other man sailed safely over the top of the attack, landing with a thrusting swerve that threw up another cloud of dirt.

The crowd let out its breath in one echoing blast of tension relief that filled the microphones that were playing the sound through to the televideo audience as the two riders fought for the control of their machines and prepared to make another death run at one another.

In the main changing-room, Doctor Karl and Marcus were unable to take their eyes off the huge monitor for a second. They knew they had to absorb every tactic and trick that was used in this first contest to learn what they could if their turn was next.

On the smaller monitor in their quiet changing-room, the two Range Guides were also watching the screens above them. For the benefit of their guards, their faces showed only a blank foolishness as if they were merely attracted by the movement and the colours that they could see, but inside, their brains were turning over, absorbing every movement, learning all they could about these machines that they would have to fight.

Carol Rabids was almost showing an interest as she commentated breathily:

'That was an excellent attacking manoeuvre, but the contestant in the yellow helmet had the better position and in this contest, position is nine-tenths of the trick. Close enough to kill is most often close enough to be killed. Now, to hit your opponent without being in a position to be hit yourself, that seems to be the trick.'

The two men were roaring around the field of battle

again, each jockeying to get the position of advantage over the other.

Deneer observed in an undertone that was low enough for only another Guide to hear: 'It takes a much finer balance and reflex and co-ordination than to ride a horse.'

Kaz was in agreement. 'And little of the instinct.'

Their blank eyes went back to the screen to observe another charge between the two men. This time the riders roared at one another, then veered away at the last moment to avert a crash that would have been fatal to them both. Neither man used the death-dealing blaster pods and both had difficulty in keeping control of their machines. Deneer was continuing to learn.

'The hand and foot controls look easy enough.'

'Yes . . . ' Kaz would have said more but his attention was suddenly elsewhere. His eyes went to look out through the tunnel and the electric shield beyond, straining his eyes at the small patch of sky he could see.

He had detected some subtle change in the natural atmosphere and he now concentrated his mind upon it, slowly letting the sound of combat and the reality of his surroundings dissolve away until he became one with the atmosphere outside. After a little while he slipped back into the present consciousness and then he reached out surreptitiously to touch Deneer on the arm, lightly, but with an urgency that at once communicated itself to the girl.

'Can you not feel the wind?'

For a moment she tried to feel what he had felt, but nothing came to her and her brow was furrowed as she turned to him.

'I feel nothing. What troubles you?'

'A Flash Wind.'

'I feel no sign of it.'

'It is there, nonetheless. It is coming towards us across the plains of the wastelands.'

She took his word unquestioningly:

'When does it come?'

'Tomorrow – I think late tomorrow.'

Deneer gave a subtle shrug. The smile on her face was wry, almost a Stateman smile.

'It is too bad that it lingers for so long. We could have used it this afternoon.'

He smiled comfort at her: 'We can use it tomorrow.'

Deneer absorbed his confidence. She was still not sure of her ability to survive this day.

'You think we will be living on the morrow?'

He was taken aback by her lack of assurance. She was not thinking like a true Guide.

'Can you doubt it?'

High above them, in the tallest tower, the Lord Zirpola was concentrating on the fight below him, trying to squeeze enjoyment from it, to combat the feelings of nausea and dizziness that now accompanied his pain. He felt as if there was a great bubble of force within his brain, that seemed about to lift his head from his shoulders.

Suddenly, it became too strong to allow him further concentration. He seized his head and groaned, his interest in the contest suddenly wiped away.

Ankar Moor turned to glare at him, half-pleased by this sudden show of weakness, but puzzled by the apparent suddenness of it just the same.

'Are you all right, My Lord?'

Zirpola shook his head in anger.

'It is nothing. Just the heat, the brightness of the light. I will be myself in a moment.'

He made himself look up, his watery blue eyes flashing a challenge at the other man, trying to prove that his weakness was but a temporary manifestation. Ankar Moor stared back at him for a moment, then turned away abruptly to renew his interest in the contest below. Zirpola tried to renew his concentration as well, but could see little with the red mist that swam before his eyes.

Below them both men were still riding and fighting for their lives. Their manoeuvres were becoming slower, more sluggish, as if the strain of driving and controlling their machines was slowly weakening them, driving the will to win from their tense bodies.

The man in the yellow helmet charged his machine almost directly under the tower that contained the Royal Box, while the man in the blue helmet gunned his engine at full speed down the hill that was in the centre of the arena, to try to cut the other rider off as he headed for higher ground.

Yellow helmet, seeing that the other man was bound to succeed in this aim if he kept to his present course, spun around abruptly and charged back the way he had come.

Taken by surprise, his opponent braked too hard to try

to cut back and follow, and in doing so, he hit a small hillock before he had regained his balance and was ready for it and, losing his moving equilibrium entirely, he flew upwards and out of control on the far side.

His landing was totally incorrect and he immediately tumbled from his falling machine, falling away and rolling over so that it would not fall on him.

A quick glance over his shoulder told the other man what had happened to his opponent and he spun round again, speeding up and moving in for what would obviously be the kill.

With certain death charging down on him, the man in the blue helmet picked himself up and lunged desperately towards his fallen machine. He had time to reach it and pull it upright as the man in the yellow helmit hit the other side of the hill and flew up into the air, his finger on the blaster button, ready for the coup de grace as he landed.

The man in the blue helmet, apparently doomed, had one chance and he took it now. He snatched up the handlebars of his machine and raised it from the ground to line up a rear shot at the point where he estimated his opponent would land.

As yellow-helmet's wheel touched the ground, he pressed the button. There came the bright green flash of the anti-matter blaster pods and, with a strangled shriek that echoed and re-echoed around the vast arena, the man in the yellow helmet, together with the Death Machine on which he rode, disappeared from Stateman sight, vaporised into his constituent atoms as he was annihilated.

A great roar of triumph went up from the crowd. The sight of complete destruction was almost as exciting and compelling to them as the sight of blood had been to their ancestors, so long ago in, the forums at the games of the great empires.

So great was the excitement that, in the changing-rooms, the prisoner Statemen cheered too, as if they did not realise that what they had watched was the annihilation of one of their number. Doctor Marcus and Karl, alone amongst their number, shuddered with a combination of fear and disgust.

The victor, after acknowledging the plaudits of the crowd, remounted his machine, started the dead engine and began to make a circuit of victory of the arena, as they rose, clapping and cheering. His circuit would bring him to a halt under the Royal Box to receive word of his reward. The commentary oozed out of Howard Koslow this time.

'Well, Carol, that was an incredible display of skill and courage, wasn't it.'

'Yes, Howard. It was one in the great tradition of the Death Sport. We'll have action replay in a moment. That man surely deserves his freedom. It was a great performance.'

Doctor Karl was disgusted by this bland dismissal of the barbaric ritual murder he had seen take place on the screen. Could not the free citizens of Helix realise that this was no voluntary duel or display of murderous skill – that the prisoners had no choice, but were forced into putting on these displays of murder? They were held on the word of the Lord Zirpola. There was no chance of trial for them, and no appeal against their forced imprisonment. This was the only chance they had to regain their freedom – and even the risk of death was preferable to rotting away in the Helix City prison complex, their lives playing out beneath the constant bright lights of their small cells.

The screen now showed the victor of the first contest coming to a halt in front of the Royal Box. He switched off his machine and dismounted to stand proudly beside it, waiting for Zirpola to acknowledge him and rise to give him the reward that was due to the victor.

Above him, Zirpola was close to screaming out from the waves of pain that were attacking him. Ankar Moor glanced across, impatient at the delay and unconcerned with any weakness in the other man; weakness was to be sneered at.

'My Lord, the victor is waiting.'

Zirpola made a superhuman effort. By clutching at the arms of his chair with his talon-like hands, he was able to push himself upright, though shaking from head to foot. He let go and staggered rather than walked to the front of the box. His face was ashen from the pain and his voice quavered as he spoke, even though he put all his strength into the effort to control himself under the eye of the cameras.

'Well done. We are proud of you.' With a great effort he managed to raise one shaking arm in a kind of benediction. It fell back to his side and even the crowd became puzzled by the pause that followed.

A minute and he was strong enough to continue:

'You have won your freedom bravely, Stateman, and your fellow citizens can be proud that you will be among them again. You have made a place for yourself on my Obedience force by the quality of your efforts. Be loyal to your lord and the State. You are, from this moment on, a free man.'

The man saluted his lord, then began to wheel the machine back to the tunnel entrance to the changing-rooms and away from the field of death.

Zirpola forced himself to stand straight as he watched the man go, clutching the front of the box to stop himself from falling and waiting for the cheers of the crowd to die down. When they were done with their acclaim, he had more to say on the subject of Triton and the Death Machines, to ram his earlier message home. The cheering died down and he forced his voice to be firm by a sheer effort of will.

'Now you Statemen of Helix have seen what the Death Machines mean, what they will do for you. With them we can have pride in our City. Triton cannot stand against us, no one can stand in the way of our destiny.'

He waved his hand once more, then backed away from the sight of the crowd as the cameras cut away from him again. The moment the red light on them had gone off, he slumped back into his chair and lay back, closing his eyes against an even more intense wave of pain.

There was to be a short delay before the next event of the Death Sport – when six men would go out on machines to fight the two Guides who had been captured. Before that time came, Ankar Moor wanted just one last chance to gloat over Kaz Oshay and Deneer. He swept from the room, not bothering to ask leave to go from the stricken man who ruled him.

As the victor reached the anti-blaster shield, it broke for a moment and he was able to wheel his machine up the tunnel and into the changing-room where his fellow-prisoners of a few moments before were waiting to greet and congratulate him. There was pandemonium as he came into view to be crowded round and applauded by the other men. Only Marcus and his father remained seated, not joining in the general euphoria.

Polna was waiting in the tunnel, taking his right to be the first to congratulate the freed man and to give him his instructions for taking up his post as an Obedience Enforcer. He grasped the man's hand and slapped him on the back –

the last time he would ever have to be nice to him.

'Congratulations – you fought and killed him fair.'

The man turned a dazed stare on his erstwhile captor.

'I'm really free?'

Polna grinned.

'Damned right you are. You are as free as the day you were born and an Enforcer now, to boot. You must be very proud.'

The irony of this method of getting out of the frying pan and into the fire was lost entirely on both the victor and the man who had spoken. But it was not lost on either Marcus or his father, who glanced at one another and allowed a shudder to pass between them as they contemplated the 'honour' of a life's entrapment in the Enforcer guards that had been thrust upon the man.

Meanwhile the other prisoners were pressing and surging round him, offering their congratulations. Polna, who had detached himself and was now standing back, the grim look returning to his face, glanced at his chronometer. Time was getting short. It would not be long before the next item on the afternoon's display of murder would be due to start.

He snapped on his communicator and talked to the men who were guarding the Guides in the other changing-room.

'Are the Guides there and waiting?'

'We have them ready. Shall we issue weapons to them?'

Polna snapped: 'No, not yet.'

'What will they have?'

'They will only have their own weapons. They will be supplied to them just before the Death Sport begins.'

The guard, who was not without humanity and was already worried by the dazed condition of his prisoners, gasped:

'But how will they defend themselves against the Death Machines? It is no contest.'

Polna snarled:

'We will be the judges of that. That is their problem and need be of no concern to you.'

He snapped off the communicator, making a mental note that the guard he had spoken to would have to be disciplined later. It was time for him to select the six men who would fight the Guides.

The prisoners were still crowding round the victor of the

last battle. Polna signalled his men to move in in case of protest and shouted:

'Right, that's enough. Move back and shut up.'

The men obeyed with reluctance, seeing the electric prods their guards held in case they were too slow to obey.

Polna waited until he had silence.

'None of you will gain the right to freedom till you have fought like this man did. But you will all have a chance. That is why you are here.'

He glanced round until he had spotted Marcus and his father. There was the young man who had instigated all the trouble at the prison, being instrumental in bringing the prisoners as close to a successful escape as they had ever been. He beckoned him over.

Marcus glanced at his father but the older man just nodded briefly, his eyes containing a message of love and blessing. Polna pointed another five men out of the group of prisoners, including the huge figure of Durc, with the vicious scars down his face.

When they were grouped round him, he said: 'Get changed and select your machines. You six will be fighting the Guides.'

Marcus felt a stab of almost physical pain through his heart. The moment of decision and truth had come at last.

CHAPTER EIGHT

Kaz Oshay and Deneer knew that their moment of testing was on the way. They had been made to stand and they had been pushed into the tunnel that led to the entrance to the arena. Now they stood together, keeping the glazed look about them, surrounded by nervous guards, their weapons at the ready in case either Guide made a wrong move.

They could still hear the commentary over the televideo and were listening harder than their guards knew, as Carol Rabids said:

'Now this next one should be very exciting. We have two of the Range Guides and, without any handicaps, they are challenging six of our own Statemen on Death Machines. The purpose of this event is to introduce you, in the most dramatic way possible, to the real power of the Death Machines. The idea of Statemen beating Guides would have been unthinkable until these machines were created, isn't that right Howard?'

'It sure is, Carol, but, now you'll see the difference the machines make this afternoon, all right.'

'Thank you, Howard. Now the crowd is waiting. Yes, I think we're about due for the start of what promises to be a very exciting contest . . . '

Behind them came strong footsteps. The guards came quickly to attention but the two imprisoned Guides turned only slowly, still keeping up their pose. The moment they saw the newcomer they could pretend to be broken no longer.

Kaz raised his blazing eyes so that they looked deep into the soul of Ankar Moor. The latter pulled his eyes away from the frank stare of hatred and laughed.

'I came to wish you farewell, Kaz Oshay, as you prepare for your journey into the beyond.'

Kaz's voice was equally harsh, full of steel.

'Ankar Moor, I wish only that I could finish the work my mother began on you.'

Ankar Moor glanced now into the blazing eyes of Deneer. He was taken aback: both the prisoners seemed full of strength and poise. What had Polna been thinking of? Was he not supposed to have given them treatment in the disorientation chambers?

On the surface he gave no sign that he was puzzled. He snapped out in challenge to the looks he had received: 'You are so close to death and yet you still defy me. I who have the power of life and death over you?'

Kaz snarled: 'We would defy you even in death, Ankar Moor.'

He laughed. 'And you are about to have the chance to make that boast true. You are doomed, Kaz Oshay, son of Oshay.'

'And you are an animal, Ankar Moor.'

The chief of the Obedience Enforcers came as close to Kaz as he could without touching him.

'It does not matter what you think of me, enslaved one. Your death will be your salute to me.'

But if he thought he had had the last word, he was mistaken. The hatred and determination of Kaz Oshay was greater than that:

'And yours will be to me when you accept the code and fight me, useless animal.'

For a moment, Ankar Moor was silent, then he threw his head back and laughed at the bravado of the imprisoned man. After a moment he got himself under control and rasped: 'Salute your mother for me, I will see you both in hell.'

He turned away abruptly and gave an order to the chief guard:

'Do not arm them until the Statemen have positioned themselves on the field.'

'Yes, Sir.'

Ankar Moor strode away from the little group and back to the elevator that would take him up again to the Royal Box. Only when he was inside did he let himself give way to his anger. He took a communicator from his pocket and tuned it in to get Polna. His assistant answered after a moment:

'Yes, Sir.'

Ankar Moor roared: 'I ordered disorientation for those Guides.'

Polna was silent. He did not understand. At last, 'I did as you ordered. Their brains are partially destroyed.'

The huge man snorted into the machine.

'They have tricked you. They have tricked all of us. Only the machines will put the matter right. Mark my words, Polna, you will pay for this after they are dead.'

He switched off the communicator as the elevator continued its upward path.

It took Polna a little time to do the same. His hands were clammy with sweat and he was shaking with fear. Perhaps he had at last made the error that he had always dreaded.

A guard ran up, holding some anti-matter blasters. Polna was so afraid he did not even see the man until the latter coughed politely and said:

'Sir?'

'What is it?'

The man was taken aback by the viciousness of his superior's tone:

'The hand blasters, Sir.'

Polna managed to soften his tone.

'Good. Put them down.'

The guard laid them at Polna's feet and the senior man watched as the six Statemen prisoners finished dressing themselves. This time there was no differentiation between them, there was no need for it. They all wore the riding coveralls and had white protective helmets. All seemed in order and Polna got their attention, pointing at the small pile of blasters at his feet:

'Each of you can take one hand blaster and lock it to your belt. If for any reason you get dismounted from your machines, do not hesitate to use the blaster.'

The Statemen went one at a time to obey the instruction. If any of them had it in their minds to use the blasters now and make a break for it, the number of armed guards around would have discouraged it successfully. Marcus was the last of the men to pick up the deadly weapon and, as he backed away with it, his father, feeling him in need of comfort and afraid of the loss of his beloved son, came up to him.

'How do you feel?' He could have told the answer from the look on Marcus's face, but still felt the question should be asked.

Marcus answered it a dull voice:

'How would you expect me to feel – with a choice between my own life and the lives of a man and woman I respect and trust?'

Doctor Karl sighed. There seemed to be little that he could say, he felt exactly as his son did.

'You must act for the best.'

'Do you mean I should kill?'

His father frowned. 'Only if you feel you must. Sit back, try to avoid the choice.' Even as he spoke he felt ashamed of his words, but there really wasn't anything else to think. His son had little choice. Either kill or be killed. It was an impossible dilemma.

Marcus seemed calmer, though he had reacted badly to his father's words.

'There may be a way.'

'How?'

Marcus even managed a smile.

'It is likely I will die, but I have a choice to make.'

'But there is no choice other than to allow yourself to kill or be killed in the battle.'

Marcus smiled more broadly, but with the sinking feeling growing inside him as he wondered whether he really had the strength to do what had come to him.

'There is a choice. That choice is what side I will be on when I die.'

Doctor Karl understood and admired his son more for his courage in that moment than he had in all his life, in spite of all the boy's good qualities. He put a hand round his shoulder and smiled bravely.

'You'll make it, son . . . You'll come back to me, I am sure of that, if of nothing else.'

They embraced, then Marcus turned away so that his father would not see the tears in his eyes. He had made his decision in his own heart already, there would be no need to review it once he was in the arena.

Ankar Moor was still smouldering with rage at the failure of the disorientation treatment on the two Guides as the elevator came to a halt and he pushed the door back to step into the Royal Box.

The situation up there had deteriorated since he had left. The members of the television crew were trembling in fear. Obviously, Lord Zirpola had gone into one of his rages during the Enforcer leader's absence. This was borne out when he saw the girls. One of them was bleeding from the mouth, her face a livid red down one side where the Lord of Helix had struck her.

As for Zirpola himself, he was slumped down in his chair, his head in his hands, sobbing and groaning with pain from his head.

'What happened?' snapped Ankar Moor.

One of the girls spoke.

'It was Marda. She saw he was in pain and went to help him. He just lashed out at her. We haven't been near him since.'

Ankar Moor turned his attention to his master, who tried to rise, fell back and groaned: 'The pain. I have to stop it. I can't stand it any more. Please help me stop it.'

Ankar Moor leant down to the chair and grasped the

stricken man by his arms, shaking him into some semblance of normal behaviour.

'Do you want me to call a doctor?'

Zirpola giggled, his breath hissing with a horrible sound between his teeth as he made the effort to reply.

'There is no doctor any more. I had him arrested, remember. He lied to me about what was wrong.'

'And what is wrong with you?'

'I'm.' Zirpola stopped himself, suddenly aware that he was about to place himself entirely in the other man's hands. 'It is nothing. Headaches brought on by the strain of waiting for our plans to mature.'

Ankar Moor did not believe this unconvincing answer. No matter, he could question the doctor, take him out of the Death Sport and torture him for the information if necessary. For now, though, it was important that the next game in the Death Sport be called – the game that would put the two Guides against the Death Machines:

'Pull yourself together. It is time for the main event to begin.'

Zirpola tried to rise, but fell back and gasped: 'I can't. You must call it for me.'

Ankar Moor let him fall back and snatched up his communicator. To hell with the crowd knowing or thinking anything was wrong when the games started. He got Polna on the other end: 'Bring on the machines.'

'But the game has not been announced.'

Ankar Moor roared: 'I'm announcing it now. Bring on the machines.' He snapped off the communicator before Polna could give him any further argument.

Polna switched off his communicator and shouted the order to the guards to get the men lined up on their machines and get them started. In a little while they were ready, the large figure of Durc at the head of them, Marcus having made sure he got the last spot.

Polna moved over to the controls of the anti-blaster shield, then turned and shouted to the prisoners on their great machines: 'All right. Give them hell.'

With that, he lifted the shield for a moment and gave the signal for the prisoners to move forward into the arena. They made their way slowly out, in single file, going across the arena so that the whole crowd could get a clear view of them. They then went up to the far end of the blaster-shield enclosed arena and stopped their machines to wait for the arrival of their opponents of the day.

Kaz Oshay and Deneer had been given helmets for protection and their Whistlers. They were to get no other help than this – and what good was a helmet against a blaster? The odds had been balanced just as the Lord Zirpola had wanted.

They glanced at one another for reassurance. Deneer said quietly:

'Our Union is real.'

His eyes locked on to hers and he echoed her with emotion:

'Our Union is real.'

Their eyes stayed together and the guard said:

'The blaster shield will rise in a moment. Run out as soon as it does – right?'

Kaz nodded. The man was not so bad. He was just doing his job and the Guide knew that at least he had pitied them.

Kaz turned his attention back to Deneer. He smiled at her now, showing real affection, a gesture that owed nothing to the code.

'I feel power from you, woman.'

In that moment, Deneer had the confirmation that their Union was truly one over the wastelands, should they ever return to them.

'And I from you, man.'

Ankar Moor's voice crackled over the loudspeakers.

'Let the combat begin.'

The anti-blaster shield disappeared from the entrance to their tunnel. At once, and in perfect co-ordination, the two Guides ran forward as fast as they could accelerate.

Kaz cried out:

'High ground.'

Deneer answered by giving the loud war whoop of the Guides as she continued the run forward.

The high ground was to one side of the huge arena and the two Guides concentrated on getting into this area as fast as they could. They took no notice as five of the six Death Machines revved up and started forward in an attempt to cut them off, Durc moving rapidly ahead of the other men with him. Only Marcus remained unmoving, astride his machine but just watching his fellow-prisoners as they progressed across the broken ground.

Kaz managed to gasp: 'One has not yet moved against us.

For the others, we must soon split the pack.'

Deneer's mind was running ahead of his own. 'We must take a machine.'

'I agree.'

They were there. As the audience both in the stands and on televideo had followed their progress, it appeared that they had moved with incredible speed. Immediately, they split and ran to hillocks that were far apart, so that each of their enemies would have to take a choice about which Guide to go after.

Their tactics worked and three cycles made for Kaz, while the other two charged for Deneer, who was now further away from them. The Guides drew their Whistlers and waited like sentinels for their enemies to come to them.

Marcus Karl sat silent on his machine, watching the drama unfold, waiting to make his own move.

Back in the changing rooms, Doctor Karl looked anxiously at the screen. Naturally, the cameras were on the spot where the action would come and there was no sign of his son. Carol Rabids was getting properly excited for the first time that afternoon:

' . . . All they have is their swords and they are just standing there, waiting for the Death Machines to come to them. They may be our enemies, but their courage is amazing, right Howard?'

'You're absolutely right, Carol. This is amazing. I think we're in for a few surprises, Carol.'

'Yes, Howard, and there seems to be one already. One of the riders hasn't moved from his position. We really are in for some strange entertainment before this fight is over.'

'O.K., Carol, now they're closing in for the attack . . . '

In that moment, Doctor Karl realised that the man who has not moved must be Marcus and he closed his eyes and prayed for the safety of his son.

As the Death Machines approached and charged in on them, Kaz Oshay and Deneer held their ground until the very last possible moment, just a split second before the prisoners fired their blaster pods. At that split second both Guides gave out with their echoing war cries and leapt high in the air, up and over the screaming machines.'

The first two Death Machines blasted their way ineffectually past under Kaz, but the third man was not so lucky. Kaz landed lightly at the side of the machine as the man roared past and the watchers could hardly see the speed with which his Whistler carved its way through the air. They could only hear the threatening whistle of it.

A second later, the still-helmeted head of the third rider was rolling across the ground, while the machine, a headless corpse still gripping the handle bars, zoomed straight on.

Another moment and the crowd were treated to a rare sight of self-destruction as the headless rider charged his machine straight into the blaster shield and, such was his speed, was not deflected but was dissolved into oblivion with an electric screech and a shower of sparks that lit up the whole field in spite of the already bright light of the sun.

As for Deneer, she made a leap equal in height to her male partner but, having only two machines coming at her, she had not the luxury of a third rider to kill.

She satisfied herself by shouting over to Kaz, 'Well done!'

Kaz glanced over to her. His cheeks were flushed with his success and the thrill of getting into action again.

'And better next time!'

With that, their minds working in perfect union, they ran across the centre of the field as the enemy righted their machines and turned to give chase again.

Bedlam had broken out in the Royal Box high above. At the start of the fight, Zirpola had recovered himself enough to sit up and watch. Now he had gone pale again at what he had witnessed, a pallor that owed nothing to his illness. He turned to Ankar Moor and snarled:

'That wasn't supposed to happen.'

Ankar Moor was engrossed in the fight, but he had his alibi at the ready. He glared at Zirpola and snarled:

'It is the prisoners, they are incompetent. But they will win.'

'They'd better do it soon.'

'They will, I guarantee it.'

Zirpola thought for a moment, then:

'And these Guides? Were they not supposed to have been adjusted by the disorientation technique?'

Ankar Moor glared again. 'Polna slipped up. He will pay for it.'

This time when he turned his attention back to the field of combat, he was determined that the argument was at an end.

Howard Koslow had taken up the commentary:

'Well, that was amazing, Carol. Now they're going up the

middle of the field again. And look at them go. Three times faster at least than any normal man.'

'Yes, Howard. It really is amazing. But another attack is about to start I think.'

On the field, with the Death Machines screaming in behind them, Kaz Oshay and Deneer split up again and bounded towards opposite sides of the great arena. Now there were two machines bearing down on each of the Guides. A moment later the silent sixth man gunned his machine and started to roar forward at Deneer, the closest Guide to his position. At this move the crowd roared. Now they would see some excitement.

Carol Rabids shouted:

'Now the sixth man's moved. I think we'll see one of the Guides go down this time.'

In the changing-rooms, Doctor Karl prayed that his son would be safe and that he had taken the right decision. Now he was shown on the televideo screen and the doctor felt alarm in his heart.

The two Guides had less time to prepare this time as the Death Machines moved faster across the open ground, faster in racing down on them. Both Guides were heading for high mounds that they knew they might never make.

Running as fast as he could, Kaz turned for a split second and saw that Durc, on the leading machine, was almost on his heels, his hand moving forward to the button of his blaster pods. Lunging forward, he dived over the top of the mound, hit the ground and, instead of rolling forward, he gripped himself to an immediate crouched halt.

This had the effect of depriving Durc of his target at the last possible moment and he saw a streak of green light pass above him. A moment later, Durc hit the mound and flew over his head, unable to slow down his machine in time.

Now, with the second machine on its way, Kaz rolled a short distance to one side and rose suddenly, his Whistler held at the ready. The second machine roared over the mound and took to the air.

This time there was no whistling sound from the great sword. Kaz Oshay merely had to hold it up and the forward movement of the rider and his powerful machine did the rest. Another head, still helmeted, rolled across the dirt, while the machine and his body roared on.

Deneer seemed to be in a lot more trouble than Kaz had

been. She too glanced back as she ran. The two machines chasing her were almost on top of her. A moment later she saw the third machine that was moving laterally towards her. There would be no time to use her Whistler; the best she could do would be to take avoiding action.

She leapt high in the air to dodge Marcus Karl's machine, but even she realised that she need not have worried. He had veered slightly away from her to avoid hitting her and now he roared on, oblivious of the moves she was making.

A moment later, taking a deep breath of fear, he pressed the button that activated the blaster pods on the front of his machine. In a great screaming flash of green anti-matter, the leading Death Machine on her tail dissolved into its constituent atoms. As both rider and machine dissolved into an empty nothingness, Marcus roared through the spot where they had been, just ahead of the suddenly confused second rider. He was quickly out of the man's range. This latter fighter was caught completely off-balance by the sudden turn of events and it took him a second to recover his speed and direction. It was this moment of hesitation that cost him his life.

Deneer was faster in her reactions. She swooped in on him with a terrible war cry. Her shrieking Whistler flashed in the sunlight and the man's head fell from his shoulders in the same manner that the two who had been vanquished by Kaz Oshay had done. But the man's machine was turning at an angle as the death occurred and it now flipped on its side, still roaring and only a few yards from her. She turned at once and ran towards it, to mount up and put herself on better terms with her remaining enemies.

On the other side of the field, Kaz Oshay ran forward and managed to grab the second machine before it whirled its way towards the anti-matter blaster shield.

Now they were both mounted and only one enemy was left on the field. To allow himself time to recover, Durc sped off to the far side of the field before making his turn; the feeling of death was upon him and he was mortally afraid.

Deneer, having mounted her machine, turned it as the man she had jumped aside from turned and roared back at her. He raised a hand to his helmet, pushing it back so that she could see who the rider was and yelled as hard as he could:

'I'm on your side.'

Her hand, that had been hovering over the blaster pod button, withdrew and instead she raised her Whistler and let it circle in the air, the strange wailing it made acknowledging his help and alliance.

Durc gunned his machine frantically as Kaz Oshay made his way across the field towards him.

Up in the Royal Box, bedlam had set in. Despite the pain in his head, the Lord Zirpola had snapped back to reality far enough to be watching the farce that it seemed to him was being played out in the arena below. His face reddened with an uncontrollable rage and he roared:

'Destroy them. I want them destroyed!'

Ankar Moor was at the edge of the box, gripping it strongly with his huge hands as he watched the disaster. He neither turned nor spoke when Zirpola yelled at him. As the ruler's rage grew, he found the strength to rise from his chair and stagger forward to grab the arm of the leader of the Obedience Enforcers.

'This wasn't supposed to happen. This wasn't supposed to happen.'

Ankar Moor glanced down into his eyes and Zirpola began to see the hatred that the big man held for him.

'No, it wasn't.' He turned back to the field, shaking Zirpola off, but the Lord of Helix grabbed him again.

'Why did it happen?'

Ankar Moor ignored him and he screamed on:

'You're responsible! Traitor! You did this to me. You did it. You caused it all. I can trust no one.'

Ankar Moor turned trembling with rage. Even Zirpola got the message this time and froze in fear. Ankar Moor picked him up bodily and carried him back to place him firmly in his chair. Zirpola sat there, trembling with fear as the man glared down at him.

After a moment, Ankar Moor turned and grabbed the microphone from the member of the televideo camera crew who carried it.

'Is it on?'

'No, sir.'

'Then switch it on.'

With a shaky hand the man complied with the order and Ankar Moor's voice boomed out, not only over the public address system but also over every video unit in the City:

'Send out the remaining Death Machines. Send them out at once. I want those Guides destroyed.'

The remaining prisoners, who had been looking in awe at the drama that was being played out on the huge colour screen in front of them, now erupted into action as Polna backed his master's booming tones by shouting at the guards to get the machines ready. Any excess machines were to be ridden by the guards themselves.

As he heard the order, Doctor Karl's heart leapt within him; here was his chance to join his son. At least they could die together, if they could not make a chance for escape.

Polna screamed: 'Get out there and kill them! You can't let them win. You've got to kill them if you're going to survive.'

Quickly the prisoners were mounted up. There was no delay for niceties such as helmets and blasters for their belts. They were being sent out to kill with speed and it didn't matter how many of them were killed in the attempt.

Doctor Karl made sure he was well back in the crowd coming down the tunnel, where they paused to wait for the anti-blaster shield to be broken for an instant.

The shield was lifted and the machines roared forward into the arena. Doctor Karl waited for just as long as it took him to get clear of the tunnel, then pressed the button of his forward blaster pods, immediately annihilating the man who was in front of him. Before anyone else could react, he broke off to the side and began to go round the edge of the arena, waving at Marcus as he went and trying to get round the edge of the arena to where he was manoeuvring.

Kaz was concentrating on pushing Durc into a smaller and smaller space in which to move and dodge him. He was not yet ready for the kill. Some of the new riders made straight for him, two of them in the lead by a long margin.

Durc chose that moment to take the desperate strategy of braking and using his rear blasters, but he scored another miss as Kaz Oshay swerved at the last moment. He then turned, did a crossover jump with Deneer, who was also speeding to his aid, then did a little rear blasting of his own. Durc, who had still had his back to the Guide and had been given no chance to make a turn, disappeared into oblivion, without even the scream of a man who knew it was happening to him.

Now it was time for Kaz Oshay and Deneer to take care

of the new danger that was bearing down on them. With a nod from Kaz, Deneer veered off to one side while Kaz moved away from them, making them come forward to chase him. Deneer charged in from the side as they reached a hillock behind which she was riding, then roared forward. She jumped over the top of the first rider, landed between the two of them and quickly fired both front and rear pods. Both riders and their machines were obliterated by her master stroke.

Now Kaz and Deneer were alongside each other and, a moment later, they were joined by Marcus and Doctor Karl.

Kaz smiled on Deneer. 'Powerfully done, woman.'

Deneer's eyes twinkled as she smiled back at him:

'Powerfully done, man.'

In the Royal Box, Zirpola, his illness completely forgotten, was almost jumping up and down like a child.

'They've ruined it. They've ruined the Death Sport. All my plans are in ruins.'

Ankar Moor roared angrily into the microphone, so the whole City knew of his discomfiture: 'I said I wanted all the machines on the field. I want them now! Hurry! They must be destroyed.'

In between his bellowed orders, the whole television coverage had gone silent. Howard Koslow had fainted and Carol Rabids, without his support, was totally devoid of words. The producer could not cut off the programme without direct orders from the Lord Zirpola and any attempt to get through to the Royal Box for clearance was blocked by the fact that Ankar Moor was bellowing over the equipment.

But the shame of the Lord of Helix had only just begun. A new batch of four Death Machines roared out from the tunnel and were instantly attacked by the four defenders, manoeuvring with greater ease as they became better used to the handling of their machines. In as many minutes, there were four fewer machines and riders in the City of Helix.

Zirpola rushed to the front of the box, screaming out obscenities at the farce below.

Then the worst blow fell. The lights of the City flickered, came on strong again, then died. A moment later the anti-blaster shield, too, melted away as the power for the City was cut off.

Zirpola whirled round.

'What's happened?'

Ankar Moor did not bother to reply, but threw the dead microphone angrily to the ground.

Polna was just entering the arena and all the men who followed him on their machines were Enforcer guards, line upon line of them. Kaz whirled round as he and his fellow fighters became aware of the brighter light and the sun beating down on them with a sudden greater heat. Kaz crowed:

'The shield is broken. Come on.'

Kaz turned and Deneer, with her faster reflexes, was hard on his heels. It took Doctor Karl and Marcus a little longer to make their turn, but the others held back slightly for the two Statemen to catch up with them. When they were in line, they all pressed the rear buttons on their blaster pods and blasted the first line of Enforcers, who were catching up on them, into oblivion, before roaring ahead across the wastelands and out of range.

Up in the box, the Lord Zirpola was purple in the face and frothing in his impotent rage. He looked as if he might burst at any moment and Ankar Moor would have been indifferent if he had. He was also almost shaking with anger, but more at the way the revenge had been snatched from him, for the way Kaz Oshay's mother had destroyed his face and banished him from the Guides, than at the way the Death Sport and the ideas behind it had been destroyed – by four brave prisoners, two Guides and two Statemen.

Zirpola ran up to him and hit him repeatedly on his chest with weak, ineffectual fists. 'Get them. Go after them. You imbecile! You let them escape! I'll have your head for this. I'll have your head!'

Coolly, under complete control, his hatred seething but not unleashed, Ankar Moor reached down and grabbed Zirpola by the collar of his emerald cloak, pulling him eyeball to bulging watery blue eyeball:

'You worthless animal. Never, never speak to me like that.'

He hurled the Ruler of Helix from him, so that Zirpola crashed in a heap on the ground. For a moment it looked as if Ankar Moor would put his foot on him to squash him like a bug, but he scuttled away across the floor, to cower by his chair.

When Ankar Moor spoke again his voice was quiet, but each word sounded as if it had been cast in steel.

'I will go after Kaz Oshay and the others because it pleases me to do so. And I will see them all destroyed because I am Ankar Moor and I wish to see them destroyed.'

With that he leaned forward and grabbed the ruler of Helix by the collar once more. He lifted him up so that the man was choking, gasping for breath, then threw him down into his chair. 'You own me no longer. I do not follow the code but in this one respect: I am my own master.'

With that, he strode away from the Lord of Helix, then made his way to the nearest staircase, which, with the elevators out of action, would get him to a Death Machine and in pursuit of his enemies as soon as possible.

Zirpola was very still for a moment, until he was quite sure that his former fellow-plotter was gone. Then he struggled to his feet again. The only people available to feel his anger now were the four girls, one of them already marked by him, and the television crew. He rose and moved towards the girls, who backed away from him, afraid for their lives.

He got only two paces forward before the tissues in his brain ruptured and exploded, throwing him to the ground. He was dead before his body was laid out before them.

Kaz Oshay smiled round at his companions. They were well out of the City now and far ahead of their pursuers. Helix City was just a spot on the horizon, the sun shining on its domes.

Marcus Karl moved his machine closer to the Range Guide, so that he was able to shout across at Kaz:

'We must get to Triton. We must warn them about the Lord Zirpola's plans for war.'

But Kaz Oshay shook his head and turned to Deneer.

'We must first look after our own. You will lead, Deneer. Tell me where the child was lost.'

Deneer nodded, pleased, but she understood Marcus's fears and smiled at him: 'The place is by the sandstone cliffs on the route to Triton. We will try to rescue Karissa, then go on to the City.'

And with that the Karls, for the moment, had to be content.

CHAPTER NINE

By the late afternoon, the City of Helix and the nightmare of the events of the past night and day had been left far behind. As he rode along at the side of his father, Marcus Karl began to recognise some of the landmarks it had taken almost a day to reach when he had originally been travelling the same trail by caravan, on his journey to Triton for his wedding. He was happier to think of this now. There was a chance he would still be in Triton in time for the wedding, perhaps even ahead of the time he had originally been expected. In the meantime, he could only pray that they would not be able to find the tribe of Mutants who had taken the Guide girl, Karissa. For, like all Statemen, he was frightened of the Mutants and did not dare to meet these misshapen men, with their sharp teeth and poisoned glands, in open combat.

It seemed that they held no fears either for Kaz Oshay or Deneer and when Marcus had indicated to his father that he would protest again about going after one little child when there was a whole City to save, his father had advised him against it:

'They have a law in their code. They take care of their own first. Respect that, they are still our best chance of getting away to Triton. Even with these machines, we could not make it on our own.'

'But they are so fast.'

His father nodded.

'But how would you survive the nights, when the Mutants are abroad?'

Marcus had agreed. His father had a point. So he had maintained his silence since the first protest he had made, when they were escaping from the Death Sport arena.

The shadows were lengthening as they came over the brow of a rise and started down towards the canyon that went past the great sandstone cliffs where the Enforcers had attacked, and Karissa, the daughter of the destroyed Guide Adriann, had been lost to them.

Kaz turned to Deneer: 'Whereabouts was the child lost?'

Deneer pointed a long way ahead.

'Over there, by the sand cliffs. Where my group was attacked.'

Kaz Oshay was gently reassuring.

'We have Union. We will find her.'

Marcus could contain himself no longer.

'Please. They will still be chasing us. We must press on and warn Triton, so that they can arm themselves for protection.'

Kaz was calm. He did not wish to hurt the young Stateman, but he would perhaps never understand the attitude of the Guides. His world was not theirs.

'You go to Triton if you want, Stateman. You are free to do as you please now.'

Marcus slapped his hand to his forehead. 'But don't you understand?'

'I understand your anxiety. Please understand ours.'

But Marcus was too anxious to listen:

'Don't you understand? There's going to be a war. Thousands of people may lose their lives. We have to warn Triton and stop it happening if we can get there in time.'

Deneer tried to explain again:

'Our first responsibility is to our own kind, Stateman. It is the way of the code.'

'But this is important to the whole world.'

Kaz sighed. His patience was running out. Anyway this pause in their flight might give Ankar Moor and his men a chance to catch up with them. 'If it is so important to you, then you go on alone.'

Marcus snorted: 'You know I can't. I'd never get there alive. But if you took us, we'd be in Triton tomorrow night.'

Now Kaz Oshay glared at him.

'Not even a fool travels the wastes at night.'

Marcus was beside himself.

'Why can't you see how important it is?'

Doctor Karl thought it was time he took a hand in the conversation. Marcus was over anxious and all he was succeeding in doing was making angry the only two people who could help them.

'I am sorry. My son is young. The girl he loves lives in Triton. Like you, he is anxious to look after his own kind first. What can you do for us, Kaz Oshay?'

Kaz Oshay smiled on the man he had come to respect during their night in the cells.

'You and your son are our friends. You have helped us regain our freedom and keep our lives. We will guide you all the way to Triton after we have found the child – not before.'

Deneer echoed him.

'I agree. It is just.'

'Well I don't – '

Marcus's father glared him into silence and snapped: 'Shut up!'

He turned back to Kaz:

'That is all we can ask, Kaz Oshay.'

They were about to re-start their machines when Deneer held up a warning hand.

'Do you hear it?'

Neither of the Karls could hear anything, but Kaz Oshay nodded:

'I hear.' He mounted his machine, started it and, to Marcus's surprise, started rapidly back the way they had come. He veered off their path and mounted a rise, stopping at the top of it, so he was outlined for them against the falling sun, like some ancient hero of the worlds.

From where he had stopped his machine, he could see the men making a rolling cloud of dust across the plain. It was the Enforcers, giving chase, and in the lead was Ankar Moor, larger than the others, his silver outfit glinting in the sun as he rode.

Kaz smiled to himself. Perhaps the time was coming when Ankar Moor would have to respond to the code and fight him alone, animal or not.

Kaz turned his machine and roared back down to join the others:

'Ankar Moor. He and his men are behind us. They follow us with ease, for he leads them. They close the gap.'

All four machines were soon throbbing with power. Kaz said. 'There will be danger, we cannot take a direct route to the sandstone cliffs and the caves, for they will follow us too easily.' And with that he led off up the side of the canyon, taking the steep wall with ease.

To the Statemen, it seemed like an impossible climb, but Deneer calmed their fears:

'I will follow you. Kaz Oshay is a kind man. He would not lead where you cannot follow.'

Even so, it came as a surprise to both Marcus and his father when the Death Machines they rode took the slope easily. Deneer followed them and soon they were spread out behind Kaz Oshay, going through rock gaps and gullies, weaving through the rubble and dust of nature.

Ankar Moor charged across the dusty plain ahead of his most trusted Enforcers. The remaining prisoners and the weaker brethren had been left far behind and the big man was not displeased.

Polna was close behind him, relieved that his master had not, in fact, wreaked any punishment on him for the events for which he had blamed him. What he did not know was that this was no sign of forgiveness, it was just that, at this moment, he needed the other man's support as he chased after Kaz Oshay and the others, bent on his revenge. All thoughts of world conquest were pushed out of his mind by the needs of his colossal vanity for vengeance and retribution.

With the two of them were only six other men, the best armed, both physically and mentally, of the guards of Helix. All were equipped with helmet microphones and as Ankar Moor observed Kaz Oshay on the horizon and knew he was on the right track, and gaining on his enemy, he rasped to the other men who followed him:

'If any of you should falter, you will be left behind. You have been warned.'

Polna answered, in an effort to make sure that his status was assured beyond the chase:

'We will not falter, Ankar Moor.'

'So be it,' rasped their leader, revving his machine and pushing it forward as the figure of Kaz Oshay disappeared from view.

The sun was low in the sky by the time Deneer felt that they were once more travelling in the right direction, making a wide sweep through the mountains that would bring them back to the sandstone caves and a chance to find Karissa.

Marcus and Doctor Karl were relieved, too, that there would soon be an end to what had turned into more of an exercise in mountaineering than anything else. The going had been tortuous and frightening for all of them, but they had laid a false trail that Ankar Moor, with constant pauses for the following of their tracks, would find it even more difficult to trace.

At last they arrived at a point where they overlooked the central part of the canyon where the sandstone caves were placed. One moment it seemed that Kaz Oshay was climbing up the side of a mountain: the next he had braked hard on the summit.

The others joined him and the two Statemen gulped as they looked at the almost sheer drop on the other side, right to the bottom of the canyon, immediately facing the caves.

Marcus said: 'You don't mean we are going to go down this?'

Kaz turned to him, his irritation at the young man's demands completely forgotten.

'We have no choice.'

He glanced behind him and the Karls, for the first time, saw something of which Kaz and Deneer had both been aware (because of their acute hearing) as they had dodged their way through the mountains – Ankar Moor, his men strung out behind him, was already near the foot of the mountain they had just scaled with the help of the miraculous machines they had stolen. Now the Karls also knew, that they had no choice and Marcus gave Kaz a grinning nod which indicated that he would make the best of it.

They all gave one more quick glance at their pursuer as he started up the mountainside after them, then all went forward at once, out into space, leaving their lives in the hands of the various gods they trusted. For the Statemen this was the old God, for Kaz Oshay and Deneer, it was the consciousness.

Kaz gave a great shout as he led them down, a shout that echoed round the empty canyon. Amazingly, they reached the bottom almost together and charged forward at high speed across the canyon.

Deneer caught up with Kaz.

'I know you did not plan that. I thought you knew the way?'

Kaz, who was not prepared to admit he had made a mistake in front of the two trusting Statemen, grinned at her:

'That is a well-known short-cut. I have often used it.'

Deneer laughed.

'And your horse rolled down at your side. I suppose?'

Kaz winked at her and joined in her laughter. Marcus had caught one word of the exchange and now said breathlessly:

'A short-cut to suicide is the best way to describe it.'

Deneer laughed again. 'But you have come through alive.'

Kaz added: 'And remember too, that if you had not, you would have become one with the infinity to which we all already belong.'

Marcus would have asked more about this last statement, but Kaz Oshay's attention had already been taken by something else behind him. He stopped his machine and stared back at the vertical side down which they had come. The others followed suit and saw what he had seen.

Ankar Moor was at the top of the slide. He had stopped his machine, obviously not wishing to descend on his own, and equally obviously not believing that any of his men would follow him. Kaz Oshay knew enough of the man to know that he was no coward, so it was only a sense of unequal danger that had made him pause. They would have time for their mission of rescue, for their pursuers would have to go some distance to find a safe place to get down into the canyon and anyway darkness was nearly on top of them.

Kaz said quietly to Deneer: 'It is too late tonight. We will have to come back tomorrow.'

'I agree.'

He restarted his machine and led them off up the canyon, away from the caves once more. They came to a slide area on the canyon wall and Kaz Oshay started up it, the others following behind trustingly. He shouted a loud encouragement: 'Darkness will be coming! We must hurry!'

At the top they found themselves in the head of a shadowed valley. They raced forward into the dusk of the wastelands.

At the bottom of the valley, there flowed a shallow stream. Marcus sighed: 'Thank God. I could use a drink.'

His father was alarmed.

'Don't touch it. The pollution. Everything in the wasteland is poisoned beyond reclaim.'

Marcus took his father's advice and merely drove slowly through the water after the others. The rumble of their machines bounced back at them from the narrowing valley walls. Eventually, it became so narrow that they had to go in and out of the stream to move down it. Round a bend, they came to a fork, where two valleys ran on. Kaz abruptly stopped his machine and signalled the others to do the same. They obeyed, then listened to the sudden silence that fell.

Doctor Karl and his son could hear nothing, but Kaz Oshay turned to Deneer. 'They still follow us.'

Deneer sighed, disappointed, as she too heard the faint sound that was carried to her on the evening breeze.

'Yes. I thought we had lost them.'

Marcus shook his head. 'That is incredible. I can't hear a thing.'

Doctor Karl put a finger to his lips. 'Hush. Neither can I.'

Kaz turned his attention to the two choices of route that were now in front of them.

'This is not my land.'

Deneer shook her head.

'Nor mine.'

'I am not familiar,' Kaz went on to admit. 'But we have a choice to make.'

'I am not familiar with this place either, but we remain close to the sandstone cliffs and that will be our right direction tomorrow. You lead and choose, we will follow.'

Kaz nodded and signalled them all to restart their machines.

'The light leaves us. Let us try on the left.' He pointed out the direction and Deneer nodded her agreement.

The four fugitives started their machines and went up the left fork in the canyon formed by the splitting of the valley. Not knowing the terrain, there was always a risk that they would find themselves in a dead end and would have to retrace their route, with the danger that Ankar Moor and his men would catch up and confront them. Kaz Oshay did not wish to avoid that confrontation if it came, but, until an attempt had been made to find and rescue Karissa, he did not want to be pushed into it.

The ground began to rise and as it did so they found that they were riding on the remains of an old rutted road that must have been there before the great devastation nine hundred years before. They were relieved, it meant at least that this valley went somewhere, the right choice had been made.

The road flattened out into a flat, grassy plain, high up and clear of obstruction, allowing more of the dying daylight to get to them, so they were able to accelerate back to high speed again for a while. Kaz turned to Deneer and grinned. 'Another one of my short-cuts.'

She laughed and pulled back the throttle on the Death Machine she was riding, to race him across the grassy plain. Doctor Karl and his son followed more slowly, looking about them. It was the first time in his life that Doctor Karl had seen any growing thing in the open – grass only, it was true, but it was something. It proved that the world was becoming less poisonous if its soil was able to support life again.

He eventually managed to catch up with Kaz Oshay and Deneer and shouted to them:

'This grass? Have you seen other places where it grows?'

Kaz frowned but Deneer leant across and smiled at him.

'This man is our friend. You can tell him.'

Kaz said, 'I am sorry. We seem to learn that men destroy all they find. Only the Guides are the guardians of the future. Yes, there are places. They are few and it has been difficult, but plants and animals were always preserved and thrive again. Perhaps, one day, they will once more cover the face of the earth.'

Deneer interrupted.

'There is a special place the Guides look after, a valley. We must keep its secret, but I will take Karissa there to be looked after when we have rescued her.'

Doctor Karl could only wish them well, though he despaired of the hope that the news had given him. But then, if anyone could preserve enough to keep the world and mankind alive, it would be the Guides.

They came to the edge of the plain where the ground fell away to a broken area below them and paused in their flight to squint down into the great fireball sunset. It was then that they saw the huge complex of buildings, below and to one side, hugging the floor of a wide canyon. The buildings were large and low, hugging the ground, but they looked battered and worn by time. The group could only speculate that perhaps it was the remains of some great military complex or manufacturing plant from before the great war. It was built so low and long that, from most angles, it would be completely out of sight of those who looked for it.

They went forward slowly to the highest point they could reach above the buildings, then turned off their machines and waited, as Kaz Oshay and Deneer listened for any sign of life.

A noise came to them, a tap-tap-tap as if someone was banging something against metal. It was Marcus who spotted the cause of it. A broken wire cable was still tied on to the roof of one of the buildings and was being blown against the roof by the sunset breeze. Other than this there was no sound.

Kaz said, 'It seems clear.'

Deneer was nervous, she had misgivings. It was not a place she knew, so she was suspicious of it.

'Perhaps . . . But it is strange that I have never heard of this place before.'

Kaz, too, now frowned:

'Nor I.'

'If you wish, we could go on.'

Kaz glanced around. The sun was almost gone and a huge full moon was pulling itself up over the horizon.

'No. Not with the full moon. The Mutants will be out for sure tonight. We need defendable space.'

'I agree.'

As they continued to look out over the area, trying to spot any sign of danger that would put the complex out as a safe place to spend the night, Marcus turned to his father.

'Father, what is it the Guides mean when they say to one another that their "Union is limited"?'

Doctor Karl, who could hardly take his eyes off their Guide companions, and who was learning so much about them that he admired and respected, pulled his concentration away to turn to his son.

'It just means that they are making a temporary arrangement for a specific purpose.'

Marcus frowned. 'I don't understand. They are of the same tribe?'

'But the laws of the code they follow teach them to be independent, relying only on themselves, never on the help or reliability of others. It is a good way – look what happens in a City like Helix when we put our reliance for government or security on someone else.'

'That is true, but it is so . . . so unfriendly.'

His father frowned to look for another way to explain it. It was not an easy concept to describe. He had, after all, been a Stateman all his life, as his ancestors had been ever since the great war.

'The Guides are taught to be fiercely independent, even from their birth. When they are old enough they leave their mothers forever. Some of them never meet their fathers, or know who they are, for their whole lives.'

'I cannot believe that.'

'Yet it is true. They don't believe in forming permanent relationships. "Our Union is limited" is a formalised way of saying, let's do something together now, for our mutual benefit, but when the job is done, each is on his own again.'

Marcus frowned again, then glanced at the two Guides, a little apart, conferring quietly.

'But Kaz and Deneer – they seem a lot closer than that. Their Union does not look temporary.'

His father agreed.

'Yes, oddly so . . . '

'Why?'

The older man smiled. It was a smile as old as the world itself.

'I guess they like each other.'

Marcus thought of his bride-to-be in Triton and reddened as he realised the turn the conversation had taken.

'Well, if they like each other . . . I mean . . . Why don't Guides fall in love and marry like anyone else?'

His father grinned. 'I think that we can see they fall in love.'

'Yes, but they will not marry, will they?'

His father shrugged.

'All their lives they roam the wastelands. They have respect for one another and none would do any harm to another Guide. Why is it necessary to claim ownership over a woman if she claims that her affection is with you? No one else will try to break that link.'

His son believed he understood. 'Then there is no need for it.'

'That is right. They do not need our reassurance. Their affection for each other is reassurance enough.'

Marcus had his mouth open to ask another question, but he closed it abruptly as the other two turned their machines and wheeled them over to the two Statemen. Kaz said:

'It seems clear we need shelter for the night.'

Doctor Karl nodded, then, cautiously:

'Should we not check it out more closely?'

Kaz nodded and pointed at the hand blaster that was attached to Marcus's belt. It was the only one that the party possessed, and had been given to him when he had been prepared to go into the arena to take part in the Death Sport game.

'I will lead. May I have your hand blaster?'

Marcus had no hesitation in handing the weapon over. He trusted the Guide completely now and would rather he, than any other, was looking out for them and was well enough armed to do so properly.

There was no need to start the Death Machines again to get to their destination. The less noise they could make, the smaller the chance of alerting anyone who might be inside the structures – nor would the sound echo away through the mountains and canyons and tell Ankar Moor and his hunters of their position.

They wheeled their Death Machines to a point on the edge of the incline above the buildings, then got aboard and coasted down to the front of the first building. Apart from the thrumming of the broken cable against the roof of the building, there was no other sound.

It was when they got down to ground level and close to the first building that they saw the damaged condition of them. The large metal double doors at the end were open a little way and rusted, as if they had been in this position for centuries. The windows along one side of this building were all smashed – whether by some blast all those centuries before, or by the vandalism of marauding tribes of Mutants since.

The others held Kaz's machine as they still straddled their own. He gripped the hand blaster and stepped forward to the doors, waiting for what seemed like an eternity before disappearing inside. He was back only a short time later.

'The first building, at least, is empty. We should enter and hide the machines before we go forward.'

Deneer nodded agreement and the two Statemen followed suit. All four wheeled their machines through the gap in the double doors, under cover at last. They found themselves in a hall only as wide as the doors, fading into darkness. They started cautiously along this corridor, still wheeling their machines, Kaz with one hand on his, the other still holding up the hand blaster, moving ahead of the others.

A door was open in the corridor and he glanced inside. The broken windows on this side faced the sunset and the room was flooded with a pink and orange glow, a reflection of the message the dying sun had left in the sky.

From ahead there came a sudden, unexpected sound. Deneer drew in her breath sharply and Kaz spun round, firing without looking at the cause of the sound. In the same second they all saw the source of it. A jack rabbit had been hopping down the corridor and now disappeared into eternity.

Doctor Karl cried excitedly, 'Life! The world is supporting life again.'

Kaz looked round at him, surprised at the outburst.

'In the places protected from the Flash Winds, such life has been supported for some time.'

Deneer laughed.

'Why did you kill him?'

His grin covered embarrassment.

'Just testing my aim.'

They all laughed, then moved forward again, still cautious but more relaxed within themselves. Each building led off into the next one and litter was scattered everywhere. One room was filled with smashed crates that had contained some sort of packaging material and these had been torn open, leaving the material scattered all over a huge room.

Deneer looked at Kaz.

'Foraging Mutants.'

'Yes. But it was long ago.'

In the third building they walked through to, they found the ramp that led to the even wider construction that had taken place below ground. From outside, it had just looked like a series of long, low buildings of the type that had been popular in the times before the third world war. Doctor Karl could remember this from his video library and the lessons he had given his son on what the old world had been like. But these buildings now appeared to have been some sort of shell for the real works underneath. It was almost as if the people who had constructed them had been starting plans for a factory complex like one of the great Cities, but had eventually abandoned the project, either from lack of time or materials. It looked as if it had been deserted for centuries.

Before exploring the pitch black underground area at the bottom of the ramp, the party hurried back to where they had hidden their machines. Never having seen them in the dark, they were unaware that the cycles had lights on the front of them, but Doctor Karl had a solution to the problem of light.

He led the others back into the room that had contained the packing cases. Then he made them break slats off the crates, before binding a mass of the compressed wrapping material to each of the slats. Marcus, who had never been searched thanks to his unorthodox method of getting imprisoned, still had his electronic fire lighter on him and the torches that the doctor had created were soon flaming, replacing the almost withdrawn light of day.

Taking some unlit spare torches along with them, they wheeled their Death Machines to the head of the ramp and started them in order to ride down. They went in single file, cautiously, with Kaz Oshay in the lead. If there were any Mutants below, they would probably be too frightened by the sound of the machines to attack and that would give the party the time it would need to get away.

But though Kaz Oshay used all his powers of smell, there seemed to be no stench in the network of underground corridors they were transversing. They went down a long corridor, small doorways opening off each side of it at regular intervals. Each door seemed to lead into small, absolutely identical rooms, all empty.

Marcus caught up with his father.

'What do you think this place used to be?'

He thought for a moment, then said, 'Probably it was a munitions factory.'

'I wonder what happened to everything?'

'The Mutants have had nine hundred years to investigate and steal away the contents.'

'No, it seems as if it was deliberately cleared.'

The line of speculation was cut short by Kaz ahead of them. He had passed a particular doorway and now halted his machine and called out, 'Stop!'

He switched off the engine and put the machine up on its stand, before striding over to the doorway. The others did likewise and crowded in behind him.

It was the first of the rooms in which they had found any trace of life. It was slightly larger than the others they had seen and some evidence of occupation was scattered around: some stained, filthy mattresses, empty cans, broken bottles and glass were littering the floor. The occupation looked quite recent. Certainly the objects were not covered in nine hundred years of dust.

Two objects, wedged in a corner between the mattresses

and the wall, caught Deneer's attention and she raced forward to hold them up. Each seemed to have something that was passable as a handle and she now swung one from each hand.

'What are these?'

Doctor Karl stepped forward to inspect them. He held one and tried to remember where he had seen it before. It was filthy and covered in rust, a large bulbous metal portion. Above it was a round of frosted glass, the handle above that again. As he swung it in his hand, some liquid slopped around in the rusty metal bottom part.

He remembered at last. It was a sort of light that had been used, a lantern that burnt oil. He chuckled in surprise.

'I've only ever seen a lamp like that in pictures. It must be hundreds of years old. It dates before the disaster.'

Deneer inspected the one she still held closely. In it, too, a liquid slopped about in the lower portion.

'Do you know how it works?'

The Doctor nodded.

'I think I can figure it out.'

It was the work of only a few minutes to get the two lanterns lit and throwing out a respectable light. Kaz took one of them from him and said:

'It seems safe for you two Statemen to rest in here tonight. I will go further to be sure.'

Marcus grunted. 'Should we not all stay together?'

Kaz glanced at Deneer and smiled at her, before turning to the youth and his father.

'Deneer and I will be close at the end. Never fear – Deneer, I will come back for you. Stay with our friends for the moment.'

He turned to leave the room and Marcus took a pace forward to protest, but his father held him by the arm.

'They deserve some time on their own and Kaz would not suggest it if he didn't think it was safe.'

Marcus nodded. His father was right, as usual.

Lifting the lantern high, the anti-matter blaster held tightly in his other hand, Kaz Oshay moved further down the underground corridor to the next rooms. As he went the sound of his light footsteps faded quickly away from the others and Marcus Karl felt a chill of fear round his heart as the protection of which he had been so contemptuous was taken away for a moment.

As he proceeded, Kaz Oshay could hear no sounds other than the footfall of his own boots on the concrete floor of the passage. The first room he inspected was another of the smaller ones. It was empty save for one mattress in the middle of the floor. He nodded. The room seemed clean, just right for himself and Deneer to spend the night.

As he entered the next room beyond, he suddenly froze at a sight that would turn even a Guide cold with shock and rage. Recovering, he stepped into the room for a closer inspection of the contents.

Someone had made an open fire out of old crates and mattresses in the centre of the room and scattered all around were the ancient remains of an obvious cannibal feast. Everywhere Kaz looked he could see charred and broken bones and skulls that had had the craniums smashed so that the brains could be taken out and eaten. He felt sickened at the sight. It was the only real evidence so far that the Mutants had ever been in the buildings, but he could see that the cannibal party must have been centuries old.

He heard a sudden intake of breath behind him and whirled round, ready to fire the blaster. But the other three stood in the doorway, and it was Marcus who had reacted in shock. Now he said, 'I'm sorry. We just came to look.'

Kaz stepped aside and said harshly, 'Then look.'

'Oh, my God, the Mutants.'

His father pushed past. 'I think I understand.'

Deneer asked, 'What do you mean?'

The doctor turned to her.

'This was obviously some sort of factory complex and these shelters down here were for the workers in case the war came. When it did, they sheltered down here. There must have been stores and living accommodation for all of them for a very long time. Then, at some time later, those who survived, or perhaps their offspring, were attacked and overwhelmed by the Mutants. The Mutants must have eaten their remains and the stores that were left, or perhaps carried the latter away with them, and the crime has remained preserved for us to find.'

'Then why are there no Mutants here now?'

'Because they know there is no longer anything left for them to find. Why would they bother to come back?'

Marcus said, 'But it would be a place for them to live.'

His father shook his head.

'It is too dry for them. They like the damp warmth of the caves. It is better for their skin. That is why they mostly hunt by night. They do not like the heat of the sun.'

Kaz Oshay agreed.

'Your father is right. The wastelands are scattered with such tragedies as this and the Mutants like their skins to stay damp. Their eyes, too, they are large and bulge out to catch all the light the moon can give them.'

There was an awkward silence, then, 'We will be safe here. Take your lantern and go to the first room you saw. Deneer, I have found a place for us.'

The Guide girl walked over and stood looking up at him. Marcus stared at them, but after a moment his father took his arm and led him away, back up the corridor to the first room they had found. The two Statemen settled themselves on the mattresses, the lamp, which Doctor Karl now turned down, between them. Marcus said, 'Do you think we will ever get to Triton?'

His father placed a reassuring hand on his arm.

'If anyone can get us there, it will be those two. I trust them.'

His son, who had been showing his impatience and lack of trust all day, now smiled and nodded.

'So do I.'

Neither man had realised, up until now, quite how exhausted they were. In a few minutes they both drifted off into the sleep of exhaustion, their breathing steady, the only other sound in the room being the hiss of the lamp that stood between them, casting its mellow glow over the pair of sleepers.

Out on the desert highland a huge bonfire sparked with a great roar into the moonlit sky as another pile of dried debris and old brambles were thrown on to it. From above, the giant face of the moon stared down, making the shadows all around doubly eerie in its reflected light.

The other Obedience Enforcers settled down next to their machines, ready for sleep, each man with his anti-matter blaster by his side, in case of an attack by the Mutants during the night. But Ankar Moor and Polna stood side by side, staring into the flames.

Ankar Moor had been lost in thought for a long time and, at last, Polna presumed himself dismissed. But as he started to turn away, his leader said, 'We must be just about half a day's ride from Triton by these machines. That is clearly where they will be heading.'

Polna shook his head.

'If it is, they sure picked a strange way to get there.'

Ankar Moor disagreed.

'No. They knew that we could catch them up and destroy them on the plain. Their only chance was to dodge us in the mountains. They understood that. Kaz Oshay is a worthy opponent.'

There was another silence between the two men. It was Ankar Moor who broke it once more.

'Those caves in the canyon. There is something about them. Something that flashed to me when they were near them. They will go back to them before they go to Triton.'

'But you just said they were on their way there.'

Ankar Moor held up his hand.

'I am no longer of the Guides, but I know their ways. The consciousness still touches me. They will go back up that valley. We must make our ambush for them there in the morning.'

'Yes, sir.'

Another silence, then the big man swore.

'Damn. If I thought that we could find them tonight I would risk the chance of an attack by the Mutants!'

Polna, who did not have quite the self-confidence in his own survival as his master, shuddered at the thought and hoped that Ankar Moor had not noticed it. There was another silence as the Obedience Enforcer leader stared up at the sky once more, then down into the fire. Polna breathed a sigh of relief as he said, 'We had better keep it bright all night.'

Relieved, he turned away.

'I will see to it.'

He left Ankar Moor alone, staring out into the darkness and planning his vengeance for the morrow.

Kaz Oshay and Deneer sat at opposite ends of their mattress, staring into each other's eyes. There was no sound in the room other than the hiss of the lamp they had taken. For the moment their eyes were locked and their minds were touching and caressing one another. At last, Deneer spoke in a soft voice:

'Be grateful for every moment there is between us, for we must remember these moments. They may never come back to us once we have moved past them and gone on.'

Kaz whispered, 'You speak truly, woman.'

They rose and moved close to one another. Their arms reached out and they entwined, the physical contact relaxing and, at the same time, exciting both of them.

After a while, they broke away from each other and, with gentle fingers, each one began to undress the other until they stood facing one another, each admiring the body of the other.

Slowly they sank down on the mattress, their bodies pressing close together, the warmth of their feelings passing between them. Kaz rolled over until he was atop Deneer and she stretched herself out beneath him, arching her back in welcome to him.

'I want you, Kaz Oshay . . . I want you.'

He whispered his answer in kind:

'And I you, Deneer . . . and I you . . .'

After that they did not speak again. They had no need of words, for, just as their souls were one in the power of the consciousness, so too did their bodies become one in the power of ecstasy.

Both would have had all the alertness of the Guides, had their powers been called upon, but danger was not near. Instead they were able to concentrate their minds on the fulfilment of the needs of their bodies. The moment for which both of them had roamed the wastelands alone all of their lives had come to them.

CHAPTER TEN

Ankar Moor had picked the point of ambush well. Even Polna had to admit that to himself. The only question was, would the fugitives come across the plain and up the valley to the place he had chosen, or would they have found some other route to their destination.

The Enforcer guards had set out with the coming of the dawn. There had been no sign of the Mutants during the night and most of them had slept soundly and were ready to face the vicissitudes of another day, driven on more by the power for revenge of their leader than by their own strength and determination.

The sun was only just over the horizon, but already the ground was cracking in the heat. In the distance, even Polna could see the heat shimmering on the dry bed of the lake that had once been across the plain.

Ankar Moor and three of the men were on one side of a hilltop overlooking the ambush point, out of sight to anyone coming across the plain from the twin valleys. He glanced down into the pass in the hills and at the ravine that ran across it, partially blocking it. Polna and the other three men were hidden in this ravine with their machines, waiting for his signal.

For an hour, the sun rose higher and the temperature of the ground and air with it. Ankar Moor scanned the horizon with his special field binoculars but so far he could see no movement, detect no sign of the fugitives.

Then he saw them. Just the glint of their machines on the horizon at first, then they sprang into prominence against the background of the dry lake bed as they started to roar across it in line, abreast, close together.

Only now did he transmit the information to Polna.

'Just as I thought. They are riding straight towards the pass. Don't make a move until I tell you.'

Polna and his men got the order over the microphones in their helmets and they waited impatiently on their silent machines.

Unaware of the enemies who lay in wait for them, Kaz, Deneer, Doctor Karl and Marcus made a race of speeding across the lake. They were all refreshed after their night's sleep and faced the ordeals of the day with a renewed spirit.

Marcus fell back a bit and observed his father's antics on the Death Machine with a boyish smile. At last, he called:

'Hey, dad!'

Doctor Karl glanced over his shoulder:

'Yes?'

'If anyone had ever told me I'd live to see my old man riding something like this machine across the desert when he was fifty years old, I'd have told them they were crazy.'

Doctor Karl smiled vaguely. He had not really heard the words that had been shouted at him.

'What was that?'

Marcus moved closer.

'Nothing! I was just saying that I think you're great.'

That his father did hear and he smiled affectionate appreciation before going into a series of manoeuvres, zig-zagging his machine to show how adept he had become at handling it. This showing off nearly ended with him sliding into the side of Deneer's machine and the girl took evasive action before shouting: 'Watch out, Doctor! We will have enough trouble with our enemies, without you going wild.'

The remark was made in the same mood that affected all four, but it did have the effect of reminding them that there might be threats to be faced ahead of them for which they must be prepared. Kaz had kept out of the general horseplay. Now he looked up at the sky and stiffened in the saddle. Deneer frowned at him and asked: 'What is it?'

He said anxiously, 'We must reach the sandstone cliffs quickly and get to the caves.'

'Why?'

'The Flash Wind. It is bearing down on us.'

Now Deneer put out all her antennae and she too got the feeling of the wind in the air.

'Yes, now I feel it too. The Flash Wind is coming faster than you said it would.'

Kaz smiled at her. He knew her teasing ways and was no longer offended when she poked this sort of fun at him.

'No one is perfect. Would you have preferred to wait in the Death Sport arena for the Flash Wind to come?'

She lowered her eyes and laughed.

'Only if you had waited with me.'

They went up the rise that took them out of the open space that had once been a lake and then came to an old road. In the days before the devastation it had been a two lane highway up to a resort area near the lake. It had been well-made because parts of it still retained their tarmac, though nine hundred years of nature and the dreadful Flash Winds had broken up sections of it and returned them to dust. They crossed on a stretch that was still flat and well impacted and Marcus grumbled:

'Too bad we can't take a road like this straight in to Triton. We could be there in an hour.'

His father frowned at him, affectionately:

'Have patience. They will get us there in good time.'

Ankar Moor rose from his position, put away his field glasses and straddled his Death Machine. The fugitives were half-way across the distance towards him. It was time to put his plan into effect. He rasped his instructions into the helmet microphone:

'Block the pass.'

He started his own machine and appeared over the brow of the hill, slightly in the lead of the three men with him, plunging down the side on to the plain, making straight for the fugitives.

Below him, Polna glanced round at his men, hidden in the ravine. They started their machines on his signal and then he beckoned the men to move, shouting:

'Come on. You can't live forever.'

As the soldiers had charged from their trenches in the ancient wars, so now did Polna and his men charge up out of the ravine on their screaming machines, fanning out in line abreast to block the pass, Polna in the centre.

Kaz spotted the movements up on the hillside at once and zoomed his machine close to Deneer's.

'They are ahead of us. They are blocking the pass.'

Deneer nodded.

'I see them.'

All four of the fugitives grouped together and slowed down their machines but, taking their cue from Kaz, they did not stop altogether. After a short run forward, Deneer said, in a voice that had slowly filled with an unwonted tension, 'We must draw them out.'

Kaz pointed.

'They have split. Some of them are coming to us, others are blocking the pass. We need more guile than that.'

Doctor Karl and Marcus glanced at each other, neither of them having an idea in their minds as to how they were to avoid death this time. It seemed that the odds were too great and Kaz Oshay was leading them merely into a confrontation that would end in their deaths.

Kaz turned to them.

'We will go forward to deal with the men who charge us.

You hold back and then head for the pass when you see us go.'

The Karls obeyed their orders and started falling back at once. Kaz smiled at Deneer: 'Divide and conquer.'

They faced front again, then, from deep within them, came the great whoop of their war cry and they throttled back their machines and charged off in the direction of Ankar Moor and his charging guards, across the desert wasteland.

Ankar Moor threw back his head in triumphant exhilaration as they came forward at him. Now he would have the vengeance that he had waited for so long. He shouted into his microphone:

'Split and attack from the flanks.'

With one of his three fellow guards he swung away to the east side of the plain, the other two men veering off from the straight line to the west. Kaz Oshay and Deneer did not split: instead they took the track that would bring them straight at the two men who had gone to the west flank.

They throttled back still further until they were both going at top speed. A collision seemed to be inevitable. Soon all four of the charging machines would be within blaster firing range. As Marcus and Doctor Karl watched, they held their breath and prayed.

Just as it seemed that the end was inevitable, the two Guides roared their machines up a mound in the same second and, flying through the air, they sailed over the heads of the two alarmed Enforcers. As they landed, both of them fired their rear blaster pods in unison and Ankar Moor lost two of his best men in a flash of green, their screams hanging in the air as they were consigned to oblivion.

Marcus looked at his father.

'You were right. They are special.'

'Let us thank God for it.'

Kaz and Deneer turned their machines and he shouted over at her:

'Nicely done, woman!'

'Nicely done, man!'

Now Kaz raised his arm and waved, the signal for Marcus and his father to follow them.

Marcus throttled back his machine:

'Come on, dad.'

'I'm coming.' He too throttled back his machine and

bumped over the open ground a little behind his son.

Ankar Moor and his remaining fighter made a broad sweeping turn and the big man shouted into his mircrophone: 'Hold your positions! You mustn't let them through.'

Polna acknowledged the order and told his men to stay exactly where they were, ranged across the mouth of the canyon, just ahead of the ravine:

'Hold it, stay where you are. You're not to move unless and until I give you a specific order.'

However nervous his men were feeling after witnessing the annihilation of their fellows, they did their best to give no sign of it and waved acknowledgement to Polna.

Ankar Moor and the other man were doing their best to get back to the mouth of the canyon, but the big man knew that he would never make it in time. Once more, Kaz Oshay had tricked him.

Kaz glanced round. Deneer was right on his tail and the other two machines were catching up rapidly, falling into line. If there was any problem, it was Doctor Karl. He was not so used to his machine, an older man, therefore perhaps a little slower. He was hanging back from the others, a wider gap between him and the rest of the group.

Kaz pointed towards the pass.

'Follow me.'

He immediately swung his machine to one side, putting up a cloud of dust between him and the Enforcers holding the shaky line. The others followed suit as they reached the spot, then saw him charge through the cloud that had been raised, up one side of the pass and at the man on the end of the line at the upper edge of the ravine.

Polna reacted and swung into action, shouting at the other two guards:

'Get them! We can't let them through.'

Kaz led the pack of fugitives straight at the hapless Enforcer, balanced on his machine at the lip of the ravine. The man was frozen in terror. Then unfroze for long enough to consider his position and decide that the wisest thing he could do at that moment would be to desert his post.

Turning quickly, he tried to get his machine round and tried to plunge it down into the ravine, but he was too late. Kaz pressed the button on his forward pods and the machine and man disintegrated together. Immediately, Kaz aimed his machine at the lip of the ravine, hit it at full speed and, lifting the nose of the great machine into the air, he flew up and across the ravine.

As he hit the far side and began to roar up the pass, Deneer passed immediately over the spot he had used and she too lifted the nose of her cycle in the air and made the leap.

It was Marcus's turn next. Polna and the others had got their machines turned and were racing to close the gap. Polna had Ankar Moor's screams of angry encouragement in his ears:

'Destroy them! They must not pass!'

Marcus reached the lip of the ravine, tried to copy the movements of the two Guides and found himself sailing through the air. He almost lost control as he hit the other side, wobbled for a moment, then roared off after them up the pass.

Doctor Karl was lagging just a little way behind. He throttled back as hard as he dared, but Polna and the others were closing the gap too fast for comfort.

The doctor roared up the path and hit the mound only a yard ahead of his nearest pursuer. He hit the mound and took to the air. At the last moment he remembered his rear blaster pods and pressed the button. In the same second, the Enforcer fired his forward pods as he left the ground. Both men disappeared in a green flash of anti-matter without touching the ground again.

Kaz was glancing back and saw the explosion that obliterated Doctor Karl, then noticed Marcus speeding forward, not turning, unaware that his father had died. He made no signal, but faced the front again and roared on, the other two survivors in his wake.

Ankar Moor flew at the mound at top speed, hit the lip and leapt the ravine before coming to an angry halt on the far side. He raised his helmet and turned his leather-clad face back to scream at Polna:

'It's all your fault. You let them get through the line. I told you to hold your positions. Why didn't you obey me?'

'They rushed us.'

'Don't argue with me. We must give chase at once.' He gunned his machine and shot off up the pass in pursuit of the disappearing fugitives. Wearily, Polna turned to the remaining two men.

'O.K., after me.' They revved their machines to take the jump across the ravine and join in the pursuit once more.

Still unaware that his father had been killed, Marcus Karl sped after Kaz Oshay and Deneer out of the top of the pass and into the broken ground beyond that would lead them back to the canyon of the sandstone caves.

Kaz, feeling that they were far enough ahead of their pursuers to allow for a little relaxation, brought his machine to a halt and Deneer and Marcus slid to a stop alongside him. Marcus glanced round and realised that his father was not with them. He glanced back and Deneer said softly:

'I am sorry.'

Marcus could not take it in.

'Where's my father?'

Kaz said quietly, 'He died bravely.'

'What?'

Deneer reached across and tried to touch Marcus on the arm, but, with the sudden onset of grief, he pushed the comforting hand away:

'He took one of them with him when he died.'

It sank in at last, Marcus started to turn his machine, to rush back and avenge his father's death:

'Those bastards.'

Kaz jumped from his huge cycle, propped it up and rushed round to grab the grief-stricken youth:

'Stop. You cannot attack them by yourself.'

Marcus's eyes were blinded by tears. He was in no condition to take good advice from anyone. Instead, he tried to shake off Kaz's firm grip, crying out as he did so:

'No, I must try. You must let me go. They killed my father!'

Kaz did not let go for an instant. He knew that the young man could not think straight for the moment, so stricken was he by his grief. He took no offence at the Stateman's behaviour.

'Your father knew the risks.'

'It should have been me rather than him.'

Kaz stayed quiet. 'Be brave like him, then.'

Deneer called across: 'He would not want you to waste your life. Here is not the place to fight them. He would have wanted you to come on with us.'

This made the young man pause as he absorbed her words. She was right, of course. He had been the one who had wanted to press on, leaving the Guides if necessary. It was his father who had advised patience, had kept him in check.

Now, with the older man's death, he realised that he had been correct in his advice.

Marcus relaxed and Kaz Oshay let his hand drop from the young man's arm. Deneer had said the right words. He would stick with them now, not throw his life away in a useless gesture. Marcus said quietly, a set determination replacing grief on his face:

'Yes. Damn it, you are right.'

The others smiled on him, sympathising with his loss for a moment. Then Kaz lifted his head and listened. There were twin threats to them now. He could sense the Flash Wind bearing down on them, and, over its faint rumble, he could hear the machines of Ankar Moor and the remaining Enforcers pursuing them.

'O.K., let's go.'

He raced back to his machine, remounted and all three started off in unison, across the great waste plain to their destination.

For an hour or more they travelled in silence, taking advantage of every downward slope to speed their passage, every gully to keep them hidden as much as possible from their pursuers. By sheer guts and personality, Ankar Moor seemed to be forcing his group on, slowly gaining on them.

At last, Kaz led the other two up the almost vertical side of a huge hill, then stopped his machine on the top of it and looked back, pointing out their pursuers, coming across the plain, perhaps a mile behind. He sighed. He was getting worried.

'They're gaining on us.'

Deneer's eye followed the direction in which he was pointing and she said firmly:

'We could stop. Stand and fight them from here. We have the high ground and that will give us the advantage.'

Kaz would have agreed with her under normal circumstances, but now he shook his head.

'Not with the Flash Wind coming. It will be on us soon.'

Marcus was alarmed. This was the first he had known of such a threat to them:

'A Flash Wind?'

Deneer said anxiously, 'We must hurry, we must reach the sand cliffs before it catches up with us.'

Marcus was puzzled. 'There is no sign of it.'

Deneer merely replied, 'We are Guides. We know these things.'

Marcus shook his head. He would believe anything now after what he had seen. Kaz turned to Deneer:

'You must lead off now. You know this land better than I. You lead the way.'

Deneer nodded.

'I will lead.'

They all restarted their machines and Deneer led off down the far side of the hill. They had reached the bottom and were moving forward again over open ground as Ankar Moor led his men to the top of the hill they had just quit. He halted them and looked around, snorting as he saw the fugitives on the plain ahead. Soon they would be at the sandstone cliffs and he must reach them almost as fast as they.

Then something stirred within him, another trace of his training within the code of the consciousness stirred and he glanced round. On the western sky there seemed to be a blood-red blanket. It was still far off, but it was moving inexorably forward.

He turned to Polna and pointed out the sight he had felt before he had seen it:

'A Flash Wind.'

Polna paled.

'We must find shelter.'

Ankar Moor glared at him, but agreed with his point of view. It was a situation in which cowardice was not to be sneered at. A Flash Wind would kill all who were not in shelter from it.

'Right. We must press on.'

Polna was alarmed; it was as if Ankar Moor was ignoring the danger:

'But where?'

'The sandstone cliffs. That's the nearest point.'

Polna glanced at the receding fugitives, the question silent on his lips. Ankar Moor went on:

'Yes, we will find them there. That is where they are going, too. Come on, ride.'

With that, he gunned his machine and started down the side of the hill in pursuit. With a reluctance that was partially countered by their fear of the approaching Flash Wind,

Polna and the other men followed him down the hillside, all moving as fast as they dared.

Behind them the oceans of dark, ominous, blood-red clouds boiled across the sky, hissing audibly as they carried their radioactive filth on their path of destruction.

Kaz, Deneer and Marcus reached the lip of the canyon and then were forced to roar along it until they found a slide down which they could go to the canyon floor. Once there, the great sandstone cliffs were facing them on the far side of the canyon. On the side they were on, there was sandstone too, and there were great gouges in it that would give shelter from the coming storm, but Deneer pointed across the canyon:

'It was over there.'

Marcus said in a panicky voice:

'But the Flash Wind.'

Kaz's eyes flashed a warning though his face and his voice remained soft and understanding.

'We have time.'

'But –'

'Be patient. We do not wish to die, either.'

Marcus understood he had been snubbed, but respected it; the ways of these Guides were strange, but he was coming to understand them and his father's praise for them, with every moment that passed, more and more.

The three fugitives drove down the canyon until Deneer held up her hand for them to stop. The two Guides got off their machines quite close to the cliffs and put them on their stands. Though he did not understand exactly what was happening, Marcus followed suit.

Even he could hear the hissing approach of the storm clouds now and he was getting frightened by them. He expected that all three of them would make for the nearest cave, but, to his surprise, Deneer walked out from the wall of the canyon. Her eyes were shut and she was breathing deeply and seemed to be waiting for something.

Marcus opened his mouth to call her back, but a firm glance from the watchful Kaz Oshay silenced him. For a while, they watched her walking up and down, with her eyes still closed, as the hissing became more and more audible.

With each striding up and down, Deneer was getting further and further out into the centre of the canyon. At last, when she was far enough away so that he believed that he could not be heard, Marcus asked:

'What is it? What is she doing?'

Kaz was quiet.

'She is looking.'

The Stateman frowned.

'Looking for what?'

'For a sign.'

Marcus bit his lip. Why did these people never answer a straight question with a straight answer? He listened to the approaching Flash Wind for another few seconds.

'Please, we have to find shelter. The wind will be on us in a minute, if Ankar Moor doesn't get to us first.'

Kaz nodded. He knew all that. It was a waste of breath and time to talk about it. He did not take his eyes off Deneer as she continued her blind walk. Marcus tried again.

'What the hell is she looking for?'

'The past.'

Deneer had entered the area where the caravan had been attacked and got the vague memories of it immediately. She stopped dead and the whole memory of what had happened slipped through her mind like the re-run of a film.

She stood with her eyes shut and watched the whole action again – the panic of the Statemen – the forming of the circle – Adriann making Karissa stay with the others – the fight itself – the death of Adriann – then Karissa moving out on her pony – and the men who crept from the caves and took her while Deneer was trying to fight off the Death Machines.

She opened her eyes and turned suddenly.

'Kaz Oshay. The Mutants. It is true. The Mutants have her. I have just seen it.'

Even Kaz paled. The chances of them finding and rescuing the girl would be small. She might be dead already. Even so, he found time to turn to Marcus. 'You see. We have found the past.'

Deneer raced back, her eyes shining. Her vision of the consciousness had told her much.

'I think that she is still alive. I feel it. The Mutants have her in their caves.'

Kaz fastened his eyes on her.

'She lives?'

'I believe it.'

'Then we will save her.'

Marcus exploded with a combination of fear and disbelief.

'What? You mean we will have to go into the caves and seek out the Mutants? You're crazy. None of us will ever come out alive from an attempt like that.'

Kaz turned and fired him a look of burning anger. There was no argument on this as far as he was concerned.

'Stateman, whether you come or stay behind means nothing to me or my fellow Guide. A Guide takes care of his own. That is the first duty of any Guide.'

He turned away and he and Deneer began to run together towards one of the cave entrances. The rumbling of the coming Flash Wind storm grew nearer and the sky seemed to be darkening as the sun was obscured. Marcus turned and, reluctant to lose his life, followed them:

'Goddammit.'

Ankar Moor coasted his great machine up to the lip of the canyon, where the fugitives had come. He looked down and he saw the three of them on the far side, too far away to catch before the storm, running towards the entrance of one of the caves. He cursed silently as he watched them go. He must find a way down into the canyon quickly, then shelter on this side until the storm had passed over. It meant that he might suffer several hours delay, though a Flash Wind had not been known to take more than that time to pass.

His straggling men caught up with him and Polna halted at his side.

'There they go.'

Ankar Moor pointed at the oncoming storm.

'We are too late for them now.'

Polna sighed.

'Then they have escaped.'

'No.' Ankar Moor felt more secure than he had that whole day. 'They cannot go anywhere either, once the storm has come. They'll be right there when the wind has passed.'

He turned his machine:

'Come, we will find a way down to shelter from the storm.'

They rode along the lip of the canyon until they found the same slide down which Kaz Oshay and the others had gone. Once on the canyon floor they made for the nearest of the sandstone hollows and parked their machines so that they might shelter from the storm, which was now almost on top of them. Ankar Moor knew now that all he had to do was wait.

Deneer led the other two past three of the lower cave entrances before she stopped before one that excited her.

'They took her in this way.'

Marcus took Kaz's arm. 'How does she know that?'

'She is a Guide, Stateman.'

Kaz put himself ahead of Deneer and plunged into the comparative darkness of the cave. With a glance of sympathy, Deneer followed and then Marcus reluctantly brought up the rear. Once they were in the entrance, both Guides drew their Whistlers and held them tightly in their hands, ready for the first sign of an attack. Kaz took the one hand blaster they had from his belt and handed it to Marcus.

Marcus gripped it tightly. He felt a little less naked with it in his hand, but he had no chance to show his gratitude for, as Kaz Oshay turned away and scanned the darkening interior of the cave, it seemed that all light was blotted out as the Flash Wind enveloped the canyon outside. The hissing was so loud and rumbling that it would be impossible for him to make himself heard. He could only give thanks that they had got into shelter in time. The fear of the Flash Wind was real – while the threat of the Mutants who might be hiding was still only a theoretical danger.

Kaz flattened himself against the wall of the cave and began to move slowly forward as his two companions followed his lead.

As they moved further into the interior of the caves and the hissing of the deadly wind receded, Marcus realised that his thought that the Mutants might not be there was a cruel self-deception. The stench that seemed to be coming towards them was almost making him choke and a glance at his two companions told him that their more sensitive nostrils were even more affected, though they were doing their best not to show their distaste as they pressed forward.

At last it was possible for them to stop and speak. There was still no sign of any Mutant look-outs and for that they could feel relieved. Kaz signalled them to stop and moved back so that they could huddle together.

Kaz spoke first to Deneer. 'I think they are close. Our hopes for our own rise.'

She nodded.

'Our Union is strong. We will succeed.'

'It is. We will.'

Kaz now turned to Marcus.

'If we run across an individual, let's see if we can silence him with our Whistlers. I don't want you to use your anti-matter blaster unless you have to. It makes too much noise. It could bring more of them swarming than we can deal with.'

Marcus nodded.

'I will do my best.'

Kaz had no irony in his tone as he said:

'For a Stateman you are as brave as a Guide.'

Marcus was flattered and answered quietly, 'Thank you, Kaz Oshay.'

'It is deserved, Stateman.'

Once more they prepared to move forward, into the almost physical barrier of stench that seemed to come towards them from the depths of the cave.

They rounded a corner in the passage and Kaz Oshay signalled to them to halt once more, before pointing forward where the shaft branched off. From one of the two choices of shaft there came a gleam of light, heralding occupation further on.

'We are on their track.'

Marcus shuddered. 'Don't they sleep during the day?'

Deneer shook her head. 'Only some of them.'

'Then they could be waiting for us?'

Kaz managed a smile. 'Let us see.'

He motioned them on. So far, Marcus had been perspiring from fear and had been ashamed of this manifestation of his faint heart; now the air was so thick and foetid that he noticed that his companions were sweating as much as he and he was relieved that he need no longer feel ashamed.

He was determined to get to Triton and he realised that his father had been right. With these two he had the best chance of getting there. But first, as they had repeatedly underlined, the Guides took care of their own. Perhaps now he could help them retrieve the little girl if she was still alive, and that would even the balance for what they would do for him.

The three of them started down the tunnel from which the hint of light was coming. They had only gone a very short distance, in silence, when Kaz signalled to them to halt again.

The walls of this piece of tunnel were honeycombed with cross-tunnels and light came from some of these as well. If they did not go very cautiously they could find themselves attacked from behind and trapped.

Marcus took the opportunity to whisper to Deneer, 'I've never smelt anything so sickening – what is it?'

It was Kaz who leant back to answer.

'Rotting flesh.'

Marcus shuddered and Deneer, who had a more understanding mind for the ways and tastes of Statemen, smiled.

'The smell troubles you?'

He nodded, embarrassed.

'Yes, I'm afraid it does.'

She reassured him. 'There is no shame in that. You must just learn to close your mind, then you will not notice.'

He nodded, though the smell was making him gag.

'That is the way of the Guides?'

'Yes. That is the way of the Guides.'

Kaz signalled violently for them to be quiet and all three pressed their bodies hard against the damp rock of the wall. A moment later two of the Mutants emerged from one of the side tunnels further on and shuffled away from them for a moment, before disappearing into another tunnel. Kaz turned and whispered: 'We will follow them.'

Deneer nodded her agreement and they started slowly forward again. Marcus brought up the rear, muttering to himself in low tones. He would have been ashamed if he had realised that the hearing of the Guides was good enough to pick up his words:

'I've got to be out of my mind.'

The moment they turned into the shaft that they had seen the two Mutants go down, they realised they were on the right track. The tunnel sloped down and was lit at intervals by torches that blazed like the temporary ones they had made when they had entered the ruined factory complex. It seemed to Marcus that this had been centuries ago, though it was less than twenty-four hours. He remembered his father showing them how to make the torches and felt sad again at the older man's death. At least it took his mind off the terrible smell, he realised, after a few moments of edging forward with thoughts of his father in his mind.

The tunnel twisted and turned as they went further and further down into the depth of the rock. In a way these caves performed the duty of a natural Helix City. No wonder these Mutants, however misshapen they were, had managed to survive the centuries since the devastation.

Kaz halted them again as he heard the strange twittering sounds that the Mutants made coming from around the next bend. This went on for a few moments, then a set of footsteps padded away into the distance. A moment later, a single Mutant started moving towards them.

He was small and very thin, almost no more than blue skin and bone, his bulging egg-like eyes the fattest thing about him. The three intruders pressed themselves in against the wall and waited for him to come on.

He shuffled slowly towards them, unaware of the trap that lay in wait for him. He was making a strange bubbling sound in his throat, which Kaz knew was the sound of a Mutant laughing. Something had amused him and the three hidden ambushers waited for him to come.

He moved one pace within their reach and Kaz reached out behind him, grabbing him by the neck and forcing his head back so that if he struggled he would not be able to inflict a poisonous bite on his captor.

The moment the little Mutant was attacked, he went rigid with fear and his mouth opened, revealing the twin rows of razor-sharp teeth and the poison dribbling from them and down his chin. It whimpered in its throat and even Marcus, who had never seen a Mutant, only heard of the horror of them, could no longer think of it as a human being.

He blurted, 'God, it's disgusting.'

Deneer gasped!

'Be careful, Kaz. It drips a poison that even we do not have a cure for. It is beyond even the power of the consciousness.'

But Kaz held the monster solidly, its chin up so that it was unable to move its head. Now with his free hand, he brought up his Whistler and held the sharp blade under the Mutant's chin, so that it touched the blue skin, rough and damp.

Kaz asked roughly, 'Where is the one of ours? The little one. The one your people took yesterday. Where?'

The Mutant braced himself again, making no response and, without hesitation, Kaz Oshay pushed the sharp blade of the Whistler against his captive's throat, not hard enough to kill it, but enough to cut the skin so that its weak blood ran down the blade like a tiny river.

Kaz clenched his teeth as he asked again: 'Where?'

This time the little creature began to twitter and point down the passageway. Still with his teeth clenched and holding the Whistler at his victim's throat, he spoke even more urgently.

'Show me, Mutant. And do not lead me astray, or I will carve you before I kill you.'

He pressed his Whistler to the Mutant's throat once more as a reminder of his power over his captive enemy, then relaxed slightly. The little creature wheezed and began to nod its head frantically, terrified out of its mind.

Kaz took the opportunity to change his grip, withdrawing his arm, then catching the little creature round the back of its neck, so that it could not turn and bite him.

He started to move forward, the little creature making its small shuffling paces in front of him, still wheezing with fear. Deneer turned to Marcus, her eyes shining.

'She's still alive!'

Marcus frowned and whispered back:

'How do you know?'

'I understand a little of their language. He has told us. He is leading us to her.'

Marcus nodded. It was not the time to disillusion her, but he thought that it was more likely that they were walking into a trap.

They went further and further down the twisting shaft, the foetid smell getting thicker, the atmosphere hotter. Marcus began to think that he would rather be outside in the Flash Wind than here in this thickening air.

The little Mutant led them abruptly off the main shaft and into another one that went down at an even more perilous angle. This shaft was less well-lit than the one they had just left and Kaz, suspicious of where he was being led, jerked the Mutant to a halt, re-introducing him to the Whistler by pressing it against his throat afresh and asking in urgent whispered tones:

'Where? Where is she?'

Almost so frightened that it could not stand up, the Mutant pointed frantically down the shaft. Reassured, Kaz withdrew the Whistler and the group pressed on down.

Marcus retched drily in his throat and gasped: 'I think I'm going to be sick.'

Deneer turned and grabbed him. Unexpectedly, she slapped him hard round the face, snapping him out of his distress.

'You must be quiet, we are all in great danger.'

The tunnel was beginning to flatten out. They were coming down to a level and, as they turned another bend in the route, the passage opened out into a huge cavern. From the noises that came from the darkened interior, they guessed it contained a large number of Mutants and was obviously their communal sleeping quarters.

The opening out was only a few yards ahead of them and the smell was beyond imagination. Kaz smashed the Mutant against the wall and held up the Whistler once more.

'Where is she?' He shook the creature again and snapped: 'How much further is it?'

Frantic with fear and pain, the little creature gesticulated wildly, even Marcus being able to read from the signals that he was telling them that the girl was just beyond this chamber, in the further recesses of the darkness.

Kaz listened to his wheezing, then turned to Deneer.

'That's a sleeping chamber just ahead of us. She's being held on the far side.'

Deneer looked into his eyes, nodded and turned round to Marcus, who was straining against the desire to retch again.

'Wait for us here in the shadow, out of the way.'

He was indignant.

'I want to go with you.'

'You look all in already. You will be safer staying here and waiting for us.'

She turned to follow Kaz and his prisoner, but Marcus, panicking, grabbed her arm.

'Wait! What if you don't come back?'

Deneer looked down. 'You have your blaster. Run with it.'

'But I couldn't just leave you.'

She smiled at him.

'That's just if we don't come back. Till then you wait for us and pray to your gods. They may bring us luck.'

With that, she turned and started after Kaz, across the chamber of sleeping Mutants and into the gloom beyond.

Marcus grasped his blaster in both hands and faded back into the shadows, his mind thick with 'ifs'.

Kaz held his Whistler at the throat of the little man as they started across the sleeping chamber. On both sides of the silent party, Mutants lay sleeping, making strange snuffling noises and letting off an odour of body heat that both Kaz and Deneer knew would finally have overcome the Stateman stomach and lungs of Marcus.

After what seemed like an eternity of special foot-placing, they reached the far side of the chamber, where the tunnel narrowed once more. The passage was again lit and Kaz lifted the hostage Mutant off his feet as they sped silently down it. There was another chamber off the passage, a little way beyond the sleeping chamber and the Mutant pointed frantically for them to enter it.

Inside was a pile of metal cages, the legacy of some long ago looting by the Mutants. There was a figure lying in one of the upper cages. The door was hanging open but it was too high up for the occupant to climb down.

Kaz held the Mutant by the entrance to the cave, while Deneer, once she had made sure that there were no other occupants, rushed forward and woke the small figure who was lying in the cage.

The little girl came straight into her arms and, as she took her down, Deneer whispered urgently:

'Ssshhh . . . don't make a sound.'

Overjoyed, but stifling her excitement, little Karissa put her arms round the Guide girl and hugged her close as she was lifted out of her miserable prison. She whispered, 'Deneer . . . I love you.'

'And I love you.'

Karissa said tightly: 'Adriann is dead.'

Deneer tried to comfort her as she carried her back to where Kaz was waiting with their prisoner.

'Don't worry. We take care of our own.'

They paused and Kaz too smiled on the little girl.

'We still have a long way to go. Stay close to us. Quickly now, we must go before they wake.'

They turned out of the chamber and back up the corridor towards the Mutant's sleeping quarters. For a while it looked as if they would be lucky. Then the worst happened.

Two of the Mutants had wakened and were now making

their way across the chamber towards them. The captured man gave an involuntary scream of warning. In one second he was dead as the Whistler cut his throat and Kaz threw him down, then shouted, 'Run. Run for your lives!'

CHAPTER ELEVEN

A moment after the first cry of warning from the captive Mutant, the sleeping cave through which Kaz Oshay and Deneer had to pass became a bedlam of twittering panic, as the sleeping creatures snapped into wakefulness and peered around in the darkness to find their enemies.

Deneer grabbed the rescued Karissa in her arms and charged through the sleeping cave, praying that speed and surprise would defend her from the sharp double rows of teeth and the poison that infused their victims when they struck. Kaz, after dropping the dead body of his captive, followed behind, using his Whistler like a flail to keep the Mutants away from their path.

Hidden in the darkness, on the far side of the cave, Marcus went rigid with fear as the noises came. He heard Kaz's order for Deneer and the girl to run and, at the same moment, there came a flurry of sound behind him. Mutants were coming down their only escape route.

He spun round and saw two of the little creatures shufffling round the corner, their mouths open, ready to attack. He went down on one knee and fired with the professionalism of an expert, a purely reflex action, a copy of what he had seen Kaz do.

The two Mutants disappeared in a green flash of anti-matter and, a moment later, Deneer was at his side. She had managed to bundle Karissa under one arm and with her free hand she drew her Whistler. She went past him, shouting, 'Run for your life!'

He was galvanised into action and started after her. Kaz had stopped at the start of the ramped tunnel and had turned. Now his blade whistled through the foetid air and he cut down the first of their enemies who charged, causing the others to pause in terror for a moment. Now he ran after the others, and, after only a moment of pause, the Mutants began to charge up the tunnel after them.

Marcus caught up with Deneer and shouted an apology.

'I'm sorry. I had to use my blaster.'

Behind him, Kaz gave a breathless laugh.

'Sorry? Why be sorry? Use it liberally, use it well!'

Ahead of them, Deneer had other things on which to concentrate. At the head of the column she had to find the way out.

'Which way?'

From behind Marcus, Kaz shouted, 'Bear right, always right.'

They raced on up the shaft, mindless of banging into the wall, intent only on getting to the surface and away from their pursuers. Suddenly the pack in full twittering cry behind them ceased to be their only problem. A group of six wailing, chanting creatures charged down on them out of the darkness ahead.

Kaz pushed past Marcus.

'Put a blast down the tunnel to hold them back.'

A moment later he was side by side with Deneer, ready to take on these new attackers. Both Guides gave their terrible war cry and began to repel the attack. Deneer dropped Karissa, who stood behind them, next to Marcus, crouched waiting for the attack from the rear. Even in the confined space, the two Guides wielded their Whistlers like the experts they were. They whistled through the air, destroying Mutant after Mutant as they charged in, but never once did the flashing blade of one Guide come within inches of the other.

Kaz, exhilarated by the fight, shouted to Deneer:

'You wield a fast blade, woman.'

She laughed.

'No faster than yours, man.'

Marcus put a second blast of anti-matter down the tunnel. It was not quite straight and gouged great slivers out of the rock that did as much damage to the oncoming enemy as did the direct hit which annihilated two of them. Kaz and Deneer had eliminated the charging men and Kaz shouted over his shoulder, 'Run! Both of you.'

Karissa and Marcus followed in the wake of the two

Guides. They turned out of the ramped tunnel into the main corridor, to the right, always to the right.

Nervous that they would get trapped in the caves until they were overwhelmed, Marcus shouted, 'Are you sure that's the right way?'

Kaz called back, brief and callous.

'If you don't believe me – don't follow me.'

Up and on they ran until they could see the first glimmerings of daylight ahead.

Running as fast as he could, Marcus could still not keep up with the special speeds of either Kaz and Deneer or even the tiny Karissa, for, while she was a child, she was also a child of the Guides. He was trailing badly as they passed the last cross-shaft and, as he went past it, he saw that the other three had reached the mouth of the cave and daylight – the Flash Wind having apparently rolled by.

At the moment he passed the entrance to the cross-shaft, a Mutant leapt out of the darkness at him, knocking into him and throwing him down on the stone floor of the cave tunnel.

Marcus cried out in his panic as he began to fight for his life. He saw a flash of the teeth, the dreadful double rows of sharp pointed teeth and the awful foaming mouth, dripping its foul poisonous saliva, and he rolled over trying to keep it out of contact with his body. In that movement the blaster was knocked from his grip and rolled away from him. He was dazed as his head came into contact with the rock.

He struggled bravely, flailing out with his arms, one fist catching the dreadful creature full in the face and knocking it back. Marcus took the opportunity to dive for his blaster. He grabbed it up, but the Mutant had already recovered himself. The little creature fell on Marcus's right leg and bit on it hard.

As Marcus screamed in agony, Kaz was at his side and his attacker fell dead, cut in half by the dreadful blade of the Whistler.

With one swift move, Kaz grabbed Marcus and pulled him on to his feet. They could hear the sound of the main group of Mutants pounding up the shaft after them. He let go of Marcus, who nearly fell, his wounded right leg taking none of his weight.

Kaz moved quickly, scooping him up under the armpits.

'Get on my back. I will carry you.'

In his terror, Marcus gave immediate obedience to the order. As the Guide bent, he got on his back and hung on with all his ebbing strength, sobbing in agony. As fast as only he could go, Kaz Oshay raced for the entrance and the waiting Deneer and Karissa.

Outside the sky was clear, the sun beating down. The Flash Wind had truly gone by. Deneer, seeing that Kaz was right behind her with his load, started down the slope towards their parked Death Machines. There was a new problem now. Ankar Moor and his men had already mounted their machines and an oncoming cloud of dust told the fugitives that their enemies were charging down on them.

Marcus's arms were beginning to weaken and Kaz had to shout at him.

'Try to hang on! Not long now.'

Marcus screamed, 'My leg! I can't feel anything in my leg!'

They arrived on the flat and raced across the intervening space to their machines. Deneer was already mounted up, revving and waiting, with Karissa ahead of her, straddling the console between her and the handlebars.

Kaz came to a halt and bent to let Marcus down. The latter managed to groan, 'I won't be able to drive my machine like this. The whole of my right leg is numb.'

Deneer called across, 'Ride behind me. I know that they have medicine for the poison in the Triton City.'

With Kaz helping him, Marcus limped across to her machine and climbed gratefully across the back of it, hanging on to her, his arms round her waist.

Kaz raced to his own machine, leapt on and started up. Ankar Moor and his men were closing fast. The Mutants had reached the mouth of the cave but had not come forward, pushed back by the sight of more enemies and the bright daylight that hurt their huge eyes and placed them at a definite disadvantage. They were no longer a problem.

Kaz glanced at Deneer and managed a tight smile to buoy her courage up:

'Go now, Deneer.'

'But Kaz – '

'I will divert them.'

For a moment their eyes locked and she tried to put all her strength into him, afraid for him, going out against Ankar

Moor and his men alone, afraid that she would never see him alive again.

As he revved up his machine, she shouted across the space that separated them: 'Be powerful, Kaz!'

'I will be powerful, woman.'

'I will be waiting for you in Triton if you show. I will see you on the other side if you do not. Our Union is strong.'

Kaz stared back, his mind assured.

'I will see you in Triton, Deneer.'

Their eyes dropped from one another. As one, they turned their machines in opposite directions and Deneer then sped away, skirting the edge of the sandstone cliffs, weaving around boulders that were at the side of the canyon, trying to stay, as much as possible, out of the view of Ankar Moor's men as she gained speed for the run towards Triton.

Kaz raced straight out from the cliffside, straight at the oncoming Ankar Moor and his Death Machine riders as they raced across the canyon, four abreast.

Ankar Moor was in the centre of the avenging group of Enforcers and, as he saw Kaz Oshay, the son of Oshay, coming towards him, he shouted into his microphone: 'Don't try to hit him straight on. Fan out and flank him – move now, quickly!'

As the line ahead of him fanned out, Kaz had to choose which of them to go for first. He decided to go for the man who was moving to his far left, on the end of the flanking movement. Exhilarated by the feeling of freedom, of fresh air pushing back the hair on his uncovered head, he shouted, more to himself than his enemy:

'All right, you fool. Let us see how good you are.'

Breaking to the left yet again, he went full throttle towards the sandstone cliffs, as if going for an 'end' run. Ankar Moor called urgently through the microphone: 'Cut him off. Dammit. Cut him off.'

Kaz had easily cleared and avoided the end man. Now he ran into an area of scrub bush and a maze of huge boulders which bordered the sandstone cliffs, arriving in that area just a few yards ahead of the panicking Enforcer. This man was alarmed to find himself now in the forefront of Ankar Moor's attack but, more afraid of his master than the enemy, he pressed relentlessly on.

In and around the scrub, up and over boulders and round screes they flew, defying catastrophe, neither of them in position for long enough to go for the kill of destruction, each manoeuvre a little more difficult to sustain and see through to the end than the one before.

At length, Kaz Oshay found himself zooming up a tiny, straight path, a huge mound at the end of it. At the very top, he cut his throttle with a sudden movement. Then, braking, he slid over the lip and a small way down the far side, pushing the machine off-balance and on to its side as he went down in the dirt. When it stopped, he lay it flat against the ground, swivelling it around so that the blaster pods faced up the dirt to the exact top of the mound. He flattened himself down next to it, his finger on the blaster button, waiting tensely. If any of his followers had seen the trick, he would be a dead Guide before another minute had passed.

But his pursuers had been too anxious about their own safety to notice this sudden change in tactics. The first Enforcer reached the top of the mound and flew in the air, roaring over him and landing far beyond before roaring forward down the path without a backward glance.

In quick succession, Polna and Ankar Moor also flew well above his head and roared on. Now there was only the last man and Kaz was determined to even up the odds, determined that Ankar Moor would be called upon to fulfil the challenge that Kaz Oshay had given to him in the torture chamber of Helix City.

The final Enforcer was trailing slightly on his companions, but at last the roar of his machine came to Kaz. He waited tensely. The man appeared at the top of the mound and, at the very moment his machine took to the air to sail over him, Kaz pressed the blaster button and the odds were reduced to three to one as the hapless Enforcer disappeared into the atmosphere in mid air and mid shriek.

Immediately, Kaz lifted up his machine, restarted it and scrambled back to the top of the rise before coming off down the far side and away from his three remaining pursuers.

Ankar Moor heard the blaster explosion behind him and slid his machine to a halt, calling through the microphone for the two men ahead of him to do the same. He shouted:

'He's tricked us. Come on, he's heading back the other way. We must catch him.'

Having shouted, he turned his machine and zoomed back, unaware that Polna and the remaining Enforcer also turned, but with noticeably less enthusiasm for the chase than their master.

Kaz dodged the boulder and scrub that dotted the area in which he was fleeing and finally burst out into the flat sandy plain that was the centre of the canyon. Once there, he turned up the canyon and started to go full throttle in the same general direction that Deneer had taken – towards the City of Triton.

Ahead of him and out of sight of the fleeing Guide, Marcus clung desperately to Deneer's waist as he sat on the back of the roaring machine, just as Karissa hung on like grim death to the front console. They had reached the end of the canyon and were now rumbling up the narrow pass. Beyond that, Deneer knew, lay the long open plain that would bring them to their destination.

Marcus's wounded leg was bleeding profusely, but the loss of blood was not affecting him as badly as the poison of the Mutants that was now beginning to course through his system. He felt dizzy and nauseous, as if his senses were slowly seeping away from him. He called out weakly, but loud enough for Deneer to hear:

'I don't know how much longer I can hang on.' He paused to get his breath, then went on, his tone even more panic-stricken: 'All the way up my right side – I cannot feel anything, my arm is going now.'

Deneer frowned. She knew the power of the poison, knew the real trouble her passenger was in.

'Hold on, Marcus. We just have to get through this pass. Triton is not far across the plain beyond. Just a short distance. With the help of the consciousness, we will make it.'

Marcus was strangely comforted by her words and the sureness with which she delivered them. He clung even harder to her as she roared on, gunning her machine to exceed what she thought would be its top speed.

Ankar Moor and the others had finally emerged from the area of scrub and boulders and were roaring over the open sand of the canyon after Kaz Oshay. The latter was just far enough ahead to be safe, but close enough to provide a tantalising target for his pursuers.

At length he thought to vary the conditions of the chase and veered to one side of the canyon, where the ground rose in a series of gently undulating dunes of sand. He started across them, leading his pursuers on, up over each crest and down into the valleys that separated one crest from the next, like an enormous natural rollercoaster.

When he was ready to make his next move, he had reached the crest of a dune and now accelerated as he went down the far side, hitting the flat, then zooming up the next, higher dune beyond. Ankar Moor and the others were hard on his heels, moving faster themselves as he put on speed and moved away from them.

It was only then that Ankar Moor realised that he was chasing one lone Guide and rapped into the microphone:

'What has happened to the Stateman and the other Guide?'

Polna answered gruffly: 'He was alone.'

Ankar Moor swore in his frustration.

'Damn him. He's been acting as a decoy, just leading us on. Hurry, we must get him.'

Kaz arrived at the top of the next dune and braked hard. Far down and ahead of him lay the flatness of the plain that was the last area to be crossed before the City of Triton would be reached. He looked forward and there, far out on the desert sand, stood Triton, a jewel in the middle of the wastelands. It was a City far more beautiful to look upon in the sunlight than Helix had been, and surrounded by the signs of experimental cultivation that was taking place as its citizens tried to emerge from their nine hundred years of hiding to move out across the face of the earth again in an effort of renewal.

There was something else to make Kaz Oshay smile as well. Far below and ahead of him on the gleaming open plain, a cloud of dust was being kicked up, and, in the centre of it, his sharp eyes could see Deneer's machine, the two extra passengers still clinging to it. In a little while they would be safe and he could concentrate on his coming battle with Ankar Moor.

Down on the plain, Marcus was marshalling every ounce of strength that was still left within him to cling on. He was looking around Deneer as he saw Triton take shape in front of his blurring vision.

'We made it.'

Deneer laughed, her voice firmer than before. For her, their safety was in truth a miracle. She had had her doubts during the journey.

'Yes, just as I said we should.'

'You have worked a miracle, Deneer.'

'It was but the will of the consciousness.'

They roared on towards their destination and their hopes of safety.

Kaz Oshay gunned the huge Death Machine and charged down the side of the dune and on to the plain for his final run.

Ankar Moor, Polna and the other Enforcer arrived at the top of the dune only seconds after he had quit the spot. They looked out across the waste and saw the City of Triton gleaming up at them, teasing them like a jewel they would never steal.

It took a second to realise the shock that they had lost their gamble of chase. Below them, Kaz Oshay had stopped on the plain and had turned his machine so that he could stare back up over the great distance at Ankar Moor, his eyes flashing the challenge of the code.

Over the enormous distance their eyes met and Ankar Moor knew that the moment of challenge had come. First he tore his gaze away and turned to face Polna.

'Truth needs no introduction. When the sun rises there is no necessity to announce it. When the moon reflects there is no need to point it out. Clearly, we have lost.'

Polna shook his head sadly. In spite of the fear he held for his master, he felt sorry for him now, feeling also that he had let the other man down.

'Yes, I'm afraid so.'

Ankar Moor pointed at Kaz, waiting for him below.

'Look at him.' The voice was filled with hatred.

Polna nodded. 'He grows arrogant with success.'

Ankar Moor absorbed this insight into his assistant's mind. Perhaps the man was not so much of a dolt as he had always thought. When he spoke to Polna it was with a new respect.

'You two should go back to Helix City. There is nothing for you to gain by coming with me.'

Polna felt a twinge of guilt. 'I serve you, Ankar Moor.'

'Then I tell you to return, out of danger.'

Polna bowed his head in acceptance and appreciation. The two men were, for a moment, closer than they had been. Whatever else he had thought of his master, Polna had never had any reason to doubt the ex-Guide's courage.

Ankar Moor stared at Kaz Oshay again, then looked back at his lieutenant.

'Man is like a candle. He must radiate life by burning himself. I have an old score to settle.'

Polna nodded. 'Be powerful, Ankar Moor.' Out of respect, he spoke in the terms of the Guides.

Ankar Moor answered him in kind.

'I will be as powerful as I need to be.'

The three of them shared a final salute to the courage of each other, then Polna and the other Enforcer turned their machines and, without further pause, roared away, back to Helix City and their future. In his mind, Polna already knew that things would have changed there beyond recognition. Perhaps the rule of the Lord Zirpola and Ankar Moor had been wrong. If he still had his position, he would help to change all that, make Helix an open City, as were the others of the plain, free and with true justice for its citizens.

Ankar Moor watched them go down the side of the dune, then up the next, until they were out of sight. Only then did he turn, gun his machine and start down on to the plain and towards what he knew was his fate, win or lose, against his enemy.

Kaz waited patiently, then watched him come, moving slowly towards him, first down the slope and then on the flat beyond. The huge man, with his frightening leather mask that covered the damage that the Lady Oshay had done to his face when she had forced him to be banished from the Guides forever, stopped his machine just outside blaster range from Kaz Oshay's own.

There was a moment of silence as the two men allowed their eyes to meet, both showing hatred and challenge. Then Kaz Oshay shouted strongly across the intervening space: 'Now we will have our duel.'

Ankar Moor nodded, a formality.

'I agree.'

'With the machines or without?'

Ankar Moor's answer was to switch off his machine and dismount before shouting, 'Without.'

Kaz nodded and he too stopped the great throbbing machine, dismounting and resting it on its stand.

'I agree.'

The two men stood, each with his legs planted astride, each studying the physique of the other, then Kaz asked, 'With blasters?'

Ankar Moor's answer was to throw his to the ground. Inwardly, Kaz breathed a sigh of relief for he had no such weapon. That had been his most difficult moment. Ankar Moor shouted, 'No blasters!'

Kaz nodded.

'With Whistlers, then?'

Ankar Moor nodded:

'With Whistlers. Just like the day that I met your mother Oshay in our battle.'

Ankar Moor took a pace forward and threw aside his cloak, revealing that he too carried the scabbard of one of the great Whistlers of the Guides. He unsnapped the cloak so that it fell to the earth behind him and drew the great fused carbon blade that flashed in the sunlight. Kaz Oshay did the same.

With infinite slowness and caution the two men approached each other, both crouching slightly, balancing on the balls of their feet as they moved like the great warriors of ancient civilisations coming at each other, ready with force, each to test the weaknesses and strengths of the other in an effort to find the point that would give them victory and the death of their opponent.

At exactly the same instant, both men held their blades up in a two-handed gesture, frozen, poised, in position for their first strikes. Locked eye to eye they stood, unmoving and unyielding, both filled with the tension of their concentration, both of them fuelling the hatred that was the dynamic of their battle.

The manner of the fugitives' entry to the City of Triton was an obvious contrast to the manner of control that was exercised for those visiting the City of Helix. Triton too had its Enforcers, but their uniforms and small hand weapons were reassuring rather than frightening and served only to single them out as officials, rather than the civilians it was their duty to help.

Deneer drove her machine to the main entry gate of the City, through an aisle of palm trees, a tribute to the re-irrigation of the land around the City after nine hundred years of decay and radioactive death. She stopped her machine and, to the surprise of all three passengers, the great door ahead of them slid open at once.

Men rushed forward to welcome them and to help them

inside and, with a groan that told of the combination of pain and numbness he felt, Marcus slid to the ground.

At once, men appeared with a trolley on to which they silently placed the stricken man. One of their number, who wore a white coat similar to the one that Doctor Karl had always worn, approached Deneer and bowed.

'Do you know his trouble?'

Deneer said quickly, 'I fear he is dying. He was bitten by a Mutant. Can you save him?'

The man bowed again.

'It is not hard. There is no danger.'

Leaving Karissa for a moment, Deneer dismounted and ran over to where Marcus was lying on the trolley. She looked down at him and smiled, gently, fondly.

'Be powerful, Marcus. I wish you well.'

Marcus managed to bring his eyes into focus, blinking hard.

'Deneer . . . I don't know how to thank you . . . And Kaz.'

The doctor gave an order, smiling an apology at Deneer at the same time, and Marcus was wheeled away for treatment.

Deneer turned to one of the guards.

'I must see your President. I carry a warning of war.'

The man paled at the word, but looking round, he breathed a sigh and pointed at a middle-aged, upright, calm man who was coming towards them.

'He comes now.'

Deneer was amazed that the ruler of a City should walk out unprotected like this. Deneer went towards him.

'My Lord, I carry a warning from Helix. That City plans to wage war upon you and your people.'

The man nodded.

'There is no need of such formality. You are Deneer of the Guides?'

'Yes.'

'We have heard of you and the good you do in the wastelands.'

She frowned. 'You must become prepared. They will attack soon.'

He shook his head.

'We owe you a tremendous debt of gratitude for the dangers you have faced in coming to us, but we have heard by video communication from Helix. The Lord Zirpola is dead and the people have risen against his rule. Their new leaders have asked to enter the Federation.'

'And what is your reply?'

'We have given our acceptance. Our technicians are already working on a plan to get fuel to them.'

'You are truly forgiving, Lord of Triton.'

He raised up her head, gently but firmly.

'We owe you a tremendous debt.'

A moment later, Karissa ran forward and, as the man put out his hand, she took it with warmth and trust. A guard ran forward.

'Sir, a duel, Sir, my men have seen it out on the plain. You can see it from the tower.'

Deneer sucked in her breath in shock and the President quickly turned to her.

'It is the legendary Kaz Oshay?'

She nodded numbly, then, 'Yes, My Lord. Our Union is one. I live or die with him.'

'Then you should watch. Come with me.'

Still holding Karissa by the hand, he led them into the first main building and thus, by an open public elevator, to the tower that overlooked the plain.

The two men had stood, crouching slightly and facing one another, for an eternity of motionless time, each willing the other man to be the first to make his move.

It was Ankar Moor who broke first, less patient than his opponent, more fuelled by the pure hatred of revenge. He leapt forward with two quick paces and slashed wildly at Kaz. The latter jumped back a step and parried with an arc of his whistling blade, causing Ankar Moor to leap up and back to avoid its swift movement.

Immediately, they spun and charged in at each other. With a loud crash their blades met just above the hand guards, sparking off each other, the spark visible even in the bright sunlight. Eye to eye, face to face, they struggled to balance each other's power and force and Ankar Moor, seeking any advantage he could snatch, rasped, 'You are not as good as your mother.'

Between clenched teeth, Kaz Oshay, the son of Oshay, forced out his response: 'But I will prove myself far better than you.'

With that the two men broke, thrusting each other back.

Kaz was the first to recover and slash forward but, as his Whistler shrieked through the air, Ankar Moor parried strongly, then scrambled aside from the oncoming enemy.

Again the two men circled, each looking for some opening, some weakness in the other, their eyes unblinkingly showing their hatred, one of the other. With a wild war cry, Kaz Oshay was the first to lunge in this exchange and the blades of the two men again crashed together, the gleaming diamond-like constitution of them flashing in the sun, like the sparkle of the jewels they resembled in all but their ability to kill and maim.

With a sudden duck and twist, Ankar Moor was behind his opponent, and turned to slash, but the other man leapt hard in time and though the blade of the big man slashed his cloak to the waist, the Guide landed unharmed and untouched.

They whirled and faced each other again, then both of these superhuman Range Guides had the same thought of attack at the same moment and leapt high into the air at each other, their blades whistling with the scream of death.

But, as they fell to the earth, it was Ankar Moor's head, cut cleanly from his shoulders, that rolled away into the dust of the desert to which all, be they Guide or Stateman or Mutant, must at length return, cut clean by the blade of the great and legendary Kaz Oshay.

Kaz landed from his leap, even his mind not at first able to contemplate the miracle that had brought him through unscathed. The head of his enemy lay on the pure white sand behind him. He turned and looked at it, as the useless body fell nearby. His mind and body were drained of all emotion as he stared at it.

He felt a sudden infinite tiredness as the hatred was drained away from him. Slowly he moved over to Ankar Moor's fallen cloak and wiped his blade clean on it before returning it to its scabbard.

Then he sat on the sand by the dead body of his enemy and, with all his concentration, he went into a trance of thankfulness of his own deliverance and for the soul of Ankar Moor, who had once been of the Guides and had come back to them again to die with honour.

High in the tower of Triton, Deneer stared out into the plain. She had been rigid with fear as she had watched the contest progress, trying to will her strength into Kaz Oshay, the Guide with whom her Union was joined and had become as one. Now, in his moment of triumph, she almost fainted away with the effort of it.

She only moved at the sound of a new arrival on the balcony. It was Marcus, still on the trolley, but sitting up now and taking notice. Truly, the medicine of Triton was powerful against the poison of the Mutants.

Marcus said, 'I have come to say farewell.'

'Farewell.'

It was the President of Triton who replied.

'We know your ways are not the ways of Statemen, though you will always be welcome at this City. But now, you would rejoin your fellow Guide, would you not?'

Dumbly she nodded and Karissa ran across to hug her, to show her oneness as a daughter of the Guides.

The Triton President went on: 'I have given orders for horses to be provided for you. Go in peace until we should meet again.'

Deneer returned his gesture, then she and Karissa, accompanied by the President, and Marcus on his trolley, went down in the lift, back to the entrance of the City. Here they were joined by the girl for whom Marcus had gone through so much danger, and he, together with her and the President, watched as Deneer mounted her horse, Karissa the new pony which had been thoughtfully provided, and a man handed the reins of a spare horse, a tall grey stallion, for Deneer to lead the little party out of the City.

Kaz Oshay did not look up from his trance until the horses were nearly on top of him.

Deneer did not dismount, but said, 'They thanked us and gave us these horses.'

Kaz rose and nodded. 'Good. I'd rather have a horse than a machine.'

Apparently with his strength renewed by his trance, he went swiftly to the great grey stallion and mounted the beast with a practised ease. He then turned casually and asked:

'Where will you go now?'

Deneer frowned. 'With you.'

Though he was not surprised, was even pleased, by this response, he made his voice questioning.

'With me?'

'Yes. Don't you want me?'

He was silent for a moment, then his answer was honest in its very simplicity. 'Yes, I do.'

Deneer smiled, relieved and happy. 'Then our Union is complete.'

He answered as a formality of the code. 'I agree.'

They rode together, the child Karissa following close behind; man, woman and child, back into the mountainous wastelands and into the starting point of their legend.

That was many centuries before our present age. All that has come about is due to them and their heirs. There were many more battles and challenges before the souls of Kaz Oshay and Deneer of the Guides returned to the consciousness, but they are not central to this tale. We must just honour their memory if we are to hold on to what we have learnt and have prospered by, in this new Golden Age for Earth and Moon.

A selection of Film Tie-ins available in Sphere Books:

STAR WARS	George Lucas	95p ☐
CLOSE ENCOUNTERS OF THE THIRD KIND	S. Spielberg	85p ☐
CLOSE ENCOUNTERS OF THE THIRD KIND PHOTONOVEL	Marcia Seligman	£1.25 ☐
UNDER THE DOCTOR	P. Buchanan	65p ☐
GREASED LIGHTNING	Ken Vose & Larry Dukore	75p ☐
MIDNIGHT EXPRESS	Billy Hayes	95p ☐
NETWORK	Sam Hedrin	75p ☐
BLUE SUNSHINE	Ken Johnson	75p ☐
THE CAT AND THE CANARY	Gerry Kingsley	75p ☐
LET'S GET LAID	Philip Massinger	75p ☐
EXPOSÉ	Philip Massinger	75p ☐
HARDCORE	Philip Massinger	75p ☐
HOLOCAUST 2000	Michael Robson	85p ☐
FUN WITH DICK AND JANE	Sam Stewart	75p ☐
FELLINI'S CASANOVA	Bernardino Zapponi	85p ☐
DAMNATION ALLEY	R. Zelazny	85p ☐

A selection of Bestsellers from Sphere Books

SARGASSO	Edwin Corley	95p	☐
RAISE THE TITANIC!	Clive Cussler	95p	☐
STORY OF MY LIFE	Moshe Dayan	£1.50p	☐
THE HAB THEORY	Allan W. Eckert	£1.50p	☐
THE CRASH OF '79	Paul Erdman	95p	☐
EMMA AND I	Sheila Hocken	85p	☐
UNTIL THE COLOURS FADE	Tim Jeal	£1.50p	☐
DR JOLLY'S BOOK OF CHILDCARE	Dr Hugh Jolly	£1.95p	☐
MAJESTY	Robert Lacey	£1.95p	☐
STAR WARS	George Lucas	95p	☐
NIGHTRUNNERS OF BENGAL	John Masters	65p	☐
THE CHINESE ULTIMATUM	Edward McGhee & Robin Moore	95p	☐
THE MITTENWALD SYNDICATE	Frederick Nolan	95p	☐
NORTH CAPE	Joe Poyer	85p	☐
THE RUSSIANS	Hedrick Smith	£1.50p	☐
CLOSE ENCOUNTERS OF THE THIRD KIND	Steven Spielberg	85p	☐
A MAN CALLED INTREPID	William Stevenson	£1.25p	☐
STAR FIRE	Ingo Swann	£1.25p	☐
FIREFOX	Craig Thomas	95p	☐
RUIN FROM THE AIR	Gordon Thomas & Max Morgan Witts	£1.50p	☐
FADE-OUT	Patrick Tilley	95p	☐

All Sphere books are available at your local bookshop or newsagent, or can be ordered direct from the publisher. Just tick the titles you want and fill in the form below.

Name ....

Address ....

....

Write to Sphere Books, Cash Sales Department, P.O. Box 11, Falmouth, Cornwall TR10 9EN

Please enclose cheque or postal order to the value of the cover price plus:

UK: 22p for the first book plus 10p per copy for each additional book ordered to a maximum charge of 82p

OVERSEAS: 30p for the first book and 10p for each additional book

BFPO and EIRE: 22p for the first book plus 10p per copy for the next 6 books, thereafter 4p per book

Sphere Books reserve the right to show new retail prices on covers which may differ from those previously advertised in the text or elsewhere, and to increase postal rates in accordance with the GPO.